GARDEN ON THE MOON

ON
GARDEN

PIERRE
BOULLE

author of *The Bridge Over the River Kwai*

Translation by Xan Fielding

The Vanguard Press, Inc.

THE MOON

ew York

Almost half a century of meditation on the subject of sins having convinced me that hypocrisy is the only one to take really seriously, I should like to make a few remarks about this book.

1. *The date of completion.* If I resign myself to inscribing a date at the foot of this text—a procedure I have always condemned as a sly attempt to inflate the importance of a novel—it is because this one is set in a future sufficiently close to create certain hazards. To describe events twenty thousand years in advance does not intimidate me unduly, but the task becomes more delicate when it is a question of only six or seven years. What disturbs me most is a still closer future, the short period intervening between the present time and the date of publication. Since the conquest of space is fairly closely linked to the politics of the nations that have embarked upon it, and since these politics are sometimes subject to rapid change, it is not beyond the bounds of possibility that two weeks after the book is published (a reasonable length of time to assume without hypocrisy that it will not yet have sunk into oblivion), some unexpected event might so affect the contents as to make them appear absurd to a contemporary reader. Now if, as I admit later, I have taken certain liberties with history, at the time of writing, these have never gone so far as to constitute an absurd contra-

7

diction of the facts. What I dread is to see the history of tomorrow bring to pass, as it sometimes does, the very absurdities I have tried to avoid. As an example of such unexpected and untoward incidents, I would cite the assassination of President Kennedy, which obliged me, toward the end of 1963, to recast a considerable part of a novel I then believed to be complete. Other such eventualities, less tragic but less improbable, might be: an agreement between the two great powers on total cooperation in the realm of space; a pure and simple cancellation of the projects for further exploration of the moon; or, on the contrary, a rapid acceleration of these projects. I have wagered against these hypotheses, but they are not inconceivable. I have therefore dated the completion of this novel so as to mitigate my responsibility in the event that surprises of this sort stamp any part of it with the infamous seal of gratuitous absurdity.

This is one of my reasons, but not the main one. At this point I must energetically exorcise the demon of hypocrisy. In actual fact, my real reason is to build up for myself the singular glory of having been truly perspicacious, should events occur more or less as I have predicted—not, of course, to the letter but in spirit.

2. *Documentation.* In a modest way I have had recourse to certain sciences like history, astronautics, and politics. My sources were historical accounts of World War II, several books written for popular consumption, a great many periodicals, and above all the daily press. I treated these materials as it seemed to me a conscientious novelist should—that is, first I worked hard to indoctrinate myself as accurately as possible, and after that I devoted almost as much energy to *forgetting* all details, preserving only the bare skeleton of the facts and ideas and often altering historical events when I thought the clarity and compactness of the narrative might be improved by so doing.

This procedure has led to some difficulties. A kind American reader has written me, for instance, that I have imagined an incident that was not only untrue but historically impossible,

8

when I had President Kennedy, on the day after his election, act as if he already possessed Presidential powers, whereas in fact a period of some two months elapses before he is so empowered. The same reader suggested an adroit and relatively simple way to resolve this problem. Would he believe me if I told him that I was quite aware of the distortion, that I hesitated a long time about whether I should correct it, and that upon receiving his advice on the matter, I spent many more sleepless nights, tempted by the idea of following his suggestion?

However, I decided against doing so. It was the Devil tempting me. I can give only one reason in support of my guilty obstinacy: that the *effect* produced seems stronger in my own version. I prefer to retain my version and ask the American public's pardon in advance.

A certain number of crimes were thus perpetrated in this book in the interests of the art of narration—a mysterious art that demands much freedom of action, at least as I look upon it. All that remains is for me to add that I did all I could to pay due respect to astronomy. Dr. Kanashima would never have forgiven me for fantasy in this realm.

P. B.

February, 1964

9

CONTENTS

PEENEMÜNDE

Stern made his way into the ruins of a deserted building, de-molished as the result of a series of unfortunate tests, and crept into a sort of alcove formed by the collapsed masonry, knowing full well that this rubble would afford him only the most meager protection in the event of an accident. His gaze settled at once on the rocket that stood less than fifty yards away, illuminated by searchlights, and for a moment he felt completely dazzled.

The familiar landscape of Peenemünde, with its forest of dark pines beginning to take shape in the light of dawn, had faded away. The workshops, the assembly plant, the test bases, the blockhouse, where the end of the countdown was feverishly awaited—these ceased to exist for him. All that remained, in his vision and consciousness, was the black-and-white rocket in the glare of the searchlights, a gigantic and at the same time elegant silhouette whose miraculously slim apex pierced the sky like a church steeple. During his many weeks of work on the de-tails of this unusual missile, engrossed in checking countless fragile parts, the spell of the whole had escaped him. Now, con-founded as though by a supernatural apparition, his nerves stretched to breaking point by the arduous labor of these last months, he was unable to suppress a tremor that shook him from head to foot.

He forced himself to close his eyes and recovered a little composure, shaking off the romantic images that the Peenemünde staff was only too inclined to evoke in connection with rockets: obelisk, church steeple, cathedral spire. Thus it was: nurtured on austere mathematical calculations or immersed in a still more prosaic world of liquid fuels, payloads and horsepower, the Peenemünde staff was romantically minded. But these unduly static comparisons did not satisfy Stern. To him the rocket was power and motion. He saw it at this moment in the form of a fish, a fantastic salmon ready to spring into space in one prodigious leap.

At dawn on this third day of October in the year of our Lord nineteen hundred and forty-two, five minutes before the dispatch of the most important missile that had ever been propelled into space, Dr. Stern was the only person on the launching pad of Peenemünde who had not retired to the shelters. The engineers, the physicists, the countless specialists required to put the new rocket into service, were all in the control center, checking apparatus or watching the image of the missile on a television screen. Others, whose presence was not needed, were also preparing to witness the spectacle but were standing more than half a mile away on the roofs of their living quarters.

Stern was fifty yards from the rocket. This was as he wished; he was disobeying the strict regulations of the base and scorning the most elementary rules of caution. The preceding tests of this model had been failures, and three of these famous salmon had ended their careers ignominiously three feet above the ground, in terrible explosions that had swept the whole launching pad with their deadly remains.

"It must succeed," Stern muttered, clenching his fists. "I have removed the cause of those accidents. It was the defective pump."

It was not only to defy fate but also because he had faith in the success of this bold enterprise—to fire a thirteen-ton rocket with a one-ton payload more than sixty miles—that he was tak-

ing this proud risk, a risk which, if he was not blown to smithereens, would at least earn him a severe reprimand from the
military commander of Peenemünde. Granted, General Schleuder felt particular respect for him, and even real friendship;
but he could not tolerate such lack of discipline and such a bad
example, even on the part of the famous Dr. Stern, the technical director of the base, the most important person, despite his
relative youth, among a distinguished group of scientists and
technicians.

Pride was inherent in his character. Aware of having contributed more than anyone else to the Peenemünde venture, he
had decided to gamble his life on this test, the culmination of
many years of relentless effort, and of prime importance for the
very future of the base. He entertained no illusions, any more
than did General Schleuder: another failure would lead to the
withdrawal of funds—already insufficient—and perhaps even to
the cancellation of big rockets. Peenemünde would be turned
into a base for conventional weapons, as some authorities had
been demanding for some time.

The hour was approaching. Stern looked at his chronometer.
He gave a sudden start and frowned angrily on discovering that
at T minus two minutes he was not alone, as he had thought, in
the ruined building. Absorbed by his vision and his dreams, he
had not noticed a figure crouching in the midst of the rubble,
one whose presence was revealed by the sound of slipping masonry.

His first impulse was to curse at the intruder. That he, Dr.
Stern, should presume to flout discipline—he had his reasons;
but he alone had that right. Moreover, this presence disturbed
his almost religious contemplation. He was about to indulge in
one of the fits of temper that were almost as famous among the
Peenemünde staff as his genius and passion for discovery, when
a head appeared above the pile of rubble and he recognized the

17

straight hair and somber eyes of Nadia, his assistant and right hand.

His anger was cut short. She alone almost always escaped the effects of his bad moods.

"You're mad," he merely said. "If there's an accident . . ."

"There won't be."

"The fuel pump . . ."

"The pump's working perfectly now."

T minus one minute. This was no time for technical discussions. It was even too late for her to get to a shelter. With a gesture he ordered her to lie flat, which she did, though she raised her head above the fragments of concrete, thus exposing her forehead and dark, strangely dilated eyes, which the romantically-minded in Peenemünde described as evoking the immensity of space. He gave a slight shrug and went back to his observation.

T minus ten seconds. Still motionless, the missile was suddenly the center of a tumultuous commotion. A dense cloud issued from the mouth of the nozzle and whirled back off the concrete, while clouds of sparks formed a sort of conflagration reminiscent of the fireworks that are seen on holidays at the bases of some monuments. Stern knew that the first control switch had been tripped. And so, immediately, was the second, for the roar became almost unbearable. The sparks poured forth in a continuous stream of flame, their color changing at every moment. With his flexed arm he went through the motion of tripping the third switch.

This was the critical moment. The rocket shuddered, seemed to hesitate, then began to rise, so slowly that it gave the impression of remaining motionless in the air for a fraction of a second. In one bound, in defiance of all prudence, Stern and Nadia had sprung to their feet. With an unconscious, ludicrous gesture, Stern flexed his arm, as though the contraction of his muscles would add a few precious pounds to the twenty-five-ton thrust required to lift the missile off the ground.

"The pump, the fuel pump! . . ." he cried, as though this fervent prayer had the slightest chance of being heard in the infernal din that made the whole of Peenemünde vibrate.

"It's off!" Nadia yelled.

The rocket was rising. Faster, faster still, it soared upward, followed by a brilliant flame, so that after a few seconds their eyes could distinguish no more than this luminous serpent in the lower, and as yet dark, regions of the atmosphere.

But the rocket itself reappeared a little later, having reached the zone already illuminated by the sun. Then suddenly, as if by magic, it blazed across the sky of Peenemünde while the flame behind it was obliterated by the sunlight.

Scarcely twenty seconds had elapsed since the blast-off. Stern had not for a moment thought of making the slightest scientific observation. It was unimportant; he would see the film that others were taking at this moment. He was too exalted by the sensation of success and could only follow the track of the missile with the spellbound eye of the artist. When he tried to grasp the binoculars hanging from his shoulder, the movement made him cry out. He had exerted such intense energy that his arm was painfully cramped.

"Come on, help me," he said with impatience. "I can't move my arm."

"And I'm trembling all over," Nadia stammered.

Her voice sounded strange. He looked at her and saw that her eyes were brimming with tears. By the time he was able to use his binoculars, the first V-2 rocket was no more than an imperceptible dot in the sky.

19

General Schleuder looked around him impatiently; Stern had not yet deigned to appear at the little party being given to celebrate the morning's success.

What the devil could the man be doing? All the others were here—"My colleagues," he called them with emphasis —the principal cadres of Peenemünde, the mathematicians, physicists, engineers, and heads of the various branches involved in the construction of liquid-fueled rockets. After the crushing toil that had culminated in the triumphant launching they were in urgent need of a rest, and now they gave vent to their high spirits. Schleuder had opened his special store of champagne, and the atmosphere became more and more jovial. Some of these men of science even appeared to have drunk a little more than was good for them. Müller, for one. But Müller always exceeded the bounds of moderation, whether he was working or celebrating a success.

As for Schleuder himself, the morning's triumph had made him years younger. He felt light and happy, as light as the V-2 that had flown off into space. If he had not played a very active part in the operation, he had had the sense to believe from the start in its importance. Above all, he had had the great wisdom of recognizing the possibility of practical achievement amid

20

the visions of a few crackpots, many of whom possessed only the barest scientific background. Unlike many of his colleagues, he had not been dismayed by the fantastic daydreams in which Stern himself sometimes indulged. He had assumed enormous responsibilities that few military men would have taken on. This he knew. He also knew that several leading figures in the Reich, even in the Führer's intimate circle, were jealous of the funds (meager enough, alas!) allocated for such an outlandish weapon and were only waiting for a resounding failure on his part to pay him back.

After the triumph of this October third, the atmosphere was bound to change. No one could deny any longer the strategic importance of big rockets. He would certainly obtain the number one priority that the Führer, badly advised, still refused to grant Peenemünde and without which nothing worthwhile could be done in wartime Germany. The presence among the guests of General von Kratz, Speer's assistant in the Ministry of Arms Production, was most encouraging from this point of view. Having arrived toward noon, Von Kratz had insisted on visiting all the installations and had seemed very favorably impressed.

A slight disappointment, however, had dampened Schleuder's enthusiasm when, still enthralled by the blast-off of the V-2, he had greeted Von Kratz as he stepped off the plane. Von Kratz had waved his arms about excitedly and embraced Schleuder as he exclaimed:

"This is a great day, Schleuder! A great victory!"

"Yes, it certainly is," said the general, beaming.

"The most important event of the war!"

"Well, I wouldn't say that," Schleuder protested, assuming a modest air.

"But don't you realize the entire Russian front is about to collapse! The Wehrmacht is on the outskirts of Stalingrad!"

They were not thinking about the same thing at all! Subsequently, however, Von Kratz had congratulated Schleuder warmly. . . . He was now polishing off the champagne and

21

seemed delighted with everything. Peenemünde would get its number one priority.

Yet that old bear Stern, the star of the day, had not turned up! Had he really been vexed, in his pigheaded way, with the reprimand that he, Schleuder, as the officer responsible for the organization of Peenemünde, had been forced to give him? That crackpot had come bursting like a whirlwind into the shelter, which he should never have left in the first place, and feverishly started questioning various specialists on the results of their observations—yes, it was then that Schleuder had pointed out what a bad example Stern was setting the others. . . . Oh, but in the mildest manner, and interlarding his reproaches with compliments that would have flattered the vanity of anyone else! Schleuder did not forget that today's success was largely due to Stern's work, work that was sometimes unmethodical but always effective, and to his strokes of genius to which everyone invariably deferred.

Stern had not uttered a single word of apology. Yes, he had vaguely mumbled "Sorry," while continuing to jot down figures with an imperious air. Then, helping himself to a handful of the record sheets, he had stalked out, followed by his shadow Nadia. He had only deigned to reappear for an hour in the afternoon to show Speer's assistant around the workshops. . . . That girl Nadia, for instance, she would not get away scot free. In a military base there must be a certain amount of discipline, damn it!

At this point in his reflections General Schleuder could not help smiling. He was well aware, of course, that the Peenemünde mentality was of a very special kind. He was equally aware that he would never make soldiers out of this irregular medly—technicians, engineers of all sorts, university men (young graduates and also students who had not yet taken a degree), and even researchers without any qualifications other than a certain gift for invention and a passion for rockets, who had been recruited by Stern from among his former friends in the Society for Space Travel. These people thought more about the moon than the war. Was not Stern himself a dreamer? However, thanks to him, a thirteen-ton rocket had risen into space.

Schleuder's smile grew more pronounced. He had been careful not to try to make soldiers of them, he reflected. Peenemünde had to preserve this strange mentality that performed such miracles. He felt younger than ever.

Müller walked by, holding a glass that he had just refilled with a slightly shaky hand.

"Do you know where Stern is?" Schleuder asked him.

"I don't know exactly, Herr General, but I can certainly tell you this: he's on the moon, that's where he is, on the moon. Stern is always on the moon, Herr General."

Schleuder shrugged his shoulders. Impossible this evening to get anything out of this whimsical fellow. Müller was another one who would never submit to discipline. Furthermore, he occasionally drank too much. But he, too, sometimes had excellent ideas and was capable of working twenty hours a day for a month at a time on any point that interested him . . . provided he could remain in bed for a week afterward.

General von Kratz was now trying to catch Schleuder's eye. He was no doubt waiting, before he could leave, for the speech that the commandant of Peenemünde was in duty bound to deliver. So much the worse for Stern. Schleuder raised his hand to request silence. His address was manifestly designed to impress the guest of honor and, through his agency, Speer and the Führer.

"It is a happy coincidence," he began, "that this test coincides with the entry of our glorious Wehrmacht into the outskirts of Stalingrad, with the dawn of a great victory. First I wish to salute our armed forces, those forces that all of us here are trying to help to the best of our ability."

23

When General von Kratz gave a nod of approval, Schleuder continued in this vein, stressing the military importance of the V-2.

"This missile can carry an explosive charge weighing one ton. This means that, once it has been perfected and put into mass production, it will provide us with artillery capable of bombarding at a distance and with firepower unknown until today. . . . "

When he wound up his speech with a word of praise for the Führer, who had enabled this research to be carried out at Peenemünde, he was greeted with cheers and Von Kratz shook him warmly by the hand, but he was painfully conscious that his "colleagues" were not entirely satisfied. They were expecting other words, it was plain to see, other words that he, Schleuder, felt a terrible urge to utter. He knew well enough what the V-2 meant to them! He knew their ambitions, their desires. He frequently went so far as to participate in their dreams. But the presence of General von Kratz precluded such digressions.

Von Kratz was preparing to leave. Schleuder accompanied him in his car to the airfield. During the drive, despite all his efforts to direct the conversation to the number one priority, his companion started talking again about Stalingrad and savoring the prospects of this victory. Before his departure, however, he promised his support so that Peenemünde might continue with its research and achieve further successes.

"It's really a very great achievement. . . . Big Bertha in the last war had a range of . . . ?"

"A range of one hundred kilometers, but it could fire only a ten-kilo shell."

"And your rockets?"

"One ton. And Bertha's unwieldiness prevented her from being rapidly moved from place to place. Moreover, mass production was impossible, whereas our V-2's . . ."

"A fine achievement, I maintain," the general concluded as he took his leave. "Don't worry, I'll discuss it in Berlin."

24

" 'A fine achievement'! Really, is that all he could think of saying?" Schleuder muttered to himself, with a trace of melancholy, as soon as he was alone.

Then, abruptly, his mood changed to icy anger at the thought of Stern's inexcusable absence, and he decided to seek him out at once. It would take only a few minutes to reach his quarters. The guests could wait.

The house that his most famous colleague occupied was unlocked. General Schleuder crossed the dark entrance hall, stopped on the threshold of the living room, and glanced inside. The door had been left ajar, allowing some light to filter through. As the fancy struck him, Stern used his living room as an office, a studio, or even as a measurements laboratory for very delicate apparatus.

Schleuder saw three figures who were too engrossed in their work to notice his presence. Stern was pacing up and down, apparently making a speech for the benefit of the other two, stopping now and then in front of a blackboard propped up on an easel to draw a diagram or jot down an equation. Nadia, seated at a drawing board, kept bending over it to add a detail, or turning to make some notes in an exercise book lying open beside her. The third figure confined himself for the time being to listening, but he, too, had a notebook open on his knees. This was Frantz, another strange individual. A simple mechanic, scarcely more than a skilled laborer when he had been first hired at Peenemünde, he had educated himself, begging to be taught and using his spare time for study. Now he possessed the knowledge of a first-rate engineer.

Stern was speaking in the tone of a schoolteacher addressing his pupils:

"One and one-half kilometers per second; that's the speed we reached today. With this type of rocket we'll never do much better than that. . . . Maybe two, maybe even three kilometers per second, by using the latest fuel. That's much too little.

25

We shall thus increase the range to a few hundred kilometers, but our missile will still fall back to earth."

"It needs an initial velocity of five or six kilometers per second to reach America," said Nadia, consulting her notes.

"Yes. But even with that velocity, our rocket will still fall back to earth."

"It will fall on America," Frantz observed.

"That's obvious. So we need a far bigger thrust. As you know. Nearly eight kilometers per second before it can become a satellite of the earth and—"

"And about twelve before it can completely escape the earth's attraction," Frantz continued, in the tone of an industrious pupil who has memorized his lesson.

"The conclusion is," Stern went on, "we need a multiple-stage rocket, three stages at least."

"That's what Tsiolkovsky thought," Nadia remarked.

"But that's not all—and this is where I want your opinion, Frantz. To reach the moon, with a crew, we shall need at blast-off a payload not of one ton but of dozens of tons. I made a small calculation the other day . . . Nadia?"

"You worked it out at about forty tons."

"That certainly won't be enough. Let's say fifty, as a round figure. That means a missile of several thousand tons and over fifty meters high, without a doubt. What do you think, Frantz? With present-day materials, is this just a utopian dream?"

"With present-day materials, I'm afraid so," Frantz replied after thinking the matter over.

"I thought so," said Stern peevishly. "Therefore . . ."

He stopped in front of the blackboard and reflected for a moment in silence.

"Therefore we'll have to find other materials," he said finally. "I'm going to form a research section to work on that problem alone."

At this point General Schleuder could contain himself no longer. He entered the room and began in an icy tone:

"There's only one thing you've forgotten, Dr. Stern . . ."

"I haven't forgotten anything," the scientist protested, without showing the slightest surprise at this intrusion. "I'm fully aware of the difficulties that have to be overcome. All I'm saying is, we've achieved a first step, an important step."

"Toward the moon?" the general asked, forcing himself to maintain his tone of severity but without being able to conceal a touch of affection.

"Listen to me, Herr General, and draw your own conclusions. First of all, we have proved that a rocket of considerable weight can take off and soar into space. Secondly . . ."

From his pocket he produced the record sheets he had purloined that morning.

"Secondly, acceleration has never exceeded five times the earth's attraction, which is perfectly safe for a man. I made some tests on myself. Without any special training, I tolerated six times . . ."

Once again Schleuder realized he would never be able to get really angry with this crazy fellow. He found himself listening to him with interest and indulging in daydreams himself. With an effort he pulled himself together.

"What you've forgotten," he said, "is that there's a war on."

"A war?" Stern echoed with an air of astonishment.

"Do you know what the Führer's main concern is today?"

"The Führer?"

"It's the Battle of Stalingrad," Schleuder yelled, exasperated by his colleague's absent-minded expression. "You're not going to tell me you've never heard of Stalingrad? That you don't know who the Führer is?"

"No, of course not."

"Well, then, you must realize that if we get the number one priority it will be in order to improve our V-2 by increasing the explosive charge—the explosive charge, do you hear?—and not to stuff it full of people like you. It will also be in order to increase its range so that it can reach any part of England and, if necessary, perhaps America as well. But in any case, Dr. Stern, it must fall back to earth, do you understand? It must fall back! What the Führer, the Minister of Arms Production, I, and the whole of Germany want at this moment is rockets that fall back to earth, not rockets that go flying off to the moon!"

Schleuder drove Stern back to the party in his car while the two assistants, looking somewhat sheepish, made their way on foot.

"If I spoke to you like that, Stern," said the general in a calmer tone of voice, "it's in the interests of your work. Himmler already suspects us, I know, of not devoting all our efforts to military ends. If he knew you spent part of your time dreaming about the moon, he'd soon clip your wings. I have to forbid anyone to regard the rocket other than as a weapon of war. Do you understand?"

"I understand," Stern growled. "You're right, Herr General. I'll comply with your orders."

"When on duty, you mean," Schleuder corrected him. "I can't prevent you from indulging in the wildest daydreams during your leisure hours."

The party was in full swing when they arrived. The departure of General von Kratz had been marked by a renewed outburst of high spirits. Stern mingled with the other guests. After a few minutes Schleuder managed to persuade himself that his order was being observed, at least technically. Since the party could not be considered duty, the conversation turned, with ever-increasing enthusiasm, to the conquest of space, satellization, and interplanetary travel. The general heaved a sigh, which transformed itself into a smile. In his heart of hearts this was how he liked to see his "colleagues."

Suddenly he wondered anxiously whether they looked upon him as a silly old fool, a dull-witted military man who was incapable of understanding their passion, still less of sharing it.

After a moment he could contain himself no longer. He requested silence and again took the floor.

"There's one point I omitted before," he said, "about today's exploit, your exploit, *our* exploit."

They all looked at him with curiosity. Müller, who was raising his glass to his lips, stopped dead without finishing the gesture. Schleuder went on, in a voice that grew progressively more animated and finally reached the level of the prevailing excitement.

"We have proved that it is possible to build heavy missiles capable of flying at a high supersonic speed, missiles soaring into space and carrying a substantial payload—a payload that one day, no doubt, will be able to be replaced by a human crew. You all know that this morning's acceleration was never greater than a man can endure."

He was interrupted by a salvo of cheers. This speech was far better understood and appreciated by the staff of Peenemünde than the earlier one. Nadia's big eyes seemed to encourage him to continue along these lines. Müller muttered in a hoarse voice: "The moon, I've always said so, the first step toward the moon. . . ." The general went on with a feeling of mounting exaltation:

"Today marks not only a decisive stage from the technical point of view, but also, and above all, it is a memorable date in the history of mankind. Today, after conquering land, sea, and air, the whole of space is opening up as a practicable route. Today we have triumphantly inaugurated the era of space navigation."

He felt in the mood to pursue this theme for a long time. But he had said enough to unleash a hurricane. His colleagues crowded around him, raising their glasses. He could add no more than a few words, carried away in his turn—he, a level-headed old soldier—by the wind of romanticism that was blowing in gusts over Peenemünde.

29

"The way is open to the moon, then to the planets and perhaps to the stars!" he cried. "I am proud of this exploit. . . ."

The rest was lost in a tumult of cries and applause, while General Schleuder, almost borne shoulder high in triumph by his delirious colleagues, muttered to himself:

"If Himmler could hear me!"

THREE

The conquest of space had been the dream of Stern's boyhood; the moon, the first reasonable material objective he had aimed for. At first he had tried without conviction to gratify his impetuous passions by systematically indulging in every sort of excess. He had done so with a lofty, fierce impatience, as if to show that since providence had decreed he should be born in the shape of a human being, he must behave like all other young men of his class. But the sooner this period was over, the better it would be for the cosmic role he felt called upon to play.

He spent eighteen months sowing his wild oats. Then, at the age of nineteen, he had looked at the bright young things with whom he consorted, as though to say: Is that enough? Are you satisfied? Am I now entitled to lead the life I want? He did not wait for an answer and decided to devote himself henceforth to the pursuit of his dream: the conquest of space.

Yet Stern was not exclusively a dreamer. He was a mixture

of sound common sense and unbridled imagination. If, as sometimes happened, he indulged in fantastic speculations on the distant stars and imagined voyages that would be impossible to undertake for several centuries, he was always brought back to present-day reality by a desire—one as fervent as his romantic aspirations—for practical, tangible, immediate results. It was then that the reasoning facet of his mind turned toward the moon.

Thus it was: To him the moon represented common sense, the specific objective of a lucid, cool, and calculating mind that refuses to be seduced too long by chimeras. Such was his outlook in relation to the scientific conceptions current at the time.

This outlook was manifested as soon as he went to an engineering college. He himself had insisted on this course, despite the disgust of his officer father, who could imagine only an army career for him. As a matter of fact, young Stern realized very soon that he had taken the wrong turn. He was not cut out to be an ordinary engineer. If he was to apply himself to the study of any science or technique, it had to be directed toward an idea, an ideal, a passion—*his* passion. If he was to take an interest in a machine, he had to be supported, upheld, by the thought that this machine could carry him into space. Being taught about the output of boilers, when he was already pondering the payload of an interplanetary rocket! Realizing very quickly the folly of the college curriculum, he no longer attended classes and began secretly taking a course in astronomy at the university. He had decided that a knowledge of the heavenly bodies was an essential preliminary to the conquest of space. Thus he spent a whole year familiarizing himself with the planets and the stars, meditating on the unusual movements of the galaxies, speculating feverishly on the origin and evolution of the universe. Meanwhile his reports from the technical college plummeted. He decided to leave it and quarreled with his father, who found him decidedly too moon-struck.

Almost without resources, freed of every restraint, his better reason asserted itself, forcing him to come down to earth. He must think of some practical means of realizing at least part of his dream, which was tending to remain a dream too long. These means existed. He had always had an inkling that they must exist, and he knew this for certain ever since a quite extraordinary book had fallen into his hands: *Rockets and Space* by Professor Roth. He read it several times and began to study with feverish intensity certain branches of mathematics indispensable to a complete understanding of the work.

When he had penetrated all its mysteries, young Stern did not hesitate. He wrote to Professor Roth, whose book, neglected by the men of science, was discussed primarily in advanced literary circles and had really interested no one except a group of film producers. The professor asked him to come to see him. He was immediately impressed by this young man who spoke of traveling to the moon as though this were feasible in the near future, a young man without a degree who seemed to have assimilated his own calculations and, in certain cases, to have extended them. Roth took him on as his assistant. Stern applied himself to more systematic reading and obtained various university degrees. At the same time he collaborated with Roth on projects for rockets designed to overcome the earth's gravity.

But Roth was essentially a theoretician and took no interest at all in the actual realization of these projects. Stern was made aware of this one day when, having read by chance an article describing a successful test by an American scientist named Clelland, he rushed to his patron and, wild with rage, waved the article under his nose.

"He has launched a rocket propelled by liquid fuel and equipped with a camera!"

"Well, that proves that my projects are not chimerical," Roth calmly replied.

"But don't you see? They are stealing our ideas!"

32

"Clelland has stolen nothing from me."

Roth told Stern that several researchers like Clelland had foreseen the future of rockets. They were mostly individual scientists who were unaware of the details of one another's work and thus came to make the same discoveries on their own. A Russian, Tsiolkovsky, had probably been the forerunner of them all, even before the end of the last century, but his works were not available in German.

Stern's anger abated a little, but his anxiety did not. So there were others following the same track as he was, and some had already reached the experimental stage. He could envision a kind of international association—an idea new to him. Instead of being encouraged by this, he felt nothing but resentment and anguish. He shuddered as he thought of the American industrial potential. Suppose the Americans reached the moon before he did!

He decided to make a thorough investigation into the work being done abroad. In the same way that he had studied mathematics in order to follow Roth's theories, so, within a few weeks, by working night and day, he learned English well enough to be able to read the works of Clelland in the original. He also mastered enough French to understand Esnault Pelleterie. He was about to embark on Russian, so as to tackle Tsiolkovsky's publications, when he met Nadia, who spared him this additional effort.

The daughter of Russian *émigrés* who had settled in Germany, Nadia had left her country at the age of four, but she spoke Russian fluently. Orphaned when still quite young, she earned her living by doing translations and at the same time attended courses in physics at the university. It was there that she met Stern, who introduced her to the small circle of eccentrics interested in space. She was immediately captivated. She and Stern embarked together on a collaboration that was to reach its highest pitch at Peenemünde, where Stern insisted that Nadia be engaged.

Less knowledgeable than Stern, less intelligent, tackling problems with less vigor and less concentration, about certain points she had a kind of scientific intuition on which he sometimes relied. Not always: for the friendly relationship that grew up between them, in which love never played any part—neither of them imagined the possibility of such a sentiment in the other—was sometimes disrupted by bitter discussions and even quarrels reminiscent of lovers' tiffs, when they found themselves disagreeing about some aspect of the nascent science of space, each of them too proud to yield an inch. On several occasions, however, Stern was forced to admit that Nadia was right. Moreover, she was an admirable draftsman and he fell into the habit, at this period, of handing over the almost indecipherable diagrams he scribbled down on bits of paper for her to render into clean copies comprehensible to others besides himself.

When he told her about Tsiolkovsky, she immediately bought all the publications, devoured them in a few days, and undertook to translate them. She was even more fascinated than he was by the work of the elderly scientist, a professor in an obscure college, who as early as 1885 had asserted that *"the heritage of mankind is not the earth but the entire universe,"* * had suggested the use of interplanetary ships propelled by liquid-fueled rockets, had already investigated some extremely precise gyroscopic mechanisms for steering these missiles through the immensity of space, and had even foreseen the installation of relay stations around the planets—all of which were discoveries and projects Stern was in the process of repeating.

---

* The statements in italics placed in the mouths of official characters were actually made. But concern for condensation has obliged the novelist to set them on dates and in circumstances somewhat different from historical reality. The letter and the spirit have been preserved, however.

The work of the Russian scientist became a topic of heated discussion between them. Commenting on certain passages, Nadia derived a strange feeling of pride in her native country. Though hitherto she had hated the Bolsheviks, now she found herself making excuses for them, simply because Lenin had dragged the old scientist from his obscurity and given him official recognition. Stern recognized Tsiolkovsky's worth and felt a sort of anxious jealousy for him, as he did for anyone else who at an earlier date had had the same ideas and aspirations as he. He soon reassured himself, however, convinced as he was that the present regime in Russia was not conducive to great achievements.

"The Slavs are admirable musicians," he would say; "chess players, I don't deny it; sometimes mathematicians of genius, I admit; in other words, theoreticians. They have imagination and intelligence. But they have no practical sense. They will never be reliable technicians, and first-class technicians are also necessary to reach the moon."

"You're just quoting from the encyclopedia," Nadia would reply impatiently. "Technique can be acquired, but not imagination, not genius."

"The most immediate danger . . ."

He did not have to finish the sentence. She was well aware what he considered the number one danger.

"The most immediate danger is certainly from the Americans. They have the technicians and they have the means . . ."

"Have they the genius?"

". . . but I don't think we're running any risk at the moment. Clelland doesn't realize the essentials of the problem. He's not yet aware of all the possibilities inherent in his recent success. He's thinking of sending only a few kilos into space, a camera and some recording apparatus, whereas many, many tons will be necessary."

There was nevertheless a risk from that direction. The age of theoretical speculation was over. Action had to be taken.

35

:

His first step was to create the Society for Space Travel, which came into being through his own efforts and those of the small circle of intellectuals who, like moths to light, had been attracted by the words "conquest of space" and "interplanetary navigation." Stern, who had recently obtained his doctorate, assumed the leadership of these young fanatics, and Nadia, who also possessed several university degrees, made a brilliant second-in-command. The others, most of whom were self-taught, had no particular qualifications.

Of these, Müller was one of the most remarkable. After exclusively literary studies, he had embarked on a writer's career. His first two works, one in verse, the other in prose, having met with equal lack of success, he fancied, at the age of twenty-five, that he heard the call of space. He abruptly changed course and began to study the rudiments of geometry and algebra. He was more interested in these than in his previous occupation and eventually gave up the latter entirely to devote himself to mathematics and the mechanics of astronomy. He applied himself to these with the same zeal and versatility he had given to writing, sometimes working for weeks on end without rest, then stopping halfway through his calculations and taking to his bed for an equal length of time, combating a morose mood with an immoderate consumption of alcohol. In a very short time he became an excellent mathematician, frequently enlivening the Society for Space Travel with his caustic wit and biting sarcasm.

For two years, with pitifully meager financial resources provided by a few wealthy eccentrics, Stern experimented with small-scale rockets—far too small for his taste, alas! With these experiments, however, he succeeded in interesting one or two genuine technicians who, for want of genius and money, contributed their manual dexterity and their practical knowledge of materials—talents painfully lacking in the original members and for which, as Stern realized more clearly every day, enthusiasm alone was no substitute. Frantz was one of these recruits.

He came to the Society out of curiosity. He stayed because he was interested in the work, because of friendship for Stern, and because of his love for Nadia. A series of daring experiments with an alcohol-oxygen combination was brought to a successful conclusion thanks to him.

At the end of two years, however, Stern was in despair. Some extremely bold plans had been mapped out, some promising tests had just been completed, but the funds at his disposal would never enable him to launch more than a child's toy into the air.

It was nevertheless one of these toys that, in 1932, attracted the attention of Major Schleuder, who was already commanding an important branch of Ordnance and who, like all his colleagues, was trying to circumvent a certain clause of the Versailles Treaty limiting the artillery of the Reich. Deeply impressed by Stern's experiments and fascinated by his strange personality, he suggested they work together. Stern did not hesitate for long. The army had little attraction for him, but it afforded him the possibility of taking a great step toward his goal. After all, if the military saw fit to replace the body that he was planning to liberate from the earth's gravity with an explosive charge, this was a mere detail, at any rate so far as the preliminary experiments were concerned. Creative science should be able to take advantage, without remorse, of the substantial sums allocated by destructive folly.

He accepted Schleuder's offer on condition that some of his friends be engaged with him. Thus it was that Nadia, Müller, Frantz, and a few others formed the original nucleus of the military rocket research center that was to be established at Peenemünde a few years later.

FOUR

Three months after the successful test of the first V-2, Peenemünde was still waiting for the necessary funds to pursue
its work but kept encountering hostile skepticism from
both civil and military authorities. All that Schleuder had received was a brief note from the Ministry informing him that a
plan was being drawn up for mass production of the new
rocket. No date had been given and no arrangement had been
made for more extensive research.

Stern roared with anger when he read this note and pitched
into Schleuder so fiercely that the latter decided, one day in
January, 1943, to request an interview with Speer and try to
obtain from him that famous number one priority they felt
they had deserved.

Having flown off the day before in his personal aircraft,
Schleuder did not return at the time he was expected and had
sent no word to explain the delay. This was a bad sign. Stern,
who for weeks had been trying to control his exasperation, felt
unable to work and decided to make a tour of the base in order
to clear his head.

He first visited the recently installed test stand, where the
combustion chambers of the big rockets were tested on the
ground. Frantz was there, surrounded by several workmen,

armed with a monkey wrench, wrestling with a nut and bolt, and swearing about the poor quality of certain materials. The sight distracted Stern and even brought a smile to his lips; these missiles, the last word in technical development and equipped with the most delicate electronic apparatus, comprised a network of metal tubing that sometimes fell apart like ordinary water pipes and necessitated the use of such primitive tools as a monkey wrench.

"This piping is worthless," Frantz groaned. "They've sent us a lot of shoddy stuff again. This isn't metal, it's butter. It melts at the slightest spark."

"I'll have a new alloy worked out," Stern replied absently.

His mind was elsewhere. He was thinking how far they still had to go. Granted, they had progressed since the Society's first fumbling attempts. In that prehistoric age a rocket consisted of a tank of liquid oxygen on one side, a tank of alcohol on the other, and two lengths of piping welded together to feed the combustion chamber. There were no auxiliary installations. Today, at least, everything looked more shipshape. The test stand, for instance, was an imposing edifice. The gas escape trench was nearly thirty feet long, and a forest of pipes of every diameter crisscrossed at the impact point of the burning gases, some acting as cooling agents, others linked to measuring devices. It was with these that Frantz was dealing at the moment.

Stern watched him work with a feeling of affection. It was through Stern that Frantz had acquired his theoretical knowledge and raised himself to the position of engineer—which still did not deter him from tackling a manual job, as he was doing at the moment; but Stern himself had learned a lot from their collaboration. If the conquest of space brought into play the noblest aspects of human genius, such as audacity, imagination, cosmic will, intelligence, and a knowledge of the most abstruse sciences, it also required men who were capable of tickling carburetors, tightening nuts and bolts properly, and assessing at a glance the resistance of a metal plate. Stern had been quick to recognize this, a fact certain members of the Peenemünde staff tended to overlook. Nadia, for instance, placed mind above all, and Müller was apt to disregard the limits imposed on theoretical speculations by matter.

With Frantz, Stern had made a thorough study of mechanics, not the mechanics that regulate the movements of the heavenly bodies but those that enable a machine to "tick." He had mastered this subject in the same spirit as he had mathematics and English, because it was necessary for the realization of his dream: The man who eventually reached the moon would be traveling in a vessel made of earthly materials.

"The general's not back?" Frantz asked, without looking up from his work.

"Not yet."

To him Frantz was teacher, pupil, and friend combined. He was well aware of his present concern.

"Maybe his interview was postponed? The ministers must have a lot on their minds at the moment."

"A lot on their minds? Certainly. But what about us?"

"I was thinking of Stalingrad. They say things aren't going so well out there."

"Stalingrad, of course . . ."

To him Stalingrad was a battle like any other. After hearing in October the report of a decisive victory, he was slightly surprised to find things dragging out much longer, but he could not work up any enthusiasm over this incident.

"Some evil-minded people even say that they're going very badly," said a sarcastic voice above the trench.

Stern raised his head. It was Müller. The tone of the remark irritated him and he was about to reply when he noticed that Müller was not alone. He was accompanied by a person who cut a very strange figure in Peenemünde, a little Japanese with darting eyes. He was the new guest at the base, Dr. Kanashima, a physicist about forty years old, the head of a delegation sent to Germany to study rocket technique and eventually to create a construction center in Japan. General Schleuder had detailed Müller, who spoke English, to show him around all the installations. He greeted Stern with respect.

"What do you think of Peenemünde, Dr. Kanashima?" Stern asked as he climbed out of the trench.

"Absolutely remarkable, Dr. Stern. Absolutely remarkable. I have never before had the opportunity to see such daring achievements."

Stern felt satisfied. During the three days Dr. Kanashima had been here, he had shown that he knew far more about rockets than his attentive pupil attitude led one to believe.

"Do you think you'll be able to create a base like Peenemünde in Japan?"

"We shall try, Dr. Stern, with Germany's help. The visit you are allowing me to make here is extremely instructive. We shall do our best with the means at our disposal, which are more modest than yours."

"Nothing escapes him," Müller remarked in German. "He asks questions I sometimes find difficult to answer."

"You must show him everything. Those are our orders."

"Perhaps the authorities foresee that one day we might be forced to go and install our bases out there ourselves."

Stern again felt annoyed by these bitter remarks. He was about to protest when he heard the sound of an airplane overhead. It was General Schleuder's plane. He excused himself and left them in order to drive to the airport. As he was getting into his car he caught sight of Nadia coming out of one of the laboratories and told her what was on his mind.

"I'm afraid he may have bad news for us," she said. "Stalingrad . . ."

"But that's not the question!" he exclaimed impatiently. "He must have tackled Speer about our number one priority."

"Yes, but this Stalingrad business must be keeping all the

ministers busy. I've been listening in on some foreign broadcasting stations . . . including a Russian one," she added, lowering her voice.

"Well?"

He was about to drive off but stopped to peer at her intently. There was a strange gleam in Nadia's eyes and he felt that she was not subscribing at this moment to the spirit of Peenemünde.

"It seems we've been told a lot of lies for the last three months," she said. "The whole world is talking about the Russian resistance at Stalingrad. They're dying on the spot rather than retreat an inch. For the last three weeks they've been attacking us; successfully, I gather."

He looked at her again. Nadia, with all her reasons for being anti-Bolshevik, seemed to be disturbed by conflicting sentiments. She went on in a low voice, with a curious sort of pride: "No one can conquer Russia."

Then she seemed to regret what she had just said, shook her head, and added: "The unfortunate thing is, our army's in a disastrous situation."

The word "disastrous" was still ringing in Stern's ears when he arrived at the airport and perceived Schleuder's wrinkled brow. The general replied to his question testily: "What do you think? The Führer won't hear of it. He regards us more or less as visionaries and feels that other weapons are far more urgent. When I started pressing the point with Speer, I was put in my place somewhat hastily. 'In view of the situation of our army in Stalingrad,' he said, 'this is hardly the moment to talk about rockets.' As though we were not working for the army!"

"So that our future plans? . . ."

"We'll have to wait and see."

"Wait for what?"

The general looked at him for a moment in silence.

"Wait, perhaps," he finally said, "until the situation is so bad—and that, I believe, is a possibility that can't be discounted—so disastrous that only a miracle can save it. Then . . . then," he added, giving Stern's arm a squeeze, "I'm willing to bet the Führer will think of us."

FIVE

It was not long before General Schleuder's prophecy was realized, and this under grave circumstances that illustrated the paradoxical manner in which the spirit of Peenemünde, so sensitive to the subtle influences of the heavenly bodies and particularly the moon, reacted to the hazards of war.

The Peenemünde spirit made its mark quickly and very emphatically on every individual who joined the base. Whether they were militarists, fanatical Nazis, or secret partisans of a speedy peace and a more humane Germany, after a few weeks spent on this misty Baltic coast almost all of them forgot their former preoccupations, their old resentments and enthusiasms, and, above all, their own points of view.

On this evening of February first, General Schleuder, sitting by himself in a corner of the mess, was reflecting in somewhat morose silence on the compelling power of the Peenemünde spirit. Dr. Kanashima was engaged in a heated discussion with Stern and Müller. Their conversation had nothing to do with what was preoccupying the dedicated German and Japanese patriots at that time, especially that particular evening. Schleuder, who understood English sufficiently to follow the debate, felt vexed by what he heard. Granted, they were not on duty, but all the same! He himself was still utterly dismayed by the speech Hitler had delivered the previous day, a speech announcing for the first time the disaster of Stalingrad where the encircled army seemed—at least to anyone who refused to visualize a shameful capitulation—doomed to total destruction.

"To place a satellite in orbit around the earth," Müller was saying, "is an easy problem. You know that as well as I do, Dr. Kanashima."

"I know it's theoretically possible, Mr. Müller," the scientist replied, with an animation that showed that he, too, was affected by the atmosphere of Peenemünde. "We only need to give our missile a velocity of about eight kilometers a second. But we haven't yet reached that point."

Schleuder noticed that he said "we," as though he were a permanent member of the base.

"It's easy with a three-stage rocket," said Stern.

He recited some equations, then quietly concluded: "I know these figures by heart because yesterday evening I amused myself by going over all the calculations."

". . . While I was listening to the Führer's speech!" Schleuder growled in fury.

"I would not presume to contradict you, Dr. Stern. Since I've been here you've convinced me that this theoretical view can certainly be realized."

"And that is why his country has sent him to Peenemünde!" Schleuder observed as angrily as before.

"It's easy to imagine," Stern continued, "such a satellite launched on a very flat elliptical trajectory and reaching the vicinity of the moon."

"After which," Müller broke in, "all that's needed is a slight impetus, a mere nudge, for the missile to become a satellite of the moon, approaching quite close to its surface."

"Very close, certainly," Stern muttered, deep in thought "But to make an actual landing is a very different matter."

"A very different matter, as you say," Kanashima agreed. "I've often thought of that myself."

"It gives rise to another problem, a problem of some consequence."

At this moment Stern became aware of Schleuder's presence and addressed himself to him.

"A very serious problem, Herr General, one of the most difficult we shall have to solve: the problem of the return."

"The problem of the return," the general echoed peevishly. "The return from where?"

"From the moon, of course."

"Really, at a time like this, all you can think of is not only getting to the moon but also of returning from it!"

He was about to add some bitingly sarcastic remark when an orderly came in to tell him that he was wanted on the telephone by the Ministry of Arms Production.

"More bad news, I'm sure."

He went out shrugging his shoulders and was away for more than a quarter of an hour. When he came back there was such an odd expression on his face that everyone stared at him. His eyes gleamed and his features seemed to brighten, as if from some deep internal satisfaction. Then he pulled himself together and resumed his stern manner, as though he had just been caught committing a misdemeanor.

"So the news isn't so bad, Herr General?" Stern eventually inquired.

"It's appalling. Worse than ever. The Stalingrad army has surrendered with Von Paulus. A hundred thousand men and over twenty generals taken prisoner."

A heavy silence greeted this announcement. But the strange gleam reappeared in General Schleuder's eyes.

"That's not all," he said, gazing at Stern.

"What else?"

45

"The Führer has just decided to grant us the number one priority and all the funds we need."

"What!"

A loud cheer echoed around the mess.

"I forbid any of you to rejoice," Schleuder resumed in a fierce tone that contrasted increasingly with his air of jubilation. "But this is the situation. I'll repeat it: the Führer has given orders for us to intensify our research. He wants more rockets and bigger, more powerful rockets. And he wants them quickly."

"Quickly . . ." muttered Stern, suddenly immersed in thought. "All the time that's been wasted! We still need . . ."

"I tell you he's granting us everything we want and even more. He wishes to see me, to see us, you and me, Stern. It seems he's singing our praises. Everyone around him is talking about Peenemünde. Speer called me up himself to tell me. What do you think of that, now?"

Stern pondered for a moment in silence, while a rustling sound, like muffled applause, filled the mess.

"I think we shall now be able to get down to some serious work, Herr General. Only . . ."

"Only what?"

"This sudden enthusiasm worries me a little. What does it mean?"

Schleuder lowered his voice so that no one but Stern could hear him.

"As you've guessed, it means that the situation is desperate and that they're beginning to think of miracles to save it, just as I said they would. Now, in spite of the criticism to which we've been subjected, we're looked upon rather as magicians. Between you and me, I'm afraid it may be too late, but we must try."

"We'll try, all right," said Stern, whose brain was already seething with fresh plans. "But every member of the staff must be informed of these decisions this very evening. I can assure you it will raise their morale."

An hour later the four thousand technicians in Peenemünde had been notified of the events of the day: the disaster at Stalingrad and the Führer's new attitude toward rockets. Thus it was that a national catastrophe was celebrated by the peculiar Peenemünde spirit with the high enthusiasm usually reserved for great victories.

SIX

The research at Peenemünde received a fresh impetus, this time with the powerful assistance of every branch of industry. But another obstacle, no less perilous than the Führer's previous lack of interest, soon appeared on the path to space: the Führer's desire to proceed too quickly and to fix unreachable goals within too short a time. When, a few months later, he summoned Schleuder and Stern to his headquarters, the former, who was aware of this state of mind from the increasingly insistent telephone calls from the Ministry, gave his colleague some urgent words of advice.

"Above all, don't rub him the wrong way. If you don't agree on any particular point, leave it to me to discuss."

"What are you frightened of, then?"

"I know his attitude toward technicians."

"Technicians!"

"Oh, I know! You're Dr. Stern, a scientist, a pioneer, an artist. I'm an officer and an engineer. But to him, scientists, engineers, generals, and artists are all technicians; it's his favorite word. And to technicians he issues orders—get this into your head—according to his own whims and fancies and without any regard for practical considerations. . . . It's useless to protest. You're rather like him yourself at times. Mind you, this often gets good results. In the case of our tank production, for instance . . ."

"We're not tank manufacturers," Stern grumbled.

"Ten tons is certainly possible, mein Führer. Personally, I think that's the next objective we ought to aim at. I had first thought of an even heavier warhead. But no, the ten-ton stage is indispensable."

"You see? I knew it. You've got to simplify the problems. Ten tons is a nice round number."

Several times Hitler repeated in an undertone, "Ten tons, ten tons," then, turning again to Stern, he asked:

"How long will it take?"

"The theoretical work is already done," Stern replied after a moment's thought. "The working plans . . ."

"I'm not interested in working plans. How long before a practical result? Do you understand? A *result!*"

Here we go, thought Schleuder, who was watching them out of the corner of his eye.

Having reached headquarters in the morning, they had had to wait two hours for the Führer to arrive. When he turned up with his staff, they found him transformed, prematurely aged, emaciated and blotchy-faced. The reversals were taking their toll on his physical appearance. Immediately he had asked to see the documentary material they had brought, including several film strips of launchings. He looked at these for more than half an hour, without making a single comment. At the end of the showing, however, Schleuder noticed that his eyes had recovered their former vivacity. He even looked excited.

It was then he had taken Stern aside to have the working of the V-2 explained to him. Now he was becoming more and more animated as he explained his own point of view.

"A practical result, you understand, Herr Stern. You have done a splendid job of pioneering, a remarkable, most important job. Thanks to you, the principle has now been worked out. All that remains is to apply it. There shouldn't be any particular difficulty in increasing the warhead. How long will it take? That's what I want to know."

"A ten-ton warhead?"

"Ten tons of explosives—I want it to have an annihilating effect."

"Let's say in three years' time, mein Führer, maybe two . . ."

"That's much too long," Hitler exclaimed, changing his tone. "You'll have to proceed much faster."

"I'm sorry, mein Führer, but it's impossible."

The staff officers, obviously expecting an outburst of temper, tried to catch Stern's eye. Hitler's face grew tense, but he managed to control himself. After a moment's hesitation he drew closer to Stern and spoke to him in a persuasive, almost wheedling tone in which there was even a strange note of entreaty.

"I've known about you for some time, Herr Stern. I've admired not only your work but the audacity you have shown. I know you're no ordinary technician. Genius is never to be found among technicians. That's why I'm asking you to do the impossible."

"We'll do our best, mein Führer," Stern replied, remembering Schleuder's advice.

"As I say, I know all about you. I for one am sure that in less than a year this rocket will be perfected and ready for mass production. You must simplify the problems, always simplify. Ten tons, one year, and two thousand rockets a month— that's a clear-cut program."

Stern and Schleuder glanced at each other. Hitler had recov-

49

ered all his former energy. They were conscious of the magnetism of his gaze, which was capable of rendering the wildest dreams plausible. Yet Stern reacted very rapidly, reckoning that it was dangerous to allow him any illusions on this point.

"It's quite out of the question, mein Führer," he said in an authoritative tone. "When I mentioned two or three years, I was thinking of *one* rocket, a prototype."

"What's the good of a prototype?" Hitler suddenly screamed, as though he had reached the limits of his endurance. "Do you think a prototype is going to stop the Allied armies? What can I do with *one* rocket, a prototype that—?"

"That will still be in itself of incalculable interest," Stern broke in, without noticing he was interrupting.

For the last few moments their ideas had ceased to coincide. As generally happened when he started talking about rockets, Stern gradually forgot the other speaker. . . . Ten tons, to him, meant a ten-ton payload, a load of scientific apparatus that was essential for preparing the flight of a human crew. Why did he need two thousand rockets for that?

". . . of incalculable interest, mein Führer. Think of all the information we lack on the higher atmosphere and that we must obtain before we can send off—"

Schleuder broke in abruptly, but in an equally firm tone.

"—before we can tell if such an explosive charge can be aimed with any accuracy at an objective. One and even several prototypes are necessary for this project, mein Führer. With all the good will in the world we can't see mass production of these missiles for another four years. Besides, at the moment we haven't enough alcohol to make them work."

An uneasy silence followed. All the members of the staff had lowered their eyes. Hitler's face had become purple. He clenched his fists. Yet for the time being, the storm did not break. He took several deep breaths and seemed to subside into himself. In a hoarse voice he kept repeating: "Four years! Four years!"

50

"Is that your opinion too, Herr Stern?" he finally asked in an almost imploring tone. "Four years?"

"That's my opinion, mein Führer. So we shall have to hurry. We've already wasted too much time, unfortunately!"

"That's true," Hitler echoed in a low voice. "We've wasted too much time."

After the Führer had asked for a particularly impressive section of one of the films to be shown again, they took their leave, having been promised increased assistance for the construction and mass production of V-2's and also for intensified research into more powerful rockets, without any definite date being fixed.

"What did you think of him?" General Schleuder asked when they were once more in their plane.

"He's very understanding."

This adjective, applied to Hitler, seemed so wildly off the mark that Schleuder looked at his colleague with a kind of admiration. Stern still had no idea, it was plain to see, that an explosion of hysterical rage had only just been averted. He went on in the same ingenuous tone:

"I'm sorry you prevented me from telling him in detail all our projects for the future."

They landed at Peenemünde in the middle of the night. No sooner had they entered the airport buildings than the sirens started shrieking. General Schleuder was not unduly worried. This was not the first time the alarm had sounded, but the installations had never been attacked. Yet after only a few minutes they heard the sound of bombs falling on the base and all the antiaircraft batteries opening fire at the same time, while the searchlights swept the sky. Tonight the target was Peenemünde.

Stern's first reaction was a fit of temper. Just as he was hoping to forge ahead at last, here was this stupid raid that was likely to cause further delays! The Reich was decidedly not a favorable spot for the conquest of space.

51

A few isolated bombs fell fairly close, but the airport was not the target. It was definitely the base. From where they stood it looked as though it were going up in flames, especially the living quarters.

"They seem to be purposely aiming at the staff," Schleuder observed anxiously. He was thinking of his colleagues.

This was partly true. Acting on sound information, the Allies regarded the scientists' quarters as a target just as important as the workshops and factories. They knew that certain brains cannot be replaced. Stern at this moment had the feeling that he himself was the main objective of the raid, and he glowed with pride.

Forced to take cover again and again, it was nearly an hour before they got back to the base, where a number of fires were raging. The fire brigade and defense personnel were completely overwhelmed. The main part of the raid was now over, and Schleuder collected some of the staff who were emerging from the trenches and asked each of them to lend a hand.

"I'm going to the engine room," he said to Stern. "You see to the assembly plant. Those are the most severely threatened points."

Stern took command of a group of men and headed for the workshops. He was about to go inside when he suddenly stopped in an agony of uncertainty. He had just thought of his personal documents. He had spent the preceding months working on a mass of calculations, investigations, and results of partial experiments in connection with the missiles of the future: a considerable undertaking, accomplished in secret. A few days earlier he had given his files to Nadia, who was to classify them, make a fair copy, and redraft the diagrams. The whole lot was at her house, in a sector that had suffered severe damage and where the worst fires were raging.

He hesitated only a second. The V-2 assembly plant was not the most valuable property. It was his projects for the future, the basis for the conquest of space, that had to be saved at all cost if there was still time. He gave some hasty instructions to a foreman and rushed off to the living quarters.

The flames cast a bright light over this sector. Nadia's house was on fire. The extinguisher he had got hold of was pitifully inadequate. In any case he could not make it work. He threw it away in fury, approached as close as he could, and caught sight of Nadia, disheveled and out of breath, as she emerged from the garden. She was followed by two men, Frantz and Dr. Kanashima. All three of them were loaded with bulging briefcases.

"Everything's saved!" she cried. "There's not a sheet missing."

As soon as the raid started, instead of taking cover in a shelter, she had begun gathering up the papers scattered all over the room. The house was ablaze and she had not yet finished when Frantz, feeling anxious about her, had arrived with the Japanese scientist, who was trying to make himself useful. Frantz wanted to drag Nadia off at once, but he soon realized she would never forgive him for the loss of even one of the documents. The three of them packed up the papers in no time and escaped from the house just as the staircase collapsed.

After thanking them profusely, Stern turned to Dr. Kanashima.

"You couldn't have done me a greater service. These papers are the most precious thing I possess. Years of work."

"That's what I understood from this lady's anxiety. I'm exceedingly happy to have been of use to you, Dr. Stern, and I'm certain of having served the cause of science today."

"Dr. Kanashima," Stern said suddenly, still under the effects of emotion, "I've never shown these papers to anyone, except Nadia. If you think they'd interest you, I'd be glad to let you take a look at them."

This was the greatest evidence of gratitude he could have shown. Dr. Kanashima gave a deep bow and showered him with thanks.

After a sleepless night and a day spent in putting things in order, Schleuder's colleagues assembled in the mess, which was still habitable. Stern had just spent several hours circling over the base in a small plane.

"The damage doesn't seem to be as bad as we thought," he said. "Some of the bombs fell into the sea. Yet they went about it in a big way! Over six hundred aircraft and about fifteen thousand tons of bombs, according to the intelligence report."

"That's just like the Americans," Nadia observed scornfully, "to send wave after wave of aircraft and drop thousands of bombs at random in the hope that ten percent will find their target."

"But what a wealth of materials!" Stern retorted, suddenly immersed in thought. "For every fifty planes brought down— that's the estimated figure of their losses last night—they build five hundred more. For every thousand bombs wasted, their factories can produce ten thousand in a few weeks or a few days."

"It seems it will not even take them two years to rebuild their Pacific fleet," Dr. Kanashima blurted out in a rather strange voice, as though he had not meant to speak.

"But a single kamikaze pilot can knock out their biggest battleship," Nadia replied.

Dr. Kanashima drew himself up.

"That's absolutely true and I'm grateful to you for pointing it out, dear lady; our pilots have heroism, just as you have genius. Only . . ."

"Only," Müller broke in, "it's one hero against one battleship. The second is more quickly replaced in America than the first in any country in the world."

"Yes, even in Japan!" said Dr. Kanashima with a sigh.

"If they took it into their heads to manufacture space vehicles," Stern muttered, as though talking to himself, "their technicians wouldn't have to go begging for funds or scraping the bottom of the barrel to find the necessary alcohol and metal. They wouldn't be reduced to pinning all their hopes on a single prototype. They'd produce twenty, a hundred. They could move ten times more quickly than we can."

"We must console ourselves with what we have," Müller's sarcastic voice broke in again. "We have genius."

Stern shrugged his shoulders and did not reply. He felt submerged by a wave of pessimism. Although not irreparable, the damage was going to cause further delays. Besides, this raid would no doubt be followed by any number of others. How could one, under such conditions, bring to a successful conclusion an enterprise that demanded peace and quiet for the research involved, and almost unlimited means for its ultimate execution? Already many materials were becoming scarce. With his nerves broken by fatigue and lack of sleep, Stern gave vent to an outburst of sheer despair.

"We'll never achieve anything, we'll never get anything done in this country!" he cried. "Oh, if only I could get my hands on half of America's industrial potential!"

SEVEN

At the beginning of 1944, Stern, who would have liked to devote himself entirely to the study of new missiles, was obliged to come back to the V-2, which was not functioning properly. In fact, scarcely ten or twenty percent of the trial shots were reaching their selected targets. Mass production, which was about to begin, would no doubt yield even worse results. The Minister of Arms Production became sharp-tongued, and Schleuder grew more and more morose. Suspecting his technical director of neglecting the present in order to prepare for the future, the general had no alternative but to take him to task after a particularly bad series.

"If this is the situation, it means our opponents are right. The rocket is not a weapon that can be relied upon. The funds we have been allocated are sheer waste. I shall be disgraced, and so will you, if you can't remedy these faults. We have launched ourselves into an enterprise beyond our capabilities and all that remains is for us to resign."

Stern accepted the reprimand because he did not have a clear conscience. It was true: for some time he had lost all interest in the V-2. Schleuder's outspokenness was deliberate. He knew his eminent colleague extremely well: given the choice of discovering the cause of the breakdowns or seeing his reputation tarnished, Stern would probably find a solution to this agonizing problem that made the best technicians in Peenemünde turn pale.

The breakdowns usually occurred when the rocket had traveled some thousands of yards. The motor would then cough and finally stop completely and the missile would come hurtling down, sometimes exploding even before touching the ground, showering fragments over land and sea. Over the shapeless remains, which were sometimes minute and almost always burned to a cinder, Stern would linger for days and nights on end, struggling to pierce the disturbing mystery. He made countless checks, dismantled hundreds of components. He was no more fortunate than his other colleagues. He found no defect.

"Yet I'm sure we've left nothing to chance," Nadia said to him, after they had both spent a whole week going over a single part of the electrical equipment.

"Chance, chance . . ." he muttered.

The word was a ray of light. When chance can no longer be blamed, the possibility of deliberate interference must be considered. Suddenly he felt it was almost certainly a question of sabotage, and determined to pursue his investigations along these lines.

Most of the V-2's were then assembled in the Peenemünde factory, since the other bases scattered throughout the Reich were not yet in operation. The task was accomplished not only by German workmen but also by foreigners, deportees of every nationality. Everyone who had any kind of qualification had been posted to secret weapons, Hitler's last hope. A fairly thorough watch was maintained by the base guards and also by agents of the Gestapo, which was increasingly concerned with Peenemünde. But the guards were mostly ignorant oafs, and the agents incapable of detecting any foul play. Schleuder had regular checks carried out by his engineers, but there were too few of them and they could not be everywhere at once.

Stern decided to keep a personal watch on the assembly plant and, guided by a kind of instinct, made a special point of following the various stages of a delicate electrical device that controlled the opening and shutting of a particular valve. At the end of a few days he discovered the cause of the breakdowns and, at the same time, the man responsible for them. He was a Russian, a former physics student and a deportee, whose papers, however, showed that he had always worked conscientiously for the Reich. He enjoyed a certain amount of trust and his job was to check some parts before passing them on to the assembly gang.

One day, when Stern and Nadia unexpectedly entered the workshop where the man was working alone, Stern noticed him trying to conceal a small bottle. He snatched it out of his hands and sniffed the contents. It was a violent acid. In front of the Russian stood a part of the mechanism, which included a very fine metal wire, immersed in some liquid. Into it a strong dose of the acid had been poured. It was a clear-cut case of sabotage: after a few hours the affected wire would no longer function. The valve would cease to work. The pressure would no longer be controlled in the tank, and the engine would stop and sometimes explode.

Caught red-handed, the deportee made no attempt to deny the crime but, grabbing the mechanism Stern was examining, flung it down on the floor and crushed it underfoot. Then he drew himself up with an air of defiance, uttering a few incoherent words in Russian.

"He says, 'That's one more that won't do any harm,' " Nadia explained.

Stern was torn between relief at having at last solved the riddle that had haunted him every night, and fury at seeing his work so stupidly sabotaged. His first reaction was to fling himself on the deportee and vent his rage; his second was to summon the guard. He was impressed, however, by the Russian's proud attitude. He remained undecided for a moment and the man spoke again to Nadia.

"What's he saying?"

"He's calling me a bitch," she calmly replied, "and other unmentionable names. He says he'll die proud and happy."

"He'll die?"

"You don't imagine Himmler treats this sort of thing lightly, do you?"

The man understood German and spoke it fairly fluently. He said, "There was a case of sabotage in the factory where I worked before I came here. Four Frenchmen. They were tortured for several hours, then strung up on the factory gates where their bodies were displayed for two days."

"It's not possible," Stern muttered.

"It's true, all right," Nadia said through clenched teeth.

"There was a similar case in Peenemünde itself. He's in for it
. . . if you hand him over to the Gestapo," she added, looking him straight in the eye.

Stern withstood her gaze and appeared to hesitate.

"What's your name?" he asked the man in an uncertain tone of voice.

"Nicholas Berchkoff."

"What was your job before the war?"

The Russian burst out laughing. "The same as yours, Herr Stern, and I'd still be doing it if it wasn't for your hirelings who hauled me off to Germany. I, too, used to amuse myself by experimenting with rockets. I even dreamed of missiles far bigger than yours—but it wasn't my intention to cram them with explosives. I must admit, though, that we haven't yet achieved anything like your V-2. Allow me to congratulate you. It's a subject in which we Russians are extremely interested. But I don't suppose you know anything about Tsiolkovsky."

"On the contrary," Stern retorted testily, "I've read everything he's written and admire him enormously."

He had completely forgotten the circumstances of this conversation and was all ready to embark on a scientific discussion.

"I translated it into German," said Nadia, who seemed anxious to justify herself in the Russian's eyes.

Stern made an effort to come back to reality. "Why did you do this?" he asked uneasily.

Berchkoff smiled but did not reply. Nadia darted another strange glance at her colleague.

"Dr. Stern, you sometimes forget that we're at war and our missiles can cause the enemy untold damage."

Stern shrugged his shoulders and gloomily remarked, "If it's a question of duty, mine is to hand you over to the Gestapo."

"I never said anything to the contrary," Berchkoff replied haughtily.

At this moment the door was pushed open and a guard marched into the workshop. He was followed by the head of the security service, who was aware of the investigation on which the technical director of Peenemünde was engaged.

"May I ask if you have found anything suspicious, Dr. Stern?"

Stern tried in vain to catch Berchkoff's eye, but the Russian seemed quite unmoved and was bending down to pick up the pieces of the broken mechanism. Nadia's gaze, on the contrary, was fixed on him relentlessly. Never had he found it so penetrating.

"No, there's nothing suspicious," he said slowly. "The work seems to be proceeding correctly."

He gave the same reply, but with a slight qualification, to General Schleuder a little later.

"Nothing suspicious. But . . ."

"But what?"

"I'm convinced the breakdowns come from that electrical device. It's so delicate that it shouldn't be entrusted to a deportee. We ought to have our own specialists on the job."

"All right. I'll give orders to that effect. But have you found any definite sign of sabotage?"

"No, only a general incompetence that might explain the breakdowns. Just take the precautions I suggest. This isn't within Himmler's province; I was wrong."

Schleuder glanced at him sharply.

"Really? You feel, in all conscience, that these precautions will be enough to eliminate the breakdowns?"

"I'll take an oath on it, Herr General," Stern replied with sudden vehemence. "You entrusted me with the task of correcting the present defects, didn't you? Well, there's the remedy. You can't ask for more than that, can you?"

"No, I can't ask for more than that," Schleuder admitted after a fresh silence and another curious glance.

EIGHT

The two Gestapo officials who called on him early one morning in March behaved with the utmost courtesy. They addressed him as "Herr Doktor" but requested him firmly to follow them.

"May I ask what I'm wanted for?" Stern inquired arrogantly.

"That's not for me to say, Herr Doktor. You'll find out when you get to Berlin."

"Berlin? But I'm working on some tests at the moment."

"I'm not in a position to discuss that point either, Herr Doktor."

"May I at least leave some instructions for my assistant?"

"We have orders to bring Fraülein Nadia with us as well, and also a certain Frantz."

This did not sound too healthy. Stern's anger was tinged with genuine anxiety. For some time Himmler had been taking a keen interest in Peenemünde. He had come and inspected the base himself, and the network of agents he had posted there seemed to multiply. Had his forbearance toward the Russian saboteur been discovered? If so, Stern knew he was lost. This would also explain Nadia's arrest, since she had maintained a guilty silence. But why Frantz?

There was no discussing the matter. It was clear that the two officials would carry out their mission to the letter. They had chosen their day carefully: General Schleuder was away from Peenemünde for a week. Had he been present, he would certainly have objected and notified the military authorities. In theory, the security of Peenemünde depended on the Abwehr and not on the Gestapo, but Himmler was growing so powerful that he could afford to overlook such niceties.

Torn between rage and anxiety, Stern packed his bag and followed the two men without another word. They seated him in their own car. Nadia and Frantz were driven off in another vehicle.

"So you're the famous Dr. Stern."

These words were uttered in a jaunty voice by the man into whose office he had just been ushered.

He haughtily replied that this was undeniably so and immediately protested his arrest.

"You're not under arrest . . . for the moment. We just want to ask you a few questions. Himmler's orders."

"I'll only answer to Himmler himself. I don't see him perfecting the V-2! Every hour I spend here is a waste of time and tantamount to an act of sabotage."

He had decided to attack vigorously, reckoning that his fate was sealed in any case if the Gestapo had proof of his behavior.

His outburst seemed to make a momentary impression on the cold-eyed official interrogating him. But the man was not put out of countenance for long. He peered at Stern for a moment and continued in a dry voice:

"It's precisely a sort of sabotage we're investigating, Dr. Stern."

"Here it comes," Stern thought. But he maintained his haughty manner.

"Would you be good enough to explain?"

The official took a file out of a drawer, opened it with deliberate slowness, and started to peruse it.

"A few weeks ago, Dr. Stern, you had a discussion with an officer in the artillery. This officer pointed out to you that the detonator of the V-2 could be improved so as to increase the blast effect of the explosive charge. You replied—it seems you were rather overwrought; 'exasperated,' I see, is the word used here—you replied: 'What interests me is not the destructive effect but how to free a rocket from the earth's attraction.' "

"I said that?" Stern asked in genuine amazement.

"There's no doubt about it. The report is explicit."

"Well, it's true. I don't know a thing about explosives. The army has specialists for that."

"I don't think such a lack of interest on your part can be much of an example to your subordinates. But those aren't the only . . . shall we say, imprudent . . . words attributed to you. A long time before, shortly after the first successful launching of the V-2, one night in the mess you said: 'This is nothing compared to the achievements that should now be our main concern, and first and foremost of these is the interplanetary rocket.' "

"Well?"

"Dr. Stern, are you asking me to believe that a man with a mind like yours does not realize that the *main concern* of every patriotic German at the present time must be the annihilation of the enemy and not the interplanetary rocket? And this is what justifies our fears with regard to your influence. Your assistant, Nadia, then clinked glasses with you and exclaimed: 'The success of the V-2 is an initial step toward the moon, Herr Doktor!' What have you got to say about that?"

"But it *is* an initial step toward the moon," Stern screamed, exasperated to the point of recklessness.

The official peered at him for a moment with his cold eyes, then went on:

"Whereupon Frantz, another of your close co-workers, added: 'One day you'll travel to the moon, Dr. Stern, and then'—it seems to have been a jovial evening—'then you'll have to take me with you, because without me you wouldn't be able to start the engine up again.' "

"And that's why you've arrested him as well!"

"Only interrogated him, for the moment, just as you're being interrogated, Dr. Stern. There are other documents here, all of which point to the same conclusion. Perhaps you now understand the attitude for which you're being called to account and which seems to be spreading in Peenemünde?"

"And . . . is that all?"

"It's quite enough as it is. It is my duty to ask you whether you admit to having uttered those words and, if so, what explanation you have to give."

The following week, upon his return to Peenemünde, General Schleuder learned of the arrest of his most valuable colleague by the civil police. He burst into a temper that prompted him to take an audacious step. Refusing to discuss the matter with subordinates, accusing the authorities of sabotaging his work, demanding to be locked up himself, he raised such a furor that he got what he chiefly wanted: an interview with Himmler.

The interview was anything but cordial. Schleuder started by repeating his request to be arrested himself, an arrogant demand that scarcely endeared him to the head of the Gestapo. The latter consented, however, to disclose the charges. The general then did his best to justify his colleagues, pleading that the choice of the moon as an ultimate target was a necessary stimulant to the special Peenemünde turn of mind. Seeing that Himmler was unmoved by these arguments, he decided to change his tone and risk his all.

"Reichsführer, it remains for me to say this: If you release Stern and the others immediately, I give you my word that within three months the V-2 will be successfully put into operation on the front, at the rate of four or five hundred missiles a month. If you persist in depriving me of my indispensable co-workers, the project will be a complete failure and our rockets will never reach England."

Himmler gave an unnerving little whistle as he peered over his rimless glasses. No one dared speak to him in such a tone.

"This is blackmail, Herr General."

"Maybe. But that's what the situation is today."

Himmler hesitated. He was interrupted in his reflections by his secretary, who came in with the secret bulletin of the latest news. He studied the text for a moment. Trained to pick out the essentials of a report at a glance, he passed rapidly over the facts he already knew: in Italy an Allied offensive was being prepared south of Rome. The Russians were likewise attacking on the Eastern front. The last piece of information held his attention: increasingly numerous signs pointed to an imminent landing in France, one likely to take place within two or three months.

He raised his head with a preoccupied air.

"You say your V-2's could start bombing England in three months' time if I release Stern?"

"Stern and the two others. I give you my word of honor as an officer."

"Three months is too long," Himmler replied curtly. "I'll give you two."

"We'll try, but I can't promise you anything."

"Let's say two and a half months, then. I also want your great specialist's word of honor."

"Ask him for it."

Himmler issued some orders to his secretary and again buried himself in the report while Schleuder observed him in silence. A quarter of an hour later Stern was ushered into the office.

"General Schleuder is vouching for your loyalty, Dr. Stern. He also asserts that you're the only man who can definitely get these damned V-2's working in the shortest possible time."

"If General Schleuder says so, it must be true."

"Can you promise me that the bombardment of England will begin in two and a half months' time? General Schleuder has given me his word of honor."

"I gave it for three months," Schleuder corrected him.

Stern thought the matter over for a few seconds, after exchanging a glance with the general.

"I give my word for two and a half months—plus the eight days I've just spent here to no purpose."

"Plus the few hours this discussion might last," Schleuder chipped in, determined to make no concession.

"Get going, then!" bellowed the head of the Gestapo, allowing his exasperation to get the better of him, perhaps for the first time in his life. "Get going at once! I suppose you're also going to ask me to put my private plane at your disposal!"

"Reichsführer, that would certainly save time," said Schleuder with dignity.

"All things considered," Stern remarked in the Gestapo plane that was flying them back to Peenemünde, "I think these eight days' rest have been beneficial. There's nothing like solitude and enforced inactivity for facilitating concentration and affording an overall view of a problem."

"Really!" the general muttered peevishly.

"Really. The problem of the return, for instance."

"The return from where?"

"The moon. I've been thinking about it in peace and quiet, which I have not had the leisure to do for some time. I've come to the conclusion that it's difficult, much more difficult than I first thought, but certainly not insoluble. Only it would need a gigantic rocket, a much heavier one than any of the missiles we've thought of so far. It's obvious: it will have to carry all the necessary instruments for a launching from the moon's surface . . ."

"From the moon's surface?" Schleuder echoed in a tone that augured no good.

"Yes, the moon's surface. This means a far greater payload than the forty tons I mentioned at the first estimate. The whole project will have to be mapped out all over again. I've started on the calculations. Unfortunately they were seized by the Gestapo. It doesn't matter . . ."

"I've got those calculations of yours."

"What?"

"Himmler handed them over to me with a smirk filled with hidden meaning. You may be sure there's now a copy in your file. . . . Yes, I've got them but I'm not going to give them back to you on any condition. Do you hear, Dr. Stern?" the general added in an icy tone of voice. "I'm going to keep them in my safe."

"It doesn't matter," Stern blithely replied. "I can easily do them again."

Then, without transition, General Schleuder burst into a frightful rage. During the last fifteen minutes of the flight he unleashed a torrent of abuse on his colleague's head, threatening to take him back to the Gestapo himself if he continued to let his mind wander like this. He did not recover his composure until just before the landing. He had barely enough breath left to ask Stern for his solemn oath not to concern himself with the moon until the end of the war.

NINE

The promise made to Himmler was kept. On the agreed date the V-2's began to fall on England, but it was too late to prevent the Allied landing. Shortly afterward the enemy captured the nearest bases on the coast. Peenemünde was bombarded without respite. Other test bases, other factories were built farther to the east. One after another, these installations had to be abandoned as a result of the Russian advance, and the materiel brought farther back toward the interior as the unconquered regions of Germany gradually lessened. Schleuder, Stern, and a few others were kept traveling all over the Reich in search of safer spots in which to set up fresh installations, harassed by Hitler, Himmler, and the Nazi High Command, who had pinned their last hope on the secret weapon.

They succeeded for a time in maintaining a precarious production, under exhausting working conditions. But for the last month all hope had been lost. On March 27, 1945, the last V-2 had been hurled into space. There was now no factory or suitable base left.

"I kept my word," Stern said to Schleuder. "I concentrated exclusively on the V-2's as long as the war lasted. Today the war is over for us."

"You seem almost pleased about it," the general growled.

"I know," Stern muttered pensively after a moment's silence. "It's a disaster for Germany."

"A catastrophe."

"As a German, as a patriot, I'm extremely upset."

"Upset? Is that all?"

"In despair, if you like, only . . ."

"Only you believe you'll soon be able to get on with your work in peace."

"That has something to do with it," Stern admitted.

"But not in Germany. We shall never again be allowed to build rockets here."

"Not in Germany, I know," Stern agreed, in the tone of voice he might have used to say, "What wonderful weather we're having!"

"That doesn't mean anything to you?"

"Does it to you?"

Schleuder did not reply. He was ashamed to admit that he did not feel the horror a German general should feel under the circumstances. There were two reasons for this: in the first place, utterly exhausted, with his mind a complete blank, he longed for rest at all costs. Secondly, since he, too, had been gradually steeped in the Peenemünde spirit, he could not help thinking of the fresh prospects that the end of hostilities would open up for the space pioneers.

By this time they had moved, with a fairly large group of specialists, to Bad Sachsa, in Thuringia, south of the Harz Mountains. They were now at loose ends and Schleuder had no objections to the plan his colleague had in mind to return to Peenemünde, recover the personal documents he had left there, and see Nadia, who had stayed behind at the base with a few others.

Peenemünde was under Russian artillery fire and threatened from the west by the British, who were advancing through

69

Holland. Stern managed to persuade a pilot, a friend of his and something of a daredevil, to fly him there.

"The Russians can take the base as soon as they like," he told Nadia. "In two days perhaps. In any case they'll be here before the British."

"That's certain."

"So you mustn't stay."

Nadia gave a little laugh.

"So you feel it's better to be captured by the British than by the Russians?"

"It seems obvious to me. Don't you agree?"

She gazed at him with the strangely tender expression that she sometimes assumed when confronted with his simplicity.

"Do you really think, Dr. Stern, that we specialists in the so-called V-2 weapon would be better off if captured by the British?"

He shrugged his shoulders, suddenly realizing the implication that had never crossed his mind before.

It had been a dangerous flight. The plane had barely escaped the Russian antiaircraft guns and, after landing, had had to pick its way through bomb craters. Nadia and the faithful Frantz had come to meet him. A few members of the old staff were still there, but most of them, including Müller, had left Peenemünde. Stern had immediately inquired about his precious documents. They were intact. Furthermore, Nadia had made a complete copy of them that she had buried in a metal box. He then suggested taking her back with him. There was only one free seat in the airplane, but Frantz might still be able to join them by car.

"Take me back where?"

"To Bad Sachsa, for the time being. Schleuder is there, with about a hundred of our colleagues."

"What would I do there?"

"Now look, Nadia, you listen to the foreign broadcasts. You know perfectly well that it's all over, despite Goebbels' speeches. Berlin is surrounded. It's a question of a few weeks, perhaps a few days."

"I know."

"Well, then, there's nothing more for you to do here. People like us can think only of the future."

"I am thinking of the future."

"The future, for us, is the conquest of space. The work accomplished at Peenemünde will be a fresh starting point. We've got to pursue our task in peace and with more substantial means."

"And for that you're obviously counting on the Americans? All you can think of is being taken prisoner by them?"

"I don't deny it. Staying here means falling into the hands of the Russians."

"I know," she repeated impatiently.

"And so?"

"And so I'm staying."

He flung his arms into the air, dumfounded by this decision.

"Nadia, don't you want to get to the moon any more?"

"Of course I do," Nadia replied.

He was more and more disconcerted and paused uncertainly for a moment, trying to ferret out her thoughts. She went on insistently:

"Do you imagine I haven't thought it all out during the weeks I've been here with nothing to do? I've listened to all the broadcasts, Russian as well as American. I've reread Tsiolkovsky. I've reread Clelland. Oh, I can assure you, I've given it a great deal of thought . . . and I'm staying."

Frantz, who was listening to the conversation, sprang to his feet in fury.

"It's her idea, and you won't make her change her mind. I've tried everything. She's as stubborn as a mule."

Yet Nadia's attitude had given Stern cause for thought.

"I certainly don't despise the Russian industrial potential, but . . ."

"They rape women," Frantz interjected in a dull voice.

"I wasn't thinking of that," said Stern, in a tone that showed he had indeed given no thought to such details.

"They may rape women, but they don't rape physicists," Nadia exclaimed impatiently. "Besides, what does it matter?"

"I meant that the Russian industrial potential can't be compared—and won't for many years—with the American."

"I know. But industrial potential alone is not enough to get you to the moon. . . . Yes, you'll be contributing your genius, I know that too, but even that's not enough. There must be the proper spirit. The Americans will send rockets into space as soon as it becomes a paying proposition or to improve their well-being."

"And you think the Russians . . . ?"

"They have proper spirit," she said with pride. "They're artists and gamblers."

She seemed to be lost in a mood of nostalgia. Stern realized he would never be able to convince her, but he continued to try, pointing out the additional risk she ran as the daughter of *émigrés*. She brushed aside all his objections with the same argument.

"They won't harm a rocket specialist."

He could not take her away by force. A mere glance at Frantz told him that Frantz would stay with her, despite his disapproval. Stern decided to go back alone. Each moment that passed made the take-off more perilous.

They opened a bottle of brandy and drank a last toast together. Stern embraced his two assistants with emotion and climbed into the airplane. His last sight of Peenemünde was Nadia waving a handkerchief. He sank back into his seat, clutching the precious documents he was taking away. He had not had time to check them, but with Nadia he could set his mind at rest. There would be nothing missing. He thought for a moment of the copy she had made, which was bound to fall into the hands of the Soviets. This vexed him slightly, but not for long.

"She's wrong," he muttered. "I've always said so. They're dreamers, sometimes even theoreticians of genius. But they're not practical-minded. That's what I need now," he went on, clenching his fists as the plane zigzagged to avoid the anti-aircraft shells. "Practical-minded men, men of action, an army of able technicians, a huge industrial potential, and millions of dollars."

T E N

Back at Bad Sachsa he found General Schleuder at grips with a Gestapo official. A truck filled with police agents was parked outside their quarters.

"You've arrived at the right moment," said Schleuder. "These gentlemen want us to go traveling again."

"Himmler's orders, Herr General," said the official. "All the Peenemünde staff are to move to the Bavarian Alps."

"Is Himmler now governing the Reich?"

The official lowered his voice and continued, but without the slightest arrogance.

"Herr General, believe me, it's in everyone's interests. The Russians won't get down there."

Schleuder conferred for a moment with Stern, who gave him the latest news from the north.

"I suppose Himmler wants to arrange for our surrender to the Americans. After all, it's probably the only way in which we can still serve Germany."

"Since our interests for once coincide with Himmler's," Stern agreed, "let's go into the mountains. We could all do with a little fresh air."

That April in the Alps was one of the most pleasant months of the war for them, despite the catastrophes overwhelming the Reich. Schleuder himself felt strangely detached. They learned, as though these were events concerning another planet, of the fall of Weimar, then of Leipzig and Nüremberg, and finally of the Russians' entry into Berlin. The circle was becoming tighter day by day. Stern never looked at a map except to calculate how much longer they would have to wait before the arrival of the Americans.

They lived in a hastily requisitioned hotel in the little village of Oberjoch. The Gestapo agents were still with them, but, horrified by the situation and almost completely cut off from the authorities, they were growing more humble every day. Schleuder took advantage of this to put their commanding officer in his place. He gave him permission to occupy an attic in the hotel, on condition that he did not show his face except at certain fixed hours, three times a day, to give a summary of the bulletins that Schleuder ordered him to listen to. The man would have agreed to any humiliation in order to hide in the shadow of the Peenemünde technicians.

"He'll soon be asking you to introduce him to the Americans as one of your co-workers," Stern remarked one day.

"As an engineer? Never. But if he continues to toe the line, maybe as an unskilled laborer for the cruder jobs . . . Well, where are our friends the Americans?" he continued, addressing the Gestapo official who had just come in with his report in his hand.

"They made contact with the Russians at Torgau yesterday, Herr General."

"Torgau? That's still quite far."

"They're moving very fast, Herr General. One of their columns has been reported driving south. They should be here in less than a week."

"Thank you," Schleuder replied with condescension. "You may go now."

The Gestapo official clicked his heels in the military manner and disappeared.

"Are you ready to confront our friends the Americans, Stern?"

"I'm ready."

This meant that he had finished work on the broad outlines of three projects, three stages in the conquest of space, that he intended to submit to the victors. Schleuder had begged him to confine himself to these three specific plans. For at the beginning of their sojourn in Oberjoch, Stern was so intoxicated by the thought of imminent freedom, by the prospect of unlimited means soon to be put at his disposal, and also perhaps by the mountain air, that he had launched into speculations on enterprises so manifestly impossible at the time that he would risk being taken for a madman if he submitted them.

Brought back to reality—his reality—Stern had thus confined himself to the three projects that he considered feasible within the following decade: artificial satellites, the moon, the planet Mars. As to the rest, he would speak only to indicate that he was thinking of the more distant future. These three conquests were the present.

Satellites, in fact, were already almost the past for him. All that was necessary was to develop the Peenemünde rockets a little further. He had forced himself, however, to map out the whole program because it was an indispensable stage before the second project, the launching of a crew to the moon.

75

The moon was the foremost objective, the masterpiece to which he had devoted most care, on which he had concentrated all the resources of his genius. Every evening he described some aspect of it to Schleuder, who never tired of listening to him, impressed by the mixture of precise calculations and impassioned comments that gradually made the wildest dream of the human mind appear relatively reasonable.

"I think we'll need a five-stage rocket, Schleuder . . ."

Schleuder had asked him to stop calling him "Herr General" when they were not on duty.

"A five-stage rocket, of which the last stage, the stage that will reach the moon, will contain within its flanks a smaller rocket, as a mother carries her unborn child. See what I mean? A fully assembled rocket, all ready for the return flight, with all the necessary launching equipment."

He unfolded a huge diagram on which he had worked for several nights.

"If only Nadia were here!" he exclaimed sorrowfully. "She would have produced something far neater, but it's quite clear just the same."

Schleuder bent over the sheet of paper avidly.

"It's very simple," Stern went on. "I was being much too timid. It's a projectile of about one hundred and fifty tons that we've got to liberate from the earth's attraction at the start of the operation. This means a booster of four or five thousand tons at least, measuring over a hundred meters."

"That's enormous," muttered Schleuder, almost in terror.

"That's what we need to solve the problem of the return."

"Don't you think, just the same, that it's a little too big, even for the Americans?"

Stern brushed aside these objections with a gesture of impatience.

"The point is to find out if they want to get to the moon, yes or no."

"Yes," Schleuder echoed pensively. "As you say, the point is to find out if they want to—"

"In which case, these are the minimum requirements. . . . And for Mars we'll have to have something a hundred times more powerful. Listen, Schleuder . . ."

He laid aside the Project Moon plans and opened another file. For three hours he explained to Schleuder the third enterprise he intended submitting to the Americans. He had worked it out in the peace and quiet of the Alps, without a glance at the green fields dotted with springtime flowers, during this last month of the war, in which the cities of the Reich were being reduced to so many piles of rubble.

A missile of forty thousand tons, assembled piece by piece on a terrestrial orbit, would be the starting point for ten cosmic vehicles, each carrying a crew of three. The voyage would last eight months, after which the cosmonauts would have to wait more than a year to find the astronomical conditions favorable for their return. The space ships would orbit around Mars as satellites, and from their flanks would be launched the rocket planes that would land in the snow of the Martian poles. Track vehicles would in turn emerge from these planes and set off to investigate the planet.

He was tortured, however, by some of the imponderables that were necessarily involved in his calculations.

"This is just a rough outline. If I had the necessary material here, the tables and instruments, I should have drawn up a specific plan. But some of the trajectory determinations would take me years; we must have electronic calculators. For that, too, we need the Americans. Even then they will probably have to build special machines."

He put his papers away.

"I'm ready, as I told you. They can come. What are they waiting for?"

They had reached this stage in their conversation when the

door was flung open. The Gestapo official burst in without knocking. He began talking in a breathless voice just as Schleuder, with an angry frown, was about to take him to task.

"Herr General!"

"We're working," Stern coldly observed.

But the news was important enough for the man to brave any reprimand.

"Herr General, I've just listened to several broadcasts. They all announce it . . . Herr General, the Führer is dead."

ELEVEN

A heavy silence followed this announcement. General Schleuder had sprung to his feet and snapped to attention. Stern did likewise, with clumsy hesitation, being vaguely aware that such an attitude on his part was ridiculous.

"He killed himself last night. His body has been burned. The Russians have occupied Berlin."

The news was not startling. For some weeks they had foreseen that this was how it would end. Nevertheless, Schleuder reproached himself for having taken so much pleasure this evening in listening to Stern. The latter was scarcely moved at all. Hitler had never meant anything to him, except at a certain period when he dreamed that Hitler's vast ambitions might facilitate the conquest of space.

"That's not all, Herr General. Admiral Doenitz has assumed

power and there's talk of an unconditional surrender. It's probably being arranged at this very moment."

Schleuder started sobbing silently. Stern went up to him and put his hand on his shoulder. The Gestapo man added timidly, "One last item of news, Herr General. An American column has been reported on its way down to Oberjoch. It will probably be here in less than an hour."

"At last!"

This time Stern gave his companion a good shake; in his own excitement, he was unable to tolerate any weakness. They had no right to waste time mourning over ruins. The past was the past. Henceforth they should think of nothing but the inspiring work to which they would at last be able to dedicate themselves. All this he blurted out incoherently to General Schleuder, who drew himself up with renewed pride and exclaimed:

"You're right, Stern! Human beings will travel through space. The moon will be conquered. Mars will be explored. And this will come about because of the work accomplished by the men of Peenemünde during this war—pioneers, Germans, whom I had the honor to command!"

Contact was established without any untoward incident. An Intelligence major who accompanied the column had his specific instructions. He was the first to arrive at the hotel, closely followed by a photographer who kept taking pictures indiscriminately until the officer grew angry and almost apologized to them for this intrusion. Then he introduced himself, subjected them to a brief interrogation to make sure of their identity, and took over the documents they had with them, all with the utmost courtesy. At Stern's request, he agreed to have the documents packaged in his presence and a list of them drawn up. The instructions he gave to the G.I.'s who carried them off were enough to show that these files were of paramount interest to him and that none of them would be mislaid.

He then requested Schleuder and Stern to be ready to leave by plane the next day, for he had orders to fly them both to England at the earliest opportunity. He advised them not to communicate with anyone or to leave the hotel, which was guarded. Before going off to arrange for the departure of the other prisoners by truck, he relaxed to a certain extent and revealed the curiosity inspired in him by certain members of the Peenemünde staff.

"I know you by reputation, Dr. Stern," he said hesitantly. "There's a lot of talk about you in the service."

It was clear that he was very eager to ask questions, but he pulled himself together and went off. Left to themselves, Stern and Schleuder packed their bags in silence. In the evening they ate the meal that was brought to them without exchanging more than three or four commonplace remarks. They seemed frightened of communicating their first impressions and hopes to each other. After dinner, which was served in Schleuder's room on the first floor, they ware about to separate when they heard someone calling outside in a low voice:

"Dr. Stern!"

He looked out of the open window and made out a figure half hidden behind a tree. Since he said nothing, the man repeated:

"Dr. Stern!"

"Yes."

The man came closer. He was wearing an American uniform.

"I'd like a word with you; only a moment, it's very important."

Stern remembered the promise he had made to the major and was about to close the window, having no wish to annoy the authorities on the very first day, when the man repeated insistently:

"Only a minute or two. I'm from the *New York Times*. . . . What are your plans?"

"Our plans . . . why, they're still the same," Stern replied automatically. "Space flight, the moon . . ."

"Fine, fine. Do you mind . . ."

He had already taken several photographs when a sound of footsteps was heard around the house.

"One last question, it's important . . ." the man said hastily.

But Stern had closed the window.

"A celebrity, my dear fellow, that's what you are," General Schleuder remarked.

Another American major interviewed them separately in London. Schleuder went into the office first and spent about half an hour there. As he came out he looked pensive but was unable to communicate with his companion, since the latter was ushered in immediately afterward.

"Dr. Stern? I've heard a lot about you."

The major was more than courteous. There was a hint of respect in his voice. He even half rose to his feet as the German entered the room, and introduced himself.

"I'm Major Wilson, technical adviser to Headquarters. A rocket specialist. . . . So you see," he explained frankly, "you have nothing to fear from me. We're on the same side, so to speak."

Stern felt completely at ease. He was at last confronting the man he had been hoping to meet: a technician in spite of his uniform. They could not fail to understand each other. His plans were spread out openly on the desk, and it was clear they had been examined. Other documents of his had been placed in a pile on a small table.

"We were enemies," the major went on. "That's understood. If I'd met you a few months ago I shouldn't have hesitated to kill you. We considered you personally as one of our most dangerous adversaries. But now that the war's over, I can't help admiring your knowledge and technical ability. A ton of explosives with a range of three hundred kilometers—congratulations!"

"Have you ever seen a V-2 intact?"

"We've captured a hundred or so, which we're sending to the United States. All our specialists are excited about your V-2. I've examined it myself in detail. What do I think of it? It's a small marvel."

"Oh, it's very small, I know, and still far from perfect! We were held up at every stage by all sorts of difficulties. . . . Otherwise, Major, I should have bombarded America before the end of the war," he added impetuously.

"Really?"

The officer seemed extremely interested in this possibility.

"But there's no longer any question of that," Stern hastily corrected himself.

"No, of course, there's no question of bombarding America," the major agreed with a smile. "But, while we're on the subject, I think my commanding officer has a proposition to make to you."

"Your commanding officer?"

"Colonel Stayman, who's in charge of our group of scientists and technicians, a very remarkable man even though he's not a scientist himself. He'll be here soon. He wants to see you. Meanwhile I wanted a word or two with you, to find out what . . . well, what your attitude is . . . what you think of America and the Americans, for instance. Well?"

"Here we go," Stern said to himself, delighted to see the conversation take the turn for which he had been hoping. It required no effort for him to state that he felt no resentment toward America and that he was very fond of the Americans.

"You ask me what my attitude is?"

He paused for a moment to muster all his powers of persuasion; then, pointing to the files on the table, he blurted out, "These plans, on which I've worked twelve hours a day for the last month, will give you an idea of my present preoccupations.

. . . You'll see from them," he went on with growing animation, "that there's an extraordinary task to undertake, an ideal that to my mind makes every political or military aspiration of today look ridiculous. I've been dreaming of this task for years. I've never lost sight of it, even during the war. It was in the hope of working on it that I agreed to cooperate with the army, since no one else in Germany could provide me with the means I wanted. My only goal, Major, my only goal is the conquest of space. It's a job of peace—I was arrested by the Gestapo because I did not concern myself enough with the war. It's far too important to allow room for the slightest feeling of hatred or rancor. I think I am, I know I am, one of the men who can bring it to a successful conclusion. I am willing to devote myself body and soul, I swear, to the country that will provide me with the means of putting it into effect."

He fell silent. The major had listened to him attentively, occasionally giving a nod of approval. If Stern had observed him more closely he would immediately have discerned a slightly condescending smile and a gesture that seemed to indicate a trace of irritation when he spoke of the conquest of space.

"Major," Stern went on, still more vehemently, "it's imperative that we get to the moon in ten years' time, in twelve years at the very latest."

"Oh, the moon!" the major exclaimed. "Yes, I've read what you have to say about that. Interesting, very interesting. You've got a lot of imagination!"

"Imagination!"

"Don't protest. It's a compliment. It's imagination that makes for genius. We've realized that for some time in America, and we respect it. But it must be disciplined at times. . . . I read your three reports in one night, like a novel. If you publish this in America, you'll have a big success. It'll be a best seller. It won't be the first time a scientist has carved himself out a successful career in literature."

Stern had no time to protest; another man had come into

83

the room. It was Colonel Stayman. He immediately showed the same cordial attitude as the major.

"I was just congratulating Dr. Stern," the latter remarked. "I know, sir, that you'll appreciate this plan and the accompanying notes as much as I do."

He unfolded the diagram of the giant rocket that was to reach the moon. The colonel bent over it and gave a whistle of admiration.

"Excellent," he said with an amused expression. "Incidentally, I've also read your statement to a journalist who managed to approach you in spite of my orders. . . . Don't worry, I know you're not to blame. One can't get rid of those devils, and one needs them sometimes. Anyway, you answered very cleverly. The conquest of space, the moon—there's nothing compromising about that and it will make a splash. If they bother you again, keep up the same story. Excellent, as I say, excellent."

Colonel Stayman thrust the plan aside and changed his tone.

"But that's not the question at hand, is it, Wilson? Have you told Dr. Stern about our proposition?"

"Not yet, sir. I thought you'd like to do so yourself. I'm sure he's ready to listen to you."

"Well, now," Colonel Stayman began, "I'll come straight to the point; that's my way. What interests us is this: a big rocket, not just one ton, but several tons of explosive, with a range up to . . . well, yes, we're not asking a great deal . . . the distance between one continent and another. You see what I mean? Can you help us to achieve this, and are you willing to? I need hardly add that we'll give you an appointment worthy of your achievements. We know your reputation."

So they still took him for a mere gunner! The effort required to suppress his indignation made him turn red. Could he have been so mistaken about the American mentality? He replied calmly enough, however, but in a faltering voice.

"Of course, Colonel, what you're asking me to do is possible, even easy, extremely easy. But what after that? What about my projects? What about the moon?"

"The moon?"

Colonel Stayman smiled once more. He seized a chair in his powerful fist, turned it back to front, sat down astride it, and insisted that Stern also be seated. At a nod, Wilson produced a bottle and some glasses.

"I like you, Dr. Stern," he said in a more familiar tone. "And now . . ."

He thrust a glass into Stern's hand.

"Now let's talk seriously."

GRAPEFRUIT

"To hell with you and your white mice!"

Almost immediately Stern regretted his outburst of temper. Such lack of courtesy on his part toward a man of science was inexcusable, especially in front of General Stayman and Meyer, a guest at La Grange. Standing some distance away on the top of the hill, these two were still contemplating the sky. They must have heard him raise his voice, even without catching the actual words.

He apologized as best he could. The young man gave a forlorn smile.

"I'm the one to apologize for bothering you like this, Dr. Stern. I know you have other things to attend to beside my mice, but this experiment on the genetic influence of cosmic rays is of paramount importance for my thesis."

"Don't fret too much. There's going to be another launching in three weeks' time. If you entrust me with another pair of your pets, I promise to find a place for them in the capsule. I hope it'll work out all right this time and that you'll get them back alive."

The young man thanked him effusively and got back into his jeep. Stern wished him good luck with his mice and, before rejoining his companions, paused for a moment to watch him drive down the hill until he was no more than a dot in the white sand.

The desert had already begun to sparkle all around him, although the sun was still low on the horizon. The La Grange rocket range, a plateau one hundred miles long and forty wide, had never looked so dazzling or so desolate, in spite of the presence of several tourist trailers on the surrounding heights and, down below, the small groups of engineers emerging from the blockhouse.

The launching itself had been successful, the rocket having reached a height of a hundred and ten miles, which was quite good for this kind of single-stage missile. Yet he gave a bitter smile as he reflected that a rocket in Peenemünde had exceeded a hundred and twenty miles thirteen years earlier. No matter; it was a relative success, for which he would be congratulated by all the technicians at La Grange. But the parachute that was to bring the recording apparatus back to earth had failed to open and the delicate instruments must have been smashed to pieces, as well as the white mice on which the biologist had pinned his hopes.

Now that he was in a slightly better mood, he could not suppress a smile at the thought of the young man's expression of dismay. During the ten years he had been at La Grange as technical adviser to the military administration, he had seen any number of these young scientists—physicists, meteorologists, and biologists—all of whom viewed space from the narrow angle of their own specialty. Eager to show the interest he took in science, General Stayman, who commanded the base, obligingly allocated each of them a small space inside the capsules for the subjects of their experiments. The military rockets thus carried into the upper atmosphere, in addition to the delicate recording instruments, various bacteria, cultures, seeds, plants, flies, and animals.

Granted, Stern reflected, these experiments were useful. It was essential to study all the influences of empty space on a variety of life before sending a man to the moon. What angered him was that this series of accessory tests seemed to have taken precedence over the essential enterprise, to the point of eclipsing it entirely.

A man on the moon! The gloomy mood that had caused the outburst this morning assailed him again. To him this was the central idea, around which all the experiments ought to revolve. In fact, however, no educated American believed in it, apart from the little group working with him at La Grange and a few other eccentrics to whom the official scientists scornfully referred as "the lunatics."

After his capture by the Americans he had quickly realized that the only way for him to pursue his experiments with rockets was to agree to the suggestion of working with the army. Certain tentative approaches to private industry had left him in no doubt about this. He was received courteously, often with cordiality, always with curiosity. He was never made to feel his position as an ex-enemy. But if his success at Peenemünde had served as an introduction, at the same time it had marked him as the V-2 man. As soon as he embarked on the problem of space on a larger scale, he came up against barely concealed smiles. The few bigwigs who may have believed vaguely in the possibility of interplanetary flight were not prepared to risk the enormous capital required for this venture unless it was a paying proposition within a reasonable length of time, which was not the case. All they envisaged was a series of small satellites that could act as relay stations for long-distance communication. As for the higher branches of the civil administration, no substantial help could be expected from them, except for projects in the interests of national defense.

For want of anything better, he had therefore agreed to place his learning and experience at the disposal of the military. Though they were not thinking of the conquest of space, they were at least interested in heavy rockets as long-distance missile weapons. Had not the V-2 proved itself? Once again, he was the V-2 man.

He had not, however, abandoned his youthful ambitions. While perfecting rockets suitable for launching an atomic bomb from one continent to another, he continued to work assiduously on his plans for the future. Moreover, by means of articles in various magazines, he tried to rouse the public's interest in the conquest of space. He had immediately found an eager audience of journalists, but many of them went to the opposite extreme: they were always inclined to magnify his methodical projects, thereby distorting them, confusing the possibilities of the present with the eventual hopes for a distant future, and thus tending to confirm the reputation of "lunatic" that he had acquired among serious scientists.

These extremes, however, were preferable to indifference. Every so often he had the feeling that his ideas were making an impression, especially among the young. He would receive enthusiastic letters. There would seem to be a movement afoot. Plans would be mapped out, ready to be translated into achievement. But this never lasted long; the spell would appear to break suddenly. The interest in space would be brushed aside by some sensational news item: tension in the international situation or the latest scandal about the current top film star.

What he still called the Peenemünde spirit seemed unwilling or unable to come into being in America. He deplored this fact each time he met Schleuder, which was infrequently, for the former general lived in New York. More often than not he would confide his bitter feelings to Maggie, his American wife, to whom he had also communicated his passion, and who was even more bitter than he about the mediocrity of spatial ambitions in her country. For this she held the government responsible (as she did whenever she discovered a fault in the United States) and, without attacking the President directly, she would remark that the group with which he had surrounded himself had the mentality of small shopkeepers fit for managing the affairs of a modest enterprise but in no way capable of presiding over the destiny of a great nation.

Whenever he had to deal with the authorities, Stern wisely refrained from mentioning the moon and instead discussed terrestrial satellites, taking care to point out that the space program could limit itself at first to small missiles weighing no more than a few pounds, which would be of immediate practical use. There, he had had some success. A precise program had been drawn up. The Army was preparing to launch one of these satellites, under his direction, and although the funds for this operation were limited, he thought he would be able to put it into effect by the beginning of 1958, just a few months away. It was far from what he had in mind. It was nevertheless an initial step.

He climbed slowly up toward the observation post, where General Stayman and Meyer were waiting for him with a jeep.

"All things considered, apart from the parachute, it went very well," said the general. "Congratulations, Stern."

General Stayman was an optimist by nature. Every time a rocket went higher than sixty miles, he was filled with delight and pride and never failed to congratulate his technical adviser. No doubt he, too, regarded him as something of a "lunatic," but a lunatic genius who only needed to be brought down to earth from time to time. No doubt he was also proud of his colleague's fame and never stopped saying that it was he, Stayman, then a mere colonel, who had recognized his exceptional worth and persuaded him to work for the United States.

Stern got along very well with him, even though he sometimes felt impatient of his methods. The general allowed him a free hand in the technical field. Frequently he even closed his eyes when some costly apparatus required for the launching of a future satellite was ordered, for want of sufficient funds, as an indispensable accessory to the national defense—a procedure to which Schleuder himself had once been obliged to resort at Peenemünde.

"What do you say, Dr. Meyer?" the general continued in a bantering tone. "What does Los Alamos think of La Grange and our wretched little chuff-chuffs?"

Meyer, a German atomic physicist, a refugee in America during the war, had formerly worked on the development of the bomb. Now, still at Los Alamos, which was not far from La Grange, he was working with a small group of scientists on the construction of a rocket propelled by atomic power. His colleagues often showed their disdain for these liquid-fueled "chuff-chuffs," which to them were missiles of the past. But Meyer was interested in any form of technical development. A personal friend of Stern's, who had invited him to spend the day at La Grange, he replied in the same lighthearted manner.

"Los Alamos thinks your chuff-chuffs have a certain charm, General . . . in spite of their somewhat old-fashioned style."

"Your outfit hasn't yet managed to send missiles a hundred and ten miles up in the air, though, has it?"

"We're not even thinking of it at the moment. Not for another ten years or so. But then . . . just you wait and see, General!"

"In that time we shall—just tell him, Stern, what we will have achieved. And not in ten years' time—in less than six months."

"A satellite around the earth," Stern said impatiently. "But he knows that. I've already told him. And in any case he would have learned about it from the papers."

"It's true, the whole of America is talking about it," the general remarked with satisfaction.

They drove down to the blockhouse. Most of the important information had been transmitted by radio and the specialists were starting to piece it together.

"There's only one thing that bothers me," said the general. "The photographs will be ruined."

Stayman, too, had his particular hobby in connection with space: high-altitude photography. He had made a personal collection of prints that he studied incessantly, admiring the extent of American territory and looking at the curvature of the earth with ever-renewed emotion.

"We'll take some more," Stern replied listlessly. "The camera will be wrecked anyway, but some of the plates, even though they're smashed, may reveal something. The recovery squads are going out now."

"Stern, I'd like you to keep a close watch on them yourself. Please do this for me," said the general. "I don't trust anyone else."

Stern, who had decided not to work that day but to devote himself to his guest, turned to Meyer.

"You come along with me. I'll take you into the desert. You're curious to know about everything that goes on at La Grange. We'll begin with the best-organized and most efficient branch of all: the wreckage-recovery service."

J

THIRTEEN

"I think that's about the lot, sir," said the foreman. "But we'll search the desert again this afternoon and tomorrow. I'm sure we'll find a few more pieces."

"Fine. Make a separate parcel of what remains of the instruments, and especially the camera."

The recovery squad had pinpointed the scene of the crash and was busy collecting the fragments: first those of the instruments, and then those of the rocket itself, which had come down some ten miles from the base. Stern and Meyer moved a short distance away to enable them to get on with their work. Stern looked on gloomily as they handled the shapeless bits and pieces with evident satisfaction, almost with love.

"Just look at them," he said to Meyer. "They're just as pleased with a failure as with a success."

"They sometimes even rush headlong to anticipate a failure."

"That's true. When I first came here . . ."

They were speaking German. When General Stayman had left them, they had continued for a moment to speak in English, a language both of them spoke perfectly and, by this time, automatically. Then, before driving off into the desert, as Stern was showing his friend some of the installations, Meyer had noticed that many of the engineers and even the workmen were using German terms when referring to certain parts of the rockets. The technical jargon of La Grange was interlarded not only with American slang but with German words that the *émigrés* had used on their arrival and that no one had ever bothered to translate. So the two friends had unconsciously reverted to their native tongue.

"When I first came here," Stern continued, "I was horrified. They had brought back from Germany about a hundred V-2's in separate pieces. Well, these pieces were assembled by engineers and mechanics. They were certainly able but they weren't specialists, and they worked with a sort of frantic haste to make immediate launchings, which were almost always marked by accidents. I had to put real pressure on them to get them to make a thorough check of every missile. Otherwise they would have launched the whole lot in a couple of weeks, out of sheer curiosity, from love of experimenting just for the sake of experimenting, without being discouraged by the failures, feeling convinced that each of these taught them something . . . which was true, of course."

"They always think first and foremost of experimenting," Meyer muttered.

"Afterward, on the other hand, they work like beavers to try to find the reason for the failure. They love *feeling their way*. We feel our way when we can't do otherwise. With them it's for pleasure. And it's the same in every field. When General Stayman dictates his letters . . . ."

They had sat down side by side in the shade of a jeep. The New Mexico sun was not too overpowering that day, and the majesty of the desert prompted them to exchange general ideas, which was not a habit of theirs. Nor were they in the habit of referring to the Americans as "they" or "them." Usually they considered themselves integrated into the nation, and indeed they were, more or less. Stern got on as well with the American technicians of La Grange as with the handful of engineers from Peenemünde who had followed him out here. Perhaps this reversion to the German language was now prompting them to make distinctions.

"When General Stayman dictates his letters, he never takes the trouble or the time to think of the wording. It's not out of laziness or intellectual incapacity; it's a system. He dictates ten, very quickly, in a sort of frenzy. But when they're returned to him typed out, then he gets down to work. He takes pleasure in seeing that they won't do at all, in crossing out, correcting, tearing up five or six successive drafts, improving them a little each time. At the last attempt the letter is written impeccably. Then he smiles with pleasure, without noticing that two minutes' reflection in the beginning would have spared him and his secretary so much work, not to mention a considerable saving in paper."

Meyer laughed soundlessly and was lost for a moment in contemplating the foreman, who was carefully packing away piles of debris and conscientiously labeling each one.

"That's how they build their cities," he said, "and it sometimes gets good results. They try to put such-and-such fifty-story building in such-and-such district of New York. If it turns out, as a result of this experiment, that the building does not harmonize with the rest of the neighborhood, they tear it down after a few years, or even a few months, and try another in its place."

"Yet they produce detailed plans and even make scale models."

"They attach no importance to them. To them there's nothing like feeling their way on the spot. Believe me, I've known them longer than you have."

"You've known them longer than I have," Stern echoed. "Yes, I know."

There was a strange intonation in his voice that seemed to indicate a slight irritation. It did not escape Meyer, who had nevertheless not meant anything derogatory by this remark. Yet it established a marked difference between the two *émigrés,* who were both naturalized. Meyer had come to the United States before Stern, at the beginning of the war in fact, fleeing from Nazi Germany and the anti-Jewish persecutions. Though the native Americans never made Stern conscious of his antecedents and regarded him now as one of themselves, the relationships he had with scientists like Meyer were usually somewhat chilly. These scientists could not forget that he had worked for Hitler and held this against him. To Meyer, however, a man of science pure and simple, these questions had no more importance than to Stern himself. So the slight feeling of uneasiness that had arisen between them for a moment did not last long.

They went on discussing American cities, remembering their own impressions when they had first arrived in New York.

"Nowhere else in the world," said Meyer, "is there an architecture that has such a character of life in perpetual evolution. What struck me most, apart from the size of the buildings, was the frenzy and passion they seemed to devote to daily demolitions."

"That's just what I would expect from people who made the bomb!" Stern muttered.

But he, too, had been impressed by the unusual ardor that animated demolition projects: a sort of fury that seemed to take possession of the whole staff, from the foreman down to the humblest laborer, each determined to get the maximum destructive power out of the strange gigantic machines that he admired as a connoisseur.

"At that time I looked upon all this activity as auguring well for my own projects. People with such a thirst for transformation that they start on the actual work without waiting for the result of lengthy research—such people seemed to me capable of the most daring achievements."

"And now?"

Stern paused for a moment and replied with a sigh, "Now I sometimes wonder whether all this frenzy isn't the sign of a sterile feverishness. There's that . . . and other things as well," he added wearily.

He felt very morose. He looked with a gloomy eye at the recovery squad, which had begun to comb the desert in search of further fragments, and made an impatient gesture.

"Let's get back to the base," he said abruptly. "There's nothing of any importance for us to do here and I've still lots of strange things to show you—our museum, if nothing else."

"Your museum?"

"The pride of La Grange. General Stayman goes and meditates there almost every day."

The rocket museum had once been open to visitors, but for some time tight security measures had barred access by the public. Stern took his friend there after lunch. The porter at once hastened toward them.

"Don't bother. We'll only be a few minutes. It's not worth showing us around. . . . No, there's no need to show us the films, either."

The porter looked hurt and returned reluctantly to his booth after opening the doors for them.

"A worthy old fellow," said Meyer. "He seems very conscious of his duty."

"Everything is old and worthy here."

Stern showed Meyer around the rooms. Most of the museum was devoted to souvenirs of Peenemünde. Framed photographs of the first launchings were on view, brilliantly illuminated by spotlights that the porter had insisted on switching on before leaving. In padlocked showcases built of costly wood, as well as behind glass, blackened and twisted fragments of old rockets, most of them V-2's, succeeded one another in order of increasing importance, from the minutest pieces of metal to whole missiles. Each exhibit bore a label, with descriptive particulars and a date. Each was set off by a spotlight and rested on a dark cloth, as though it were some precious stone or valuable work of art.

Stern stopped in front of each case, immersed in his own thoughts, apparently oblivious to the presence of his companion, a prey to the ominous sensation that overwhelmed him every time he entered the museum. When they had made a complete tour of it, he put his hand on his forehead as though his head were aching.

"Let's get out of this place. I was wrong to bring you here. Do you like this graveyard atmosphere?"

Meyer did not give a direct reply.

"I had a somewhat similar sensation near Boston," he said eventually, "while visiting a seventeenth-century iron foundry, the first industrial concern of its kind to have been built in America. It has been restored to its original state, transformed into a museum and put on show, with its ancient bellows, furnace, and original instruments. Hundreds of thousands of dollars were probably spent on reconstructing those workrooms and preserving their historical aspect. . . . Your museum must have cost a tidy sum, too."

"Yet they refuse me funds for a two-hundred-and-twenty-pound satellite! Do you think this idolatry of ancient remains is compatible with great projects?"

Since Meyer did not reply, he went on in a dull voice:

"Have they really become a senile people, Meyer? Is their feverish activity in certain fields merely a spasm of transitory revolt against the sclerosis threatening them? . . . Let's get out of here. I don't suppose you want to see the films—they're almost all of the first Peenemünde tests."

"What about you?"

"Me? . . . Not today. But I have a confession to make. I sometimes come here and have them shown just for myself . . . so does General Stayman."

"I understand."

"Well, I don't understand!" Stern exclaimed in a sudden outburst of rage. "I don't understand anything, except that I'm growing senile myself, senile at the age of forty-six, senile as everyone else now is in this country. Meyer, I was wrong. The moon is not for them!"

FOURTEEN

For the rest of the day Stern showed his friend around the La Grange installations. He felt slightly more cheerful as they visited in turn the powerhouse, the workshops, the assembly

belts, the various offices and laboratories. A whole industrial city had come into being out here in the desert.

"All the same, it's not so bad," said Meyer, looking at him closely.

"No. It's not so bad. I sometimes fly off the handle," he admitted ruefully.

He reproached himself for doubting both himself and the American potentialities. Especially just when a satellite program was about to be put into effect after years of patient toil. The Army's missile, his missile, would be the first to be launched, in the following February. It would be a success, he felt certain. It would weigh about forty pounds—his plans for a heavier missile had not been accepted because of the expense —but it would still be the first body launched by man to gravitate around the earth: a date in the history of mankind.

And it would be followed by other, bigger and heavier ones, culminating in the space craft about which he had dreamed for thirty years. Patience was needed. The public had taken to the idea. This was evident from many signs, even from the passionate interest people were beginning to show in the preparatory stages. Ultimately, public opinion was sure to shake the authorities from their inertia.

"It's time we went back," he said to Meyer. "I promised Maggie I'd be home early. We're having Walker to dinner this evening—a young engineer who works for the Navy, on rockets as well. A nice boy and sharp as mustard."

The cooler evening air and the thought of seeing Maggie and his son again served to put him in a mellow mood. He abandoned the jeep they had used all day and drove back in his car to his quarters, which stood on a height several miles from the base. During the drive Meyer could at last spare a glance for the impressive and grandiose landscape of La Grange. He had hardly had the leisure to look at it until then. Two lofty mountain ranges fringed the polygon—the left-hand "hedge" and the right-hand "hedge," as the rocket men disdainfully called them. The sun was sinking below the higher of the two, whose rocky, strangely patterned spur looked like a gigantic church organ. The desert wind had risen and accompanied their journey with a melancholy dirge as it whistled through the gulleys.

On arriving at the bungalow they paused for a moment in the garden that overlooked the desert. Exotic flowers bloomed there in profusion.

"This is Maggie's department. I don't know how she manages to get things to grow in this climate."

When they had first settled here he had teased her a little for her tussles with the military administration and her imperious demands to General Stayman to obtain more water for her garden. He had also watched with a condescending eye her efforts to transform the commonplace house they had been allocated into a proper home. He now admitted she had been right. He had come to attach more and more importance to comfort, to the decoration of a living room and the cheerful aspect of a garden, which would never have crossed his mind before. Was this another sign of senility? He refused to let himself relapse into those gloomy thoughts and showed Meyer into the bungalow.

Maggie had just gone to dress for dinner. She shouted apologies and greetings to them from her bedroom. Stern was pleased to see that his son William was not watching television. He found him lying on the sofa in the living room, deep in contemplation of a picture book. The seven-year-old boy flung his arms around his father's neck, greeted Meyer, then immediately immersed himself again in the book, which seemed to fascinate him.

"Look," said Stern, with a wink at his guest.

They both smiled; the book was an illustrated children's story in which the hero visits, one after another, the moon, various planets, and even the distant stars.

When Stern came back into the living room after a quick

change, he found no one else there. Meyer, who was spending the night at the bungalow, was still in his bedroom.

William was probably having dinner with his governess. For a moment Stern amused himself by thumbing through the book that the boy had left on the sofa. He reflected, with some displeasure, that William was a hundred percent American; he did not even speak German. He himself, Stern, though he sometimes felt alien to his surroundings, on the whole had quickly adapted himself. Maggie had obviously had a great deal to do with this. He had married her three years after arriving in the United States, and there had never been a moment's discord between them. Even before his naturalization, for which he had had to wait several years, he had felt closely attached to this country. When, a few months earlier, he had been given official recognition for exceptional services to the Army, he had felt intensely proud, without even thinking of the irony of this reward being given to the inventor of the V-2. He had played the game fairly. If, as often happened, he cursed the civil and military authorities, it was in the same spirit that he had once inveighed against the German government. Maggie was even harsher than he was about some of her compatriots.

Meyer rejoined him just as the darkness outside was pierced by some headlights. A car drew up in the garden. Maggie shouted from her room:

"I'll be ready in five minutes, darling. Give everyone a drink in the meantime."

Both Meyer and Walker, the engineer who had just driven up, were friends with whom the Sterns did not have to stand on ceremony. The men went outside to greet the new arrival. The introductions were quickly over. Walker gave a little whistle of surprise on hearing that Meyer was one of the Los Alamos atomic physicists.

"You're another of those people who are trying to cut the grass from under our feet!"

"And what's happening about that famous Navy satellite?" Meyer asked Walker.

"Really, Dr. Meyer, are you people at Los Alamos worrying about our little chuff-chuffs?"

"We're wildly jealous of them!"

For the Navy, too, was preparing to launch a satellite, several satellites, as were the Air Force and several private concerns. The idea having finally been accepted, every big organization, whether military or civil, wanted to have its own satellite. This was yet another aspect of spatial politics that made Stern fume with rage. The government, anxious not to put all its eggs in one basket, did not rely exclusively on him and a few others who had proved themselves in the field of rocketry. It preferred to scatter its financial aid among several bodies working independently of one another.

The result? A cloud of miniature satellites were being prepared, among which there were bound to be many failures. "Always the same method," Stern lamented once again; "feeling their way at random." Some of the projected operations would succeed. The rest would be started all over again.

"Let's be serious," said Walker. "Our Vanguard rocket won't be ready for another six months. The Army will leave the Navy at the post; we've resigned ourselves to that."

"I should hope so," Stern growled.

Barely thirty years of age, Walker was already an experienced technician. Although he worked for a rival service, he felt unbounded admiration for Stern, whom he had known for some time and all of whose publications he had read. Taking advantage of a few days' leave, he had come to spend them at La Grange. This had not met with the approval of General Stayman, who lived in terror of having some secret stolen by his rivals. But Stern, who greatly appreciated the young engineer's enthusiasm, had managed to persuade the general that his fears were groundless. In fact, Walker was just as scathing as

Stern about the stupid division of effort that held up progress, and, unknown to the authorities, both of them occasionally exchanged valuable information.

Meyer continued in the same bantering tone, "Mind you, we don't stop the children playing, as the Chinese used to do a thousand years ago. We even let them have a few dollars to do it with."

"You're right to say 'a few dollars,' " Walker grumbled. "We'll always be the poor relations. Ever since your damned bomb, if a scientist wants to get financial backing in this snob-ridden country, he has to inscribe the words 'atom' and 'disintegration' in fiery letters at the top of his projects."

Stern sighed. This was partly true. The program he had in mind, based on gigantic rockets propelled by a propergol, was impeded not only by the limited outlook of the military, the utilitarian attitude of big business, and the ignorance of politicians, but also by the most famous scientists. They believed in the conquest of space, but they regarded liquid-fueled missiles as outdated and maintained that the whole financial effort should be concentrated on research into the most modern methods of propulsion. Since they were in a strong position, following the success of their bomb, their opinion generally prevailed. This was another bone of contention between the Los Alamos staff and that of La Grange, about which friends like Stern and Meyer freely joked together, but which gave rise to bitter arguments at official meetings.

"Oh, well," said Stern, once again pleading his cause, "I know atomic energy is the hope of the future, but our rockets already *exist* and have been perfected. Your missile, you tell me, won't see the light of day for another ten or twelve years. In ten years, if I were given a free hand . . ."

"I know, you'd be on the moon. You're preaching to the converted. To my mind, clearing the ground as you are doing can only be beneficial."

"Clearing the ground!"

Stern was about to protest against this expression. He was prevented from doing so by a child's cry in the adjoining room.

"Daddy!"

There was a disturbing, almost tragic, note in this call. Just as the three men were rising to their feet, young William flung open the door and rushed into the room, which was unlike him, for he was well brought up and a rather shy boy.

"Daddy!"

His voice betrayed such emotion that Stern did not think for a moment of reprimanding him. Behind him, his governess was trying vainly to restrain him.

"What's the matter, William?"

"Daddy, the Russians have launched a satellite!"

FIFTEEN

"The bastards!"

"Die Schweine!"

The three men had remained dumfounded for a moment; then their rage was expressed simultaneously in a curse, the two former Germans reverting instinctively to their native tongue. A muffled cry reached them from Maggie's bedroom and a few seconds later she burst into the living room, without completing her make-up and in the throes of an indignation that surpassed even that of the men.

She had heard her son's cry and now rushed over to him.

"What did you say?"

"The Russians have launched a satellite around the earth," the boy repeated. "It's just been announced on TV."

"It's true," the governess confirmed. "I heard it, too. A special announcement."

William was standing very upright, but his face was distorted by a strange grimace. His first cry had been one of rage. Now it was plain to see that he was on the verge of tears. Stern, who was the first to recover his composure, went into the adjoining room, giving his son a friendly pat as he passed, and came back with the television set. In heavy silence they listened to an announcer repeating the news with a few additional details. Stern forced himself to listen calmly, but when the weight of the Sputnik was announced he sprang to his feet.

"Two hundred pounds! That was my initial plan, but I was limited to thirty-eight!"

"Damn them!" Maggie exclaimed, without revealing whether the abuse was directed toward the American government or the Soviet people, and without a thought for the language she was using in front of her son.

Dinner was served in an atmosphere of gloom. Stern was plunged in a morose silence from which the others did not dare to drag him. Two hundred pounds was the first project he had submitted twelve years before, and he considered this merely a preliminary experiment that could have been put into effect within three or four years. They had laughed in his face. Meanwhile the Russians had been silently at work. The Russians, a nation of musicians and chess players!

He recalled the last conversation he had had with Nadia and clenched his fists as he thought of her. She had kept copies of all his papers. He was sure the Russians had made use of these documents for their intercontinental rockets. Today it was satellites; soon, perhaps, it would be the moon. Not that they lacked scientists capable of making the same calculations and proceeding with the same experiments. Unlike many Americans, he entertained no illusions on this point. Tsiolkovsky's splendid work was still ripe in his memory. But his patient speculations, his own research, and the series of tests at Peenemünde must have constituted a powerful help and a considerable saving of time. The Americans had had the same material at their disposal and an even greater number of experienced technicians, not to mention himself, Stern!

Never before had he felt so humiliated. He was humiliated as an American; humiliated as was Maggie, who nervously smoked cigarette after cigarette between courses; as was Walker; and William, whose sorrow visibly exceeded the bounds of a child's sorrow and who had had to be consoled with assurances minimizing the incident before being sent off with his governess. And beyond all, he was humiliated as a man: Stern, the universally known rocket specialist whom the papers and magazines called the high priest of astronautics; Stern, the father of the V-2's; the recently naturalized Stern; the proud and also scrupulous Stern, who at this moment was reproaching himself for not having fulfilled the terms of the gentleman's agreement between himself and America.

He was roused from his gloomy meditation by the telephone ringing. It was General Stayman. His fury made the instrument vibrate.

"Have you heard?"

"I've heard, General."

"The bastards!"

"Yes, of course, the bastards. But they've been working, and working intelligently. Also, no doubt, their scientists were granted sufficient funds," said Stern, who could no longer conceal his bitterness.

"Maybe it's a bluff?"

"I'd be surprised if it was."

"Maybe they haven't launched a thing. It's just a propaganda broadcast."

"It's going *bleep-bleep,*" said Stern.

"What?"

"I said it's going *bleep-bleep!*" Stern bellowed. "Our stations are recording this cry of triumph and are now broadcasting it on every wave length."

"Bleep-bleep!" the general echoed furiously. "It's true, I heard it. But it doesn't mean a thing, *bleep-bleep.*"

"And it weighs two hundred pounds."

"Two hundred! It's all propaganda, I tell you. They're trying to fool us."

"They're fooling us, but I don't think they're lying. It's a reasonable weight, the same as my first project."

"Ours will weigh how much in the end?"

"Thirty-eight pounds."

"And you can't add a few more on? Increase it to . . . a round figure, say, a hundred or at least fifty pounds?"

"Impossible with the rocket we have in mind."

"And you can't change the rocket?"

"Yes. But it would take time and money."

"How much time?"

"Over a year."

The general gave an angry grunt and fell silent for a moment. Only his labored breathing could be heard in the earpiece. Then he went on:

"Good. Now listen to me. We're going to launch that thirty-eight-pound job of yours. Then . . . but actually, yours is entirely different . . . a whole factory in miniature, an absolute marvel. Only forty pounds, perhaps, but forty pounds containing a wealth of valuable instruments that will make some sensational discoveries."

"No doubt," said Stern. "But theirs still weighs two hundred pounds."

"A two-hundred-pound cannon ball—that exists already. It

has no scientific value. Ours has far greater scientific value, you must admit."

"Possibly," Stern agreed in a weary tone of voice.

"Good . . . As I was saying, this is what we're going to do. We're going to launch our forty-pound job as soon as possible. . . . Incidentally, when will you be able to launch it?"

"In February."

"February!" the general yelled. "You mean next year? It's not possible!"

"I'm sorry, but there are still any number of preliminary tests to be made."

"To hell with the preliminary tests! Can't you go whole hog . . . a final test . . . tomorrow . . . in a few days?"

"Impossible," Stern replied curtly, beginning to lose his temper. "I absolutely refuse . . ."

Maggie, who had come up beside him, motioned him to adopt a different tone. He made an effort to pull himself together.

"It's really not possible, General. We'd be heading for certain failure."

"Good, good . . . If you say so, I believe you. I know you're one of our best specialists. I submit to your decision."

"Maybe in January," said Stern, after thinking the matter over, "on condition I'm allowed to work freely and permanently with the Cape Canaveral outfit and all the firms taking part in the construction of the various components."

"I give you my word that as of tomorrow you can do whatever you like. Whatever you like, do you hear? I've got confidence in you. I've always backed you up and even defended you."

"I know, General."

This was true. In spite of his sometimes exasperating remarks, Stayman had always supported him. It was not his fault, but the High Command's, that the initial projects had not been adopted.

"So we're going to launch your forty-pound job in January,

111

since there's no way of doing it any sooner. And you get down to work immediately on the preparation of another one of . . . of at least two hundred and fifty pounds. Is that possible?"

"Not only is it possible, but the plans are all ready. Later on we must make arrangements for far bigger launchings. In the region of several tons."

"Tons!"

"Tons. Do you think the Russians are going to stop at a mere two hundred pounds?"

"The bastards!" the general exclaimed.

"Only it's going to cost a great deal."

"We'll have all the funds we need, I swear. I'll make it my business to see that we get them. Get down to work at once. There's not a second to lose."

Stern shrugged his shoulders. This was not the first time that such promises had been made.

Stayman had hung up. Stern was on his way back to the dining table when the telephone rang again. He turned around and picked up the receiver with a gesture of annoyance.

"Dr. Stern. I'm the science correspondent of the *New York Times*. You've heard the news, of course?"

"Of course."

"I wanted to ask you a few questions, since you're the greatest rocket specialist."

"Go ahead."

He was in no mood to discuss the event, but his orders were to treat every journalist politely, without disclosing any secret information.

"Isn't America preparing to launch a satellite?"

"Several."

"When?"

"Next year, 1958, the so-called Geophysical Year."

"Could you give us a rough date?"

"The Army missile, with which I'm directly connected, will be launched in February, if all goes well. That's all I know."

"That is, five months after the Russians."

"So it seems."

"How much will your satellite weigh?"

"Thirty-eight pounds," said Stern, whose hand tightened slightly around the receiver.

"The Russian Sputnik weighs two hundred, according to their report. Do you think that's true?"

"I think it's very likely."

"To what do you attribute the fact that the Soviets have launched a much heavier satellite five months before us?"

"To the fact that their rockets are more powerful than ours," he replied, trying hard to be patient.

There was a moment's silence on the other end of the line, during which he pictured the journalist hastily jotting down his answers.

"So it would seem that they're ahead of us in this field?"

"That strikes me as obvious."

"How far ahead, in your opinion?"

Thereupon, in spite of his irritation, Stern automatically embarked on certain calculations.

"At least a year. And that's on the optimistic side."

The correspondent asked a few more questions, to which he forced himself to reply with the best possible grace, then the journalist thanked him and hung up. Stern went back to dinner.

"A newspaperman," he explained as he sat down. "I . . ."

He was interrupted again by the telephone ringing.

"To hell with it!" he exclaimed. "I'm not going to answer."

"You can't do that," said Maggie. "They know you're here."

He picked up the instrument again, muttering under his breath. It was a senior White House official who took an occasional interest in La Grange and who had once come there to give a speech. He had already spoken to Stayman, but this was not enough. He hardly allowed Stern to say a word.

"Listen, Dr. Stern. I've just been talking to the general. But he doesn't understand a word; he's just an old brass hat. I want to have your opinion, the opinion of a technician, a scientist, the greatest rocket specialist, isn't that so? I want to know what I'm up against. I want to be enlightened. It's not true the Russians are ahead of us, is it? Or is it? They have no highways, not enough houses, almost no automobiles. Their railroads are ridiculous, as you know. Well, then? Just a bit of propaganda, that's all it is. I want to have your confirmation that their missile, their *bleep-bleep,* as people are beginning to call it, doesn't prove a thing . . . and I want you to say so to all the journalists who are sure to interview you. As for our satellite . . . yes, the general told me, you can't go any faster, you have to keep to a set program. . . . You scientists always have programs. That's quite understandable, of course. Only you're going to draw another one up straight away, a much bigger one. . . . You understand? I must be able to announce the imminent launching of a much heavier and more perfected satellite. Say three hundred or even four hundred pounds . . . Funds? The general mentioned them. You'll have them. Just say the word. Don't worry about that. I'll see to it myself. Meanwhile go ahead, go straight ahead, Dr. Stern. All America has her eyes fixed on you . . . on you and the Navy as well. Good heavens, I almost forgot! They've also got a program. . . . What do they call it now? . . . Ah yes, Vanguard, that's it. Maybe they'll be able to launch it a little sooner? I'll call them and see. Meanwhile, go ahead, Dr. Stern, go ahead."

"To hell with him!" Stern muttered again as he slowly replaced the receiver.

This time he did not even have time to take a step toward the dining table. The telephone rang again. He picked it up once more with an exasperated and at the same time appealing glance at his guests. It was General Stayman again. He had absolutely nothing new to say but his excitement was such that he had to get it out of his system. He turned instinctively to the telephone, as to some psychological safety valve capable of restoring a faltering nervous equilibrium.

"Have you had that bore on the line? I know he called you. He doesn't understand a thing, but he has confidence in you, too, in you and no one else. . . . There's also the Navy, damn it—that Vanguard project of theirs. And the Air Force? They must be working their guts out, too . . . Provided . . . but no, I tell you, you're the only expert of any value. I'm sure you'll be the first to succeed. Have you thought it over? You're sure you can't add a few more pounds? Good. . . . See you tomorrow, and don't forget the new program."

Every telephone line in America was busy, from New York to Washington, from Washington to La Grange, from Washington to Cape Canaveral, from Washington to the Vandenberg Base, from La Grange to Cape Canaveral, from all the big newspapers in the United States to La Grange, to Washington, and to Cape Canaveral, and a substantial part of these frantic calls ended with Stern. Between one call and another Maggie had time to remark:

"It's a good sign. Public opinion has been alerted. I'm sure they're going to get busy."

"Maybe."

"Dr. Stern?"

Another call.

"Dr. Stern, *Time* magazine . . . the science department. You gave me an interview last year. . . . A few specific questions I've jotted down; I don't want to take up too much of your time. First, do you think we're really lagging behind the Russians in the space race? Second, how long do you estimate it will take us to catch up with them, that is, if we are lagging behind? Third, to what is this due . . . ?"

Most of the big newspapers and magazines phoned, giving the impression of taking turns in order of importance. The telephone did not give him a moment's peace.

". . . What are your projects for the future?"

"The moon!" Stern screamed in exasperation. "The moon, as you know perfectly well!"

115

This was no more than the truth. But a stifled laugh at the other end of the line showed how seriously the journalist greeted this announcement. Yet not for anything in the world would he have tried to prevent the "lunatic" from continuing on such a promising track. On the contrary, he urged him on, in an encouraging tone of voice.

"The moon, yes, of course, Dr. Stern. And after that?"

"After that Mars, and then Venus, and then . . ."

"You're serious, I assume?"

"I need ten years to land a man on the moon," Stern bellowed, enraged by the imperceptibly mocking tone. "I need ten years and you can announce this to all your readers. If they had listened to me and given me the necessary means in 1945, an American would be on the moon at this very moment. I still say so today and I can prove it: an American will set foot on the moon in ten years' time, in 1967, on one condition—on condition that they provide me at once with all I need and abandon this stupid policy of establishing a balance between the Navy, the Air Force, and the goddamned Army of this goddamned country! Can you hear me, at least?"

"I can hear you all right, Dr. Stern, and I'm taking it all down, don't worry."

"And also on another condition, namely . . ."

He was once again recalled to order by the frantic gestures of Maggie, who was standing by his side at this moment.

"You were saying," the journalist eagerly persisted, "another condition?"

"No, that's all. Just·on condition that I'm allowed to work in peace."

"Darling, you mustn't get so overwrought," Maggie said when he had hung up. "It doesn't get you anywhere."

"I'm not so sure," said Meyer, who had not uttered a word until then. "In this country, when you want to get anything done, you first have to alert public opinion. Your statements are going to kick up a fine shindig tomorrow; as a result of this, maybe they'll provide you with the means you want."

"Or maybe they'll throw you out on your ear," said Walker.

"I shouldn't be surprised. But I can always get a job as a fitter."

SIXTEEN

They did their best to overcome their dismay by trying to chat lightheartedly, and dinner ended in a seemingly more relaxed atmosphere. They had even stretched stoicism so far as to switch off the television and did not mention the event any further. But Maggie's nervous gestures and precipitate speech contrasted with this feigned detachment.

At the end of the meal, unable to bear it a moment longer, she switched on the set. They gathered around the screen just as the Moscow announcement was being broadcast, to which all America was listening that night with a heavy heart and the feeling of having suffered a humiliating and undeserved defeat.

"For some years research and experiments have been under way in the Soviet Union, aimed at the construction of artificial earth satellites . . ."

"For some years!" Stern echoed.

"The dispatch of the first satellites was envisaged within the framework of the International Geophysical Year . . ."

117

"Damned hypocrites!" Walker exclaimed. "As though they needed an excuse!"

"The intense work of the research institutes and investigation centers has culminated in the construction of an artificial earth satellite, the first satellite to have been constructed in the world . . ."

"The bastards!" Meyer in his turn muttered.

"Our television shouldn't broadcast such things," Maggie exclaimed, springing to her feet.

She had drunk a great deal during the meal. She had never stopped smoking, throwing away her cigarettes half consumed. She poured herself some whisky, knocking the bottle against the glass with her shaky hands. Stern motioned her to calm down. He had recovered his composure a little and wanted to hear the rest.

"The first observations confirm that the booster rocket gave the satellite the required velocity—a velocity of eighty-eight hundred yards per second, approximately . . ."

With Walker immediately following his example, Stern produced a notebook and started jotting down this information.

"The satellite is flying at an altitude of five hundred and sixty miles and it completes one revolution around the earth in ninety-five minutes. The satellite is spherical in shape, with a diameter of twenty-three inches. It weighs one hundred and eighty-four pounds . . ."

"Not two hundred, after all!" Walker observed.

The announcement came to an end. A young girl appeared on the screen extolling the virtues of a certain brand of cigarettes. Stern was making calculations in his notebook.

"This probably means a three-stage rocket," he said, "weighing about a hundred tons at blast-off."

He was pondering on these figures when the telephone rang again. It was General Stayman. He had no more reason to disturb him than before, but the broadcast had revived his fury.

"Did you hear? The first in the world. It's unbridled propaganda. Stern, I can't stand this!"

"You'll have to nevertheless, General."

"Good. You're right. They've announced that some of our leading figures, scientists and politicians, are going to give their views. That might be interesting."

"Yes, it might. With your permission, I'd like to listen to them."

The first of the leading figures was an old professor of the University of Ohio, laden with degrees and honors. There was nothing to prove, he declared, that the Russians had actually launched a satellite. Speaking for himself, he was extremely skeptical. Everyone was too accustomed to hearing them give false information, for purely propaganda purposes, to accept this announcement without proof.

The Sterns and their guests looked at one another in a silence fraught with indignation.

"Let's hear the others," Meyer finally said. "Maybe the politicians will be a little less idiotic than the scholars."

The first political figure who gave his opinion on the screen was not an American but a British guest, and an illustrious one: the Secretary for Foreign Affairs. The television reporters had pounced on him as he landed in New York, where he had come for reasons totally unconnected with space. He had only just heard the news. Interrogated by a journalist, he merely declared:

"I don't think many people are terribly interested in this." *

This time a fourfold exclamation punctuated the broadcast. Maggie almost knocked over a small table as she sprang from her armchair. Meyer, a little calmer, raised his clenched fists in the air.

"He doesn't think!" Stern began. "He doesn't think . . . Maggie, this time I'm the one who can't stand it!"

* See note, page 34.

119

They forced themselves, however, to listen to the rest. The second politician was none other than the Vice President of the United States. Although he had no definite proof, he personally felt that the news was accurate, although he did not blindly accept the characteristics claimed for the missile.

"But," he added in a firm voice, *"this achievement must not in any way disturb us Americans, for we are well ahead of the Soviets in the fields of education and science."*

"The poor fool!" Walker growled. "He thinks . . ."

He had no time to finish his sentence. The telephone interrupted them again. Again it was General Stayman. He seemed somewhat reassured and his voice sounded like a chant of triumph.

"Well, Stern, what about it? Didn't I tell you we shouldn't lose heart? Did you hear what he said? We're well ahead of the Soviets . . ."

Stern preferred to slam down the receiver rather than answer him. He was opening his mouth to utter a curse when another figure appeared on the screen. It was an economic adviser to the White House. He shrugged his shoulders in a surly manner, uttered a few trite phrases, and proudly concluded:

"I'm very glad my country wasn't the first to launch this ludicrous bauble."

Before Stern and his guests could react, the Secretary of Defense came on. He advised Americans to sleep peacefully, promising them with a facetious air that the Sputnik would not drop anything on their heads.

"And Ike? What has Ike got to say about it?" Walker bellowed in fury.

"He'd say the same thing," said Maggie in a faltering voice. "It's an utter disgrace! This gang of grocers is driving us to ruin."

Stern forgot his own anger for a moment to observe his wife with anxiety. She had become livid. Her lips were pinched and a strange puckering of her nose, which he had noticed before in

120

two or three exceptional circumstances, augured nothing good. She went on drinking and smoking to excess. She poured herself another whisky and drank it in one gulp, before he could stop her. He came up to her, but his attention was once more held by the appearance of another celebrity on the screen. It was the Secretary of State. The television company had had the bright idea of contrasting his interview, given some time before and in a different place, with that of his British counterpart.

He confined himself initially to generalities and pointed out that America had a well-established satellite program about which everyone would be hearing very soon. Then, as his interviewer, a brash reporter, mentioned the moon and the conquest of space, he grew more animated and declared vehemently that the United States should not think of going to the moon, since such an enterprise would be too costly.

At this, Stern felt on the verge of committing any folly. He unbuttoned his collar and tore off his tie with a violent gesture. He was about to give vent to a stream of abuse when he looked at Maggie again. She was at the end of her tether. What she had had to suffer this evening went beyond the limits of her endurance. Her lips were discolored; every feature in her face was tense. Her body was shaken with spasms, which she tried in vain to suppress. She burst into tears and collapsed, completely shattered, into an armchair.

SEVENTEEN

One month later, on November third, the launching of the second Russian satellite and the brief odyssey of the dog Laika revived the bitterness of the space fanatics at La Grange and the other few bases scattered throughout the United States. This time Stern refused to make the slightest comment, forbidding himself, even with pride, to spare a thought for his rivals' exploits. He needed all his faculties to put the finishing touches to his own satellite. Even so, he was sufficiently disturbed by repeated calls from General Stayman at every hour of the day and night, wanting to know how he was progressing.

The tests were satisfactory. He hoped to be able to save a few weeks and effect a launching sometime in January. Little by little he managed to recover his peace of mind and equilibrium by concentrating on this task every second.

Toward the end of November, while he was working on a series of measurements in a laboratory, he was interrupted by the noisy intrusion of General Stayman, whose indignation that day was so strong that he had scorned the telephone and called in person.

"Do you know what they're asking me to do—asking you to do, Stern? And I'm obliged to agree to it. The order comes from the White House. They called at least a dozen times. I can't refuse."

"Refuse what?"

"The Navy has been up to its tricks. . . . You know, their famous Vanguard, that missile they're being so mysterious about."

"What of it?"

"Well, they say they're ready to launch a satellite within the next few days."

"It's not possible!"

Stern felt a painful twinge in his chest. The Russians, well and good, it was now an accomplished fact—but to be outdone even in America seemed to him the worst of defeats.

"I had dinner with one of their leading engineers, Walker, less than two months ago, the very day the Sputnik went up. He told me they had at least another six months' work to do. And he's not the sort of man to try to fool me."

"They must have found some means of going ahead more quickly. In any case, the date of their operation has now been put forward to December eighth or thereabouts. The devils! What if they succeed! What would we look like, I ask you? Well, anyway, it seems it's our duty to wish them good luck and to do everything we can to help them. So I finally agreed."

"Agreed to what, may I ask?"

"To your giving them a helping hand."

"Me?"

"You. It was Walker, in fact, who went down on his knees and begged for you. He has managed to convince his admiral that you're indispensable. The admiral—I know him, he's a manipulator—succeeded in persuading the authorities, and the White House insists that you leave at once for Cape Canaveral. . . . In one way, mind, I can see their point. If America could launch one of these projectiles before the end of the year, it would be better for all of us. And on the whole it's rather flattering for us—for you—that they should turn to you, the eminent expert, at this crucial moment."

"Ten days before the launching!"

"Yes, I know. It's cutting it a bit fine. But do what you can to help them. It doesn't matter, after all, if it's a success. We'll point out that it was thanks to your assistance."

Stern arrived at Cape Canaveral in an ugly mood and what he saw there only served to increase his fury.

He had spent the whole trip fuming against Walker, the Navy, the Army, the White House, and all the government departments that seemed in league to retard the execution of his own project.

His project was a satellite of thirty-eight pounds—it was not his fault that it was no bigger!—propelled by a four-stage rocket, one of *his* rockets, based on a Peenemünde model, a powerful, relatively simple missile that had already proved itself. A *simple* missile was what was needed to put this satellite into orbit: an elementary operation, in his opinion. This was what many American technicians refused to admit.

Without knowing all the details, he knew that the Navy's Vanguard rocket contained far more complicated components: interesting components, granted—the Navy, as he also knew, had some excellent engineers, as did the other services—but ones he would have to study for several weeks before being able to give a considered opinion. All he asked was to work with them within the framework of a general program. But there was no general program and now, ten days before the launching, he was being dragged away from his own work to be asked his advice about materials he did not know! He swore he would tell Walker what he thought of him and his methods.

It was Walker himself who came to meet him at the airport. He had not seen him since the famous Sputnik evening. He was struck by the change in his appearance, so much so that he refrained from showing his resentment. The engineer was hollow-cheeked and his complexion was pasty. His dark-ringed, bloodshot eyes bore evidence of lack of sleep and inhuman overwork. His dull gaze, which was painful to see, was that of a sleepwalker. He greeted him, however, in a tone of intense excitement.

"Come on, Stern. I'm taking you right away to the launching pad. The rocket's already there and everything's ready."

"Ready?"

"Yes, as I said. Of course, there are still a few little details to see to. But in eight days everything will be okay."

He dragged him off to his car before Stern could speak a word and drove off to the launching site.

"From what you yourself told me, I thought you were not going to be ready before March," Stern eventually remarked, looking at him with a reproachful air.

"And I meant it at the time. I wasn't trying to fool you, I assure you. But we discovered a means of going ahead more quickly, by simplifying. Of course, this entailed a few modifications of detail, but I'm certain it's going to be all right."

"Look, Walker, if you want me to help you—and believe me, I'll do my best—you must give me a general idea of your project. Could I first of all see the plans and study them?"

"Later on," said Walker in a rather embarrassed manner. "I'd first like to have your impression of the actual material on the spot. Then I'll take you to see the admiral."

"Is that necessary?"

"He insists. He attaches the greatest value to your help, as I do—as we all do."

"All right. But if I could see the plans before, I would be able to discuss . . ."

"Listen," said Walker, as though preparing himself unwillingly to make a painful confession, "listen and try not to get angry. The plans aren't ready yet, we're still working on them. You'll have to do without them for the time being."

Stern groaned.

"You say there are no plans!"

He wondered suddenly whether he had come upon a group

of maniacs or whether the whole thing was not a put-up job to make fun of him.

"I was talking of the new plans. . . . Of course, we drew some plans originally but, as I said, in order to launch before the end of the year, we've had to modify quite a lot of details. . . . Let me explain it all in a nutshell. What held us back more than anything was the fuel pump. Yes; one of our engineers had invented a perfect model, an incredibly light one. Only this model wouldn't have been ready by March. So we decided to drive our Vanguard with an old pump, one of the ones you're using."

"Who decided?"

"The admiral; after conferring with various specialists, of course. I assure you it's possible. . . . But when an essential part in these missiles has to be replaced, it involves a whole lot of other changes, as you know perfectly well."

"I can just imagine," said Stern, taking the engineer's side.

"Nothing important, but a mass of small details . . . the piping, for instance; you see, it didn't fit the new pump. Luckily the firm in New York managed to make us another set very quickly. We received it a few days ago and we've finished assembling it. . . . Only the weight isn't the same . . . the weight and also the space it fills. We're having to shift a lot of instruments. . . . But it's the weight more than anything else. The pump itself is heavier. To cut a long story short, we've saved what we can by changing a few metal plates. Yes, thinner plates . . . with smaller rivets. It'll work. . . . Furthermore, and this wasn't at all easy, we've also had to reduce the weight of our satellite. It weighs only four and a half pounds."

"Four and a half!"

"Not quite; three and a third, to be exact. . . . So you see now why the original plans don't correspond to reality. In fact, they're way off. To save time, we decided to start without them, but a whole army of draftsmen is working on them now. They'll be ready . . ."

"After the launching, I suppose," said Stern, looking him straight in the eye.

Walker did not reply. His excitement had suddenly evaporated. He remained silent, glum, until they reached the launching pad. From far off Stern caught sight of the rocket standing beside its gantry and could not take his eyes off it. As the car drew closer, he was unable to suppress an exclamation of surprise.

Granted, he was familiar with the commotion that always precedes an important launching, but he had never seen anything to compare with this feverish activity. The whole pad was occupied by a mass of vehicles of every type, forming a huge circle around the rocket: jeeps, workshop trucks, tankers, tractors with electric generators in tow, all connected to one another and to the rocket by a maze of cables and pipes. But it was the men who astonished him most of all, for there were swarms of them around the machines, and these men showed every sign of madness.

They never walked; they ran, waving their arms in a frenzied manner. Whether it was to rush from one vehicle to another, or to plunge into the gaping hole at the base of the rocket, or to hop onto one of the gantry lifts, no movement was performed calmly. When the men had to wait a minute for the arrival of one of the lifts, they paced back and forth restlessly, muttering and cursing.

Trying to discern some sort of order in this apparent chaos, Stern at last made out what he took to be a group of specialists, but it was such an odd-looking gathering that he could scarcely believe his eyes. In order to save time, to accomplish in eight days a task that would normally have required several months, representatives of the various professions were assembled there; they got in one another's way and tussled among themselves to be the first on the job. He might have burst out laughing if he, too, had not suddenly been affected by the atmosphere of tragedy underlying this incoherent commotion.

127

Cheek by jowl with electricians and electronic technicians carrying extremely delicate instruments were welders and fitters busily riveting the base of the metal carcass, amid the deafening din of their machines, entangling their compressed-air lines with wires and electric cables and exchanging an endless round of curses.

The car drew up. Stern turned to Walker to express his astonishment. The engineer sat motionless, with his head still sunk on his chest. Stern realized he had plunged into a deep sleep, almost a faint. He had to give him a good shake to rouse him.

EIGHTEEN

Walker awoke from his torpor with a start that shook him from head to foot and sat blinking for a moment or two.

"It'll work," he stammered, even before he had fully recovered consciousness.

Then he pulled himself together, gave a wan smile, and muttered: "I'm sorry. I take advantage of these trips to snatch forty winks: that's why I have a driver. Otherwise I couldn't keep going."

"I know what work is, believe me," said Stern, feeling a surge of pity and patting him on the shoulder. "I, too, have been pushed to the limits of my strength. But when one has reached the stage you have, there's only one thing to do: go to bed and sleep for ten hours. That's the first piece of advice the rocket expert gives you."

"Thanks," said Walker, smiling again. "I appreciate it and I'll follow it—some other time."

Stern frowned as he saw him take a small box out of his pocket and swallow a couple of pills. The engineer seemed to revive and soon recovered his feverish energy. He jumped out of the car and dragged his companion toward the rocket. As they picked their way through a tangle of pipes and cables, they were stopped several times by technicians. All of them had the same dark circles under their eyes and talked in the same jerky voices.

"There's nothing to be done, sir," a foreman protested. "I need a weight of two hundred and twenty pounds for these sheets and rivets, and not a pound less."

"Walker, I keep telling him one hundred and ninety," said a youthful engineer, "but he's as stubborn as a mule. I've cut it as fine as I could. If he puts on two twenty, this damned missile will never get off the ground, that's for sure."

"And if I don't have my two twenty, do you know what's going to happen? Your damned Vanguard will fall apart even before it reaches the height of a shed."

"All right," said Walker, trying to satisfy them both, "we'll try to save thirty pounds somewhere else. I'll see about it this evening."

He jotted a reminder down in his notebook, which was already full of scribbles. Another man came up to them, flinging his arms in the air.

"Gremlins, sir! Not one, but thousands, millions of them. Short circuits in every coil. It'll be a regular fireworks display!"

"We'll have to check the insulation of each section, one by one," Walker said patiently.

"And how do you expect me to manage that, sir?" the man went on in a plaintive, almost tearful voice. "They're making me shift a whole panel and reduce another by half! . . . And this fellow here with his damned blowtorch keeps burning up my insulations! Goddammit, he thinks he's working in a foundry!''

Walker, who appeared to be more animated since arriving at the site, calmed them all down with a word or a promise and they went back to their tasks, shaking their heads, clenching their teeth, but stubbornly intent on making a good job of the work in hand, striving constantly and feverishly to find miraculous solutions to insoluble problems.

"It's certainly a miracle," Stern said to himself. "They actually manage to get things done in this indescribable chaos. No workman of any other nationality would be able to do it."

They were indeed working with everything they had, with all their muscles and concentration, as though their very lives depended on the result of their efforts; with anguished eyes, wrinkled brows, and clenched teeth, each was desperately striving to get the utmost out of his human machine, the impossible output demanded to make a chimerical enterprise successful.

"There are still a few details to see to," Walker said once again, as though by way of apology, "but everything will be arranged in a few days. Come and see inside."

Before entering the gantry, Stern paused for a moment to examine its shape. In a glance he checked the general characteristics he already knew: total height, seventy-three feet; diameter at the base, a little over a yard. But already Walker was impatiently ushering him toward the opening. Two or three workmen who were milling around the hatch stepped aside, grumbling, to let them pass.

Inside, the situation was much the same as outside. Fitters were at work in the base while, slightly higher up, electricians were trying to check the system that had been hastily installed to satisfy the new conditions. Big lamps, whose own circuit added to the general confusion, illuminated faces streaming with sweat, while loud curses echoed around the great metallic cylinder like claps of thunder. Stern refused to look at anything else for the moment and went out, followed by Walker.

"Well, what do you think of it?" the engineer asked.

He spoke in the tone of a patient questioning his doctor and dreading a fearful diagnosis. Stern looked at him directly.

"Do you really, seriously, intend launching this thing eight days from now?"

Walker's pasty face went livid.

"Of course. We're in a hurry."

Stern looked at him even more sharply.

"And you feel, honestly and truly, that it will be a success?"

Walker looked away and did not give a direct answer.

"There's no harm trying," he eventually said in an uncertain voice.

Stern could not shed the sensation of astonishment that had overwhelmed him. It had needed a mere glance for him to grasp the situation. His thorough knowledge of rockets, both theoretical and practical, the experience acquired in the course of countless tests, made it quite plain to him that the project was doomed to utter failure. In this field, as he knew, as he had learned to his own cost in his youth, nothing could take the place of minute and methodical preparation. No power on earth, no miracle, could transform in eight days' time this pile of conflicting materials into a harmonious entity subject to human will. What disconcerted him most of all, perhaps, was Walker's attitude. He knew him very well. He knew he was a first-rate technician, experienced and extremely conscientious. He was heading for certain failure, jeopardizing his reputation, perhaps even his whole future. Everyone would blame him afterward. It was his duty to open Walker's eyes to this. How could he so deceive himself?

The reply came suddenly: *Walker was not deceiving himself at all.* And immediately, as he looked more closely at the men around him, he realized no less clearly that not one of them, not a single one, entertained the slightest doubt about the outcome of this wild attempt. It was a brutal enlightenment that at once dispelled the exasperation this chaos had caused him. All these engineers, who knew their jobs perfectly, all these foremen, who had considerable practical experience, all these workmen, who were capable of gauging the resistance of a material by the mere feel of it, all of them *knew* perfectly well that they were heading for failure. And yet they were rushing headlong into it. They were rushing, flying into it with a sort of morbid energy, all of them fiercely refusing to admit the obvious and confess themselves beaten.

He vaguely detected the presence of a mysterious and perhaps sublime sentiment in this willfulness. He felt moved by Walker's wretched appearance and reproached himself, as though for a crime, for the cruelty of his last remark. He no longer had the courage to utter point-blank a brutal diagnosis. He merely echoed in a dull voice:

"No, of course not, Walker, there's no harm trying."

"Walker! Walker!" a frantic voice bellowed behind them.

It was the admiral who had just driven up, completely unescorted. The workmen went on with their jobs without paying the slightest attention to him. Since a state of emergency had been declared at Cape Canaveral by the Navy, he had forbidden them to waste even a second by saluting him. He came up, stretching out his hand, and greeted Stern with jovial excitement.

"You're very welcome, Dr. Stern. As you see, there's still quite a lot to do here. I'm extremely grateful to you for agreeing to help us. . . . Everything all right, Walker?"

"It'll be all right, sir," said Walker. "Still a few details to see to."

"Well, anyway, the most important part is ready," the admiral announced triumphantly. "I drove over especially to tell you. The satellite's arrived. It can be put in place . . . tomorrow, I should think, don't you, Walker? I've seen it. The experts are looking it over now. It's a beauty, Dr. Stern . . . not very big, perhaps, but covered in a sort of gold plate. Eh? It'll sparkle in the rising sun."

He was like a child who had just been given a long-coveted toy. Stern shrugged his shoulders in a somewhat disrespectful manner.

"If you want me to be of any use," he said, "I shall have to see the plans of the rocket, the old ones for want of the new . . . and also to be told by someone how it works."

He spent the rest of the day studying the original plans of the Vanguard and trying to get someone to tell him what the last-minute alterations were. From his inquiry he derived the painful certainty that no one really knew what the situation was. The initial modification involved an endless host of others —details, as Walker insisted on calling them, but details demanding serious study, specific plans, and a testing period of several months. Instead, it was in the very belly of the rocket that new arrangements were decided upon, and orders to put them into effect were forthwith given to the workmen.

It was sheer folly. After dinner—Walker had consented to have this meal with him, which was contrary to his habits, for he generally ate a sandwich on the site—they went back to the launching pad, illuminated by searchlights for night work. Walker looked at him with pleading eyes. It was clear that he now wanted advice, some sort of action. Stern began by flying into a temper.

"I'm not God Almighty, Walker. I can't perform miracles. I can't even be of any help to you in this venture, such as it is. I would first have to think the matter over, make plans, study them, and then carry out some tests. That can't be done in eight days."

"I know we're working rather queerly at the moment, but there's no time to do anything else. If it succeeds, we shall have launched a satellite in the same year as the Russians. If not . . ."

"No need to dot the *i*'s," Stern grumbled. "I know what you mean."

"And there is a chance of its succeeding. I beg you, Stern, to help us even under these conditions. Abandon the usual routine."

"The calculations, the drawings, the plans . . . you refer to all that as routine!"

He hesitated a moment, ready to wash his hands of the whole business. But the young engineer sounded so desperate that he could not bring himself to do so. Once again his bad mood melted into a strange emotion compounded of pity and secret admiration.

"That's how it is, is it?" he exclaimed. "Well, let's get down to work!"

He had suddenly been overcome by a wave of affection for this gang of madmen. He felt their folly in every fiber of his body. He paused for a moment to contemplate the carcass of the rocket, which looked like a disemboweled body with its entrails scattered all around it by clumsy surgeons. He stood thus for a few seconds, hypnotized, spellbound by the sight of a chaos beyond the bounds of human understanding. But the perverse desire to participate in this monstrous absurdity himself urged him on.

"Let's get down to work!" he repeated. "At the stage we've now reached, you're right; to hell with the plans!"

He rushed toward the rocket, almost breaking into a run, thrust his way through the workmen who were still milling around the entrance hatch, tore off his coat, flung it on the ground, and demanded furiously:

"Get me some overalls."

A few minutes later, clad in working clothes, he entered the body of the rocket.

NINETEEN

He remained inside it for eight days, emerging only to bolt a sandwich, take one or two tablets of a stimulant that all the engineers ate incessantly, or snatch an hour's sleep on one of the camp beds installed in a temporary hut. He remained inside it for one hundred and ninety-two hours, cursing and swearing, inveighing against men and inanimate objects in a mixture of German and American slang, abusing both, sometimes criticizing violently what had been done, yelling at the senior technicians as well as the humblest laborer, often snatching a tool out of a workman's hand when the latter was not fast enough for his liking, and tackling the recalcitrant material himself.

He refused to make any calculations. He forbade himself to think or to assess the consequences of any decision taken on the spur of the moment and its fatal repercussions on other parts of the machine. He felt he could not allow his mind to take precedence even for a moment over the automatic movements of his muscles, for then he would have been obliged to conclude that he was acting like a madman. Like everyone else, he now refused to admit the idiocy of his efforts. It was all he could do to consent to listen for a few seconds to the intuitive suggestions of his experience, in order to find some makeshift solution to the problems that kept cropping up constantly.

And the others obeyed him. Such was his reputation that a fresh gust of hope had blown into the rocket when he entered it, while the inhuman thirst for work redoubled. If the famous Dr. Stern ordered this or that to be done, he had definite reasons, inspired by genius, and this was what had to be done if the venture was to succeed. They all competed as to who could carry out his instructions most quickly. He cursed them for this blind confidence for which he was suffering martyrdom. He realized that at every moment he was assuming a larger and larger share of the responsibility for the attempt. He was gambling recklessly with his reputation. At other times he found himself thinking, against all the evidence, that there must be some justification in their hope and that, without being aware of it, he was the man ordained by destiny to redeem a hopeless situation. For nothing in the world would he have abandoned his task. Thus he spent a week in a state of semi-hallucination, striving to find, among the infinity of possible combinations, the one mysterious harmony of materials— a harmony that is only achieved, finally, by time and trial and error.

One evening, as he emerged from this inferno to take a few breaths of fresh air, filthy dirty and with his forehead streaked with stale sweat, he came face to face with the admiral, who had arrived with a bottle and two glasses and insisted on pouring him a drink.

"Well, how's it going?" he asked.

"I can't tell yet," Stern muttered, turning away.

The date fixed for the launching was three days off.

"It'll be all right," said the admiral with a fine air of authority. "I've asked all the journalists."

"The journalists!"

"There'll be quite a lot of onlookers, too. It can't be helped. We do everything quite openly in this country. It must succeed."

"It must succeed," Stern echoed, spluttering.

"And the success will be mainly due to you."

"Please!"

"Yes indeed, I insist on announcing it. The help you've given us since your arrival has been incalculable. I like people like you, Dr. Stern, who don't mind pitching in and getting their hands dirty when it's necessary. It's what I expected of you."

This indeed was what the ingenuous admiral expected of him: that he should don some overalls and show the workmen how to connect two wires or put in a screw. This was how he visualized the work of the country's most celebrated rocket specialist. Once again Stern was too deeply moved to lose his temper. But did the admiral really imagine, was he the only one to believe, that this shapeless monster was going to take to the air in three days' time?

The admiral continued, convinced that he was pleasing Stern and flattering his vanity.

"I'll tell General Stayman . . . I used to see a lot of old Stayman; it can't be much fun being with him; a silly old fogy, if you ask me. But I'll tell him how you've devoted yourself to the job. And without a sign of reluctance, without the slightest jealousy, which, after all, would have been quite natural. . . . Oh yes, I know you people are also working on one of these machines, one of these satellites. You might have been furious at our lead. Well, now I know that's not the case and I'll broadcast it so everyone can hear: Dr. Stern plays fair."

Dr. Stern made no reply but, abstemious though he usually was, poured himself out another swig of whisky and drank it in one gulp. He then made a gesture that resembled a military salute and rushed back into the belly of the rocket, as though seeking asylum.

On the eve of the launching everything was ready, in theory, and the "little details" had been fixed. The satellite in its dazzling gold plate had been carried onto the pad by the admiral himself. Opening its case, he raised the fragile instrument into the air at arm's length, like a priest consecrating the Host. Scarcely bigger than an orange, the projectile threw off a thousand sparks. With utmost satisfaction the admiral handed it to the specialists, who fixed it in position. Stern had felt his heart miss a beat.

A gloomy lassitude had overcome him when he finished his work. He had forced himself to the limits of his strength, but he was incapable of remembering exactly what he had done and was assailed now and then by remorse.

That night, as on so many others, he was unable to sleep in spite of his fatigue. The countdown, which began at dawn, was a calvary for him. The presence of a multitude of eyewitnesses added to the intensity of his torment. Journalists from all over the world had indeed collected that morning around the Vanguard rocket; journalists and also a crowd of onlookers who had arrived in a convoy of cars and been greeted by smiling hostesses wearing on their breast the badge of this exalted spot: C.C., standing for Cape Canaveral.

The countdown lasted all morning instead of the two hours predicted. A defective instrument kept causing delays while a repair team repeatedly worked on it. But each time, at the first sign that the instrument appeared to work properly, without waiting for confirmation, without quickly checking it again, the procedure was immediately continued. The atmosphere was so tense that the man responsible for the blast-off had to restrain himself several times from pressing the button long before the countdown reached zero, long before this travesty of verification had been completed.

"It'll work," said Walker in the blockhouse.

Stern did not reply. For the first time in his life the launching of a rocket roused in him no cosmic emotion, no curiosity. He felt only terribly tired and deeply depressed. When the countdown reached zero he buried his head in his folded arms.

A frantic exclamation from Walker and the other engineers forced him to look at the television screen.

"She's off!"

They looked like a crowd of pilgrims gathered in some holy place and trying to bring about a miracle by the fervor of their prayers.

The machine shuddered above the ground in that fatal fraction of a second they all knew, when, motionless, it struggles against the earth's attraction with all the power of its motors.

"She's off!"

A gust of madness swept the blockhouse. A wild hope made Stern's heart beat faster. He grasped Walker's shoulder so tightly that the engineer winced.

The rocket was indeed off, but did not go far. The cheers that had begun to ring out were abruptly stilled and replaced by groans of anguish.

"It's a trick of the light," Walker stammered in a choking voice. "An optical illusion. I've seen this sort of thing before."

It was not an optical illusion. They were all too experienced not to recognize, even in their delirium, the symptoms of death. The snake of flame had fallen away, separating into several sections, while the retarded rocket began to oscillate around its vertical axis. Presently the tottering motion increased. Dipping its nose, the rocket came crashing down in the roaring, raging inferno that always accompanied such accidents.

The feverish excitement was followed by a tragic silence. Stern remained prostrate, hanging his head. He raised it only when he heard the sound of sobbing.

A hysterical scene was taking place in the blockhouse. Most of the men were weeping like children. The admiral flung his cap on the floor and trampled it underfoot. One of his staff officers lay flat on his face, his shoulders shaken by sobs. Stern

139

went up to Walker and with an effort, in an expressionless voice, said:

"I'm sorry, old man. I did everything I could."

"I know. I also . . . all of us . . . everything we could."

"The next one will be a success."

"The next one, yes. But it won't be this year."

He raised his head, however, with an air of defiance.

"We're planning *ten* satellites for next year."

"I have a confession to make," Stern continued in a strangled voice.

He felt a strange, long-forgotten sensation. His lips trembled. He made a violent effort to master his emotion and at last managed to speak, with a curious note of exultation in his voice.

"I'm a former enemy, am I not? I did you a lot of harm in the war with my V-2's."

"You know that's all dead and buried ages ago. The Army has officially recognized your services."

"I know, but I wasn't satisfied with that. I have often had occasion to feel ill at ease and uncomfortable. You know what I mean? . . . Only today, at this moment, after what I've done here, Walker, do I feel I've really paid the price!"

The engineer clasped his hand in silence. Only then did Stern turn away and burst into tears himself. It was the first time he felt really American.

THREE

THE TURNING POINT

TWENTY

Toward the end of 1958 the astronauts of the whole world held a meeting in Amsterdam. (By then the term "astronaut" was beginning to replace "lunatic" and "moonstruck" in the mind of the general public.) It was not the first time they had thus gathered, but this session was of exceptional interest in view of the successful exploits that year in the realm of space.

The quality of the participants was likewise remarkable. Stern had come at the head of the American delegation. The first evening, the most important one, he was in the big conference hall listening to a speech by Zharov, the "father of the Sputnik." Zharov was just coming to the end of his brilliant talk. He concluded it with these words:

"I hope a Soviet rocket will reach the moon in the very near future."

Immediately, in the midst of the outburst of applause, Stern rose furtively to his feet and crept toward the exit without attracting anyone's attention.

He heaved a sigh of relief on finding himself outside and seeing that no journalist had followed him. His official role was more or less over. He had already said that morning what he had to say about satellites. In the afternoon it had been the turn of the Russians. He had prepared himself for this session as for an arduous test. He had suffered as he had expected; suffered especially to see the eyes of friendly delegates fixed alternately on the Soviet scientists and then on the American delegates with a touch of anxiety and reproach.

Granted, he had some interesting results to report. The United States could glory in four successes: four satellites still orbiting the earth, three of which were his own brain children (the first, as foreseen, was one of his), launched by his rockets. Numerically they had beaten the Russians, who had only three. And yet . . .

And yet he had felt the blood rushing to his head and the eyes of the members of the congress burning into him when Zharov, in an offhand manner, reminded them of the weight of the three Russian projectiles and the following progression: 182 pounds for the first, 1237.6 for the second, which had the dog Laika on board—the Russian had mentioned this quite casually—and 2919 pounds for the third, an absolute flying laboratory. The four American projectiles together did not exceed 110 pounds!

He had never in his life felt so humiliated. All he could think of was revenge. This could only be the moon. The American people realized this. Hundreds of thousands of letters had been sent to the White House demanding a gigantic effort in this field. But the political bigwigs were not easy to move. The weight of the last Sputnik having roused anxiety among the military, who suspected the Russians of conceiving such a projectile only as a carrier of atomic bombs, some slight additional funds had been allocated. But the coherent program, which was indispensable for the grandiose schemes of which he dreamed, was still hanging fire, and the recognition of the manifest Russian lead gnawed at his heart.

He walked quickly down the steps of the institute in which the congress was being held, eager to take a short stroll by himself before rejoining his colleagues, who were busily discussing in

144

the corridors or granting interviews to the press. Someone gave him a light tap on the shoulder. He turned around and gasped with astonishment.

"Nadia!"

She had not changed very much. A few lines at the corners of her eyes were the only signs of the work she had accomplished during these last few years. The eyes themselves had retained their unusual depth, which contrasted with her somewhat homely face. Stern's first reaction was to fling his arms wide and they embraced like two old friends meeting after a long absence. Then he stepped back a pace or two and looked at her in silence, not knowing quite what to say. After a moment a gleam came into his eyes.

"You're here for . . ." he began, pointing to the institute.

She nodded.

"I'm part of the Russian delegation . . . oh, a very modest position. I'm one of Zharov's assistants. Yes, I've concentrated especially on the Sputniks."

"I congratulate you," he said, without being able to hide his vexation. "It's a prodigious success."

"You mustn't hold it against me."

"I don't hold it against you . . . even though you let the Russians have all my Peenemünde documents."

"Didn't you make use of the works of Tsiolkovsky? . . . The main thing is the conquest of space, as you used to say. What does it matter if we're the first to reach the moon?"

"In the first place, you're not going to be the first to reach the moon!" he exclaimed. "We'll have our revenge."

"We?"

"I'm an American."

"I'd forgotten," said Nadia. "And I'm a Russian. But seeing you again, I can't help thinking of Peenemünde. I haven't changed. I still have the same enthusiasm. I still have the same admiration for you. Can't we forget what we've become and chat like friends?"

"Of course we can," he said, changing his tone. "But not here, unless we want all the journalists on top of us in five minutes."

"On top of you, you mean. I'm not the celebrity."

"Let's go and have a quiet drink somewhere. Unless . . ."

He stopped and peered at her closely.

"Unless you're being kept under observation?"

She burst out laughing.

"You really are an American! The fact that I'm here means that I'm trusted."

He took her by the arm and led her some distance away from the institute. They sat down in a quiet café.

"I've never lost sight of you," she said. "I've read everything you've published in the last ten years. I think it's remarkable and I'm not the only one in Russia who does."

"So you get the American periodicals? The ones I write for aren't very widely distributed."

"Whatever pertains to space, whatever appears on this subject, not only in America but all over the world, is immediately translated, analyzed, and filed in the library of our academy . . . about seven thousand foreign publications a year," she specified with emphasis.

"That must require an enormous staff."

"Several thousand translators, scientists, and technicians are employed on that alone," she replied in the same tone.

He lowered his eyes. When, as a result of the Russian triumphs, the American government had decided to investigate the Russian scientific periodicals, it was discovered that in the whole of the United States there were less than a hundred qualified translators. The result? At the present time there was still a backlog of several thousand valuable documents. There was talk of building a special electronic device to tackle the job.

"I'm afraid I've never kept abreast of the Soviet projects," he confessed gloomily.

"They're no more secret than yours are. Some time ago one of our magazines published the main outlines of our space program and dealt in particular with our first satellites."

"I know. We found out too late."

"And you heard Zharov today? No one could state more clearly and openly that we will land on the moon one day."

"So will we!" Stern exclaimed, his bitterness suddenly revived. "So will we land on the moon. In 1952 I published the detailed plan of such an expedition."

"I know. As I told you before, we read everything you write."

They fell silent for a moment, then he changed the subject. "May I ask you a question? Don't answer if you don't want to."

"Go ahead."

"Do you belong to the Party?"

She shrugged her shoulders.

"I'm not even a Communist. I don't care about politics and I've never concealed the fact."

"And they let you move about freely in this foreign country . . . have dealings with Western colleagues?"

"Zharov trusts me," she said with a smile. "I contributed a little to the success of the Sputniks."

"Zharov, perhaps, but what about the police?"

"In Russia," she declared with a strange emphasis, "men and women of science don't have to have a political opinion."

"Have you always enjoyed such a degree of freedom?"

"Not to begin with. The police used to watch me then. But it didn't last long."

"Tell me about your first encounter with the Russians."

Nadia's eyes misted over for a moment, then she went on in her precise voice: "It almost turned out very badly, and it did turn out very badly for poor Frantz."

"Frantz? Of course, he was with you, I'd forgotten."

"He was killed trying to defend me," she said. "I grieved

over him. He was a wonderful man. But perhaps it was best for him. I don't think he would have adapted himself to Russia, and he would have refused to leave me."

"What about yourself?"

"I was born there. And I went back. I was accepted. I'm a Soviet citizen."

"Tell me about it."

"I had taken refuge with Frantz in the measurements laboratory, the only building that was still intact. The Russian troops were accompanied by police officials and also scientific delegates whose job was to prevent the looting of Peenemünde. But it was an isolated group of soldiers that turned up first. They weren't expecting to find a woman there. One of them, a corporal, flung himself on me. Frantz tried to stop him. The corporal mowed him down with a burst from his submachine gun. I can't hold it against him; he had witnessed the atrocities of Stalingrad."

She described this soberly, without any apparent emotion, as though these memories did not concern her.

"I was saved first of all by Nicholas."

"Nicholas?"

"Nicholas Berchkoff; that was the name he went by then. Don't you remember? The deportee who committed sabotage in the V-2 workshops and whom you didn't denounce."

"I've never regretted it. Still less so today, believe me."

"He was waiting for his countrymen. He came in just as the corporal had hurled me to the ground. He cried out that I had prevented him from being hanged. The corporal hesitated. The soldiers intervened. While they were discussing the matter the security officials arrived with the technicians. I was saved."

"A good act is always rewarded," Stern muttered. "What became of Berchkoff?"

"He became my husband, first of all," Nadia replied. "That made a lot of things easier for me. After that . . ."

"After that . . . what?"

"Berchkoff was only his assumed name. He resumed his real one."

"Who is he?"

She smiled.

"Didn't you recognize him? His name is Zharov, but he wasn't a celebrity then."

"The father of the . . . !"

She gave a nod and went on with her story while he gazed at her in amazement.

"I was first of all interrogated by the police. When they discovered my parents were *émigrés,* they put me in solitary confinement. Zharov once again came to my rescue. He went to see the head of the scientific commission, who came back and interrogated me himself. He was a scientist of repute. I told him about our work, our intentions, our hopes. I told him I had been one of your principal assistants. That helped me a lot."

"I'm glad to hear it," Stern said.

"Of course, I handed over all your documents to him. The next day I was sent to Moscow. A few days later I was released and attached to the Space Research Center."

"And the police let you go?"

"At the simple request of the president of our academy," Nadia declared proudly. "In Russia the police comply with justified demands of scientists. I was lucky they considered me a useful agent for putting their plan into effect."

"Because at that time they already had a plan for . . ."

"For the conquest of space. More or less the same as yours. First of all satellites, then the moon, and finally the planets."

"Who had drawn up this plan?"

"The president of the Academy of Sciences himself."

"And the government—at that time Stalin—Stalin agreed to the plan and financed it?"

"Without hesitation and without making the slightest modification."

Stern fell silent for some time. Nadia continued:

"After that I was still kept under observation, just the same. Then I married Zharov, who also had shown himself to be a useful agent. He had learned our techniques by working in our factories. He gradually came to be regarded as one of our greatest scientists. . . . You've seen the result."

"Poor Frantz. . . ."

"Poor Frantz, yes. . . . Incidentally, the corporal who killed him was court-martialed and shot."

This was the final straw for Stern, who was already amazed, to say the least, by certain details of her story.

"You mean to say a Soviet soldier was sentenced to death in 1945 becaue he tried to rape a German woman? You were German then. And so soon after Stalingrad? And under the Stalin regime? I can't believe it!"

"It wasn't because he tried to rape me. He would have been forgiven for that, as I forgave him myself. It was for killing Frantz."

"That's almost more unbelievable!"

"It was because Frantz would also have been a useful agent for the realization of the plan. The Academy insisted on making an example of his killer."

"And the military complied!"

She drained her teacup and looked at him with a smile.

"Without a murmur. Even Stalin wouldn't have dared to refuse what the Academy of Sciences demanded."

TWENTY-ONE

Nadia left him and went back to her hotel, where Zharov was expecting her for some urgent work. Stern returned to the institute, musing on the conversation he had just had with her. He made his way toward one of the smaller rooms that had been put at the visitors' disposal.

The first person he met was Schleuder. He had not seen the general for a long time. The latter was now employed by a New York firm interested in small satellites as instruments of telecommunication. He had come to Amsterdam in the hope of gleaning some valuable information and also to hear people discuss the conquest of space other than for utilitarian purposes. He had only arrived that afternoon and had not yet met Stern.

Schleuder hailed him as soon as he saw him and immediately left two delegates with whom he was conversing in order to come over and greet him. He congratulated him warmly on his latest success. Stern replied in an absent manner. He was still thinking of Nadia. He was going to tell his friend about his meeting with her when his glance happened to rest on the two people who had been talking to Schleuder. They had both got up and were smiling at him. One of them was an Asian and he felt he had seen him somewhere before, without being able

151

to remember the place or the circumstances. But the second man was already coming over toward him, stretching his hand out and greeting him in German.

"Herr Stern, Dr. Stern! Or should I say Mr. Stern nowadays?"

Stern gave a start. He had recognized the incurably supercilious voice and features of Müller.

Nadia, Schleuder, Müller, not to mention Zharov, alias Berchkoff! It was the spirit of Peenemünde all over again, and it revived the keenest memories of his career. Müller had disappeared some time before the 1945 debacle, and Stern had heard nothing more of him. He only knew he had not been taken prisoner by the Americans.

"Müller! Where have you been all this time?"

"Before telling you my adventures, haven't you anything to say to an old friend of yours?"

Müller had broken into English, standing aside to make room for the Asian, who was smiling. Since Stern remained undecided, Schleuder exclaimed:

"Come now, he's also a veteran of Peenemünde. Can't you place him? It's Dr. Kanashima."

Stern gave an exclamation of delight. Another memory of the past! The Japanese bowed ceremoniously.

"It's always a great honor for me to meet you, Dr. Stern."

"For me, Dr. Kanashima, it is not only an honor but a pleasure. I haven't forgotten the night of the raid when you risked your life to save my files."

"Nor have I forgotten that you did me the untold favor of letting me look at those documents."

"Dr. Kanashima," said Schleuder, giving Stern a wink, "has just been appointed president of the Japanese Astronautical Society."

"I read about it and I also have the summary of an extremely interesting lecture that he's going to deliver at the congress. But you must forgive me, Dr. Kanashima, I didn't connect you with the name. . . . As though I could ever forget! . . . You were planning to build V-2's in Japan. And now?"

"I'm as fascinated as ever by rockets," said the Japanese, still smiling modestly.

"Dr. Kanashima and I are working together closely," Müller chipped in.

"Which means you're now living in Japan?"

"I settled there shortly after the liberation."

"The liberation?"

"I mean the signing of the peace treaty in 1951," Müller corrected himself. "Excuse me, I'd completely forgotten you were American."

"Our aims are modest, Dr. Stern," said the Japanese. "A program in proportion to our means. Thanks to Dr. Müller's invaluable advice, we hope to be in a position to launch a satellite in a few years' time. A small satellite, of course."

"Dr. Kanashima's being too modest. He doesn't need any advice from me. It's thanks to his genius and personal efforts that our country will launch her satellite. And that's a certainty."

"Your country?"

"Why, yes, I'm a citizen of Japan. . . . But I contributed only a small stone to the edifice."

"Don't you believe it," said the Japanese.

Kanashima and Müller bowed to each other in mutual homage. Stern rubbed his eyes as though he were dreaming and looked at Schleuder in amazement. He could hardly recognize Müller in this display of deference and humility. For two pins he would have bent in half in the Japanese manner.

"There are more surprises in store for you," said Schleuder with a smile. "I've seen several other old acquaintances here."

"Stern!"

Yet another voice from the past! He swung around. It was

153

Böhme, likewise a Peenemünde veteran, an engineer specializing in radiophonic transmission.

"What the devil are you doing here?"

Böhme replied in English, with a slight Oxford accent.

"I'm accompanying the president of the Royal Interplanetary Society. I admired your talk this morning very much. Stühl, who was sitting next to me, was just saying the same. It's easy to see . . ."

"Easy to see what?"

"I said, Stühl was saying . . ."

"Stühl's here as well?"

"There he is," said Schleuder. "With Schiller."

Two men were weaving their way through the tables. They greeted Stern jovially, with the touch of respect due a former chief. Stern quickly learned what had happened to them: during the fall of the Reich Böhme had instinctively moved westward in order to avoid the Russians. After being taken prisoner by the British, his position as a Peenemünde technician had served—even in England—as an introduction to the scientific authorities. He had gradually won their confidence and had felt so at home in that country that he settled there for good.

The story of the other two men was very much the same. Stühl, a remarkable mathematician, had found himself near Berchtesgaden after a series of epic adventures and had been captured by the French forces. He had never regretted it. After a short period under surveillance he had adopted France as his country. He worked there in the National Astronautical Research Office, his one regret being that this institution so far was interested only in the problems of space navigation. But he had hopes for the future. As for Schiller, he was now working for the Egyptian government.

"So the spirit of Peenemünde has been scattered all over the world," Stern remarked with a sigh.

154

He then told them he had met Nadia.

"I thought I saw her face," said Schleuder, "but I wasn't sure. What is she doing?"

"You'll never believe it. She's not only Zharov's principal assistant, she's also his wife. She helped him produce the Sputniks!"

A shadow fell over the group while everyone's eyes were fixed on Stern, a shadow fraught with imperceptible embarrassment. Schleuder dispelled the uneasy atmosphere by suddenly exclaiming:

"I propose giving a dinner for all the old Peenemünde hands the day after tomorrow. You're my guests. We have so many things to talk about and we can't talk quietly here."

They applauded the suggestion and all accepted with enthusiasm.

"I include you, of course, Dr. Kanashima. You're also a Peenemünde veteran."

"It will be an immense pleasure for me, Herr General."

"Could you ask Nadia?" Schleuder said to Stern. "I'd very much like her to come. But perhaps it may not be acceptable to her government."

"Wait for me here a moment. I'll go and phone her."

He went off and came back a few minutes later.

"Well?"

"Well, she's with her husband at the moment. She began by saying she had some important work to do for him the day after tomorrow. But then he interrupted her and picked up the receiver. First of all he wanted to thank me . . . an old story, I'll tell you about it some time. . . . But, as for the dinner, he told his wife to accept your invitation at once. He would never forgive himself, he said, if he cast the slightest shadow on a meeting of Peenemünde veterans. He sends us all fraternal and friendly greetings. I returned the compliment. So Nadia, Zharov's wife, will be coming. . . . Oh, yes, one other thing:

when I suggested calling for her or sending a car, she told me not to bother. She added with a laugh that every Soviet delegate, even the humblest, has a car at his disposal."

Schleuder gave a little whistle of astonishment, then slapped him on the back.

"It's as I always said: the spirit of Peenemünde can never die."

TWENTY-TWO

Schleuder had not felt so happy for a long time. His "colleagues" had given him an enthusiastic ovation before taking their seats at the table, and he felt he was once again General Schleuder, head of Peenemünde, the strangest collection of scientists and dreamers assembled on this planet.

The dinner had started in a jovial atmosphere of old friends meeting again in their native land after a long exile. In fact, it was not their land, but Holland, a country which, with England, had been showered with V-2's. But none of the guests thought of that.

"Dr. Kanashima," said Schleuder, "we owe you an apology. We can't stop speaking German when we're among ourselves."

This was true. After a little hesitation they had reverted to their native tongue, which many of them now spoke with a slight foreign accent.

"Dr. Kanashima understands German," Müller protested. "He reads Goethe in the original."

"I understand it, but I speak it very imperfectly, in spite of Dr. Müller's lessons."

"Come, now, Müller, tell us how you turned up in Japan." Müller's story was somewhat different from the others. At the time of the defeat he had hidden in a small provincial town occupied by the Russians. He managed to conceal his true identity, lying low and letting time slip by, and it was some years before he succeeded in crossing over into Western Germany. By then the Peenemünde experts were no longer in great demand with the Allies. Müller found himself at loose ends. This former man of letters who had switched to the study of space on the spur of the moment wondered what on earth he could do. He thought of resuming his literary career but soon gave up this idea, being unfavorably disposed to any kind of work. His only regular occupation was drinking. He left for the Far East in a fit of depression. A chance visit to Japan led to his meeting Dr. Kanashima again.

Japan was still living under the proconsulate of MacArthur and could not openly do research on rockets, but Müller soon realized that Kanashima and a few others were actively engaged in theoretical work and were even doing practical experiments secretly. This revived his old Peenemünde enthusiasm and he suddenly felt ashamed of his idleness. The Japanese scientist knew he could trust this Bohemian character who was still opposed on principle to official authority. He suggested he work with him and with the small group he had formed, unknown to the occupying forces. Müller accepted at once. It was typical of him to make such a decision. He was attracted by the zest of the adventure and also dazzled by the importance of the position he was offered. Even in America he would probably never have had such material advantages. He set to work with the fervor he had always shown when not in a fit of depression or idleness.

In 1952, after the departure of the Americans—the "liberation," as he called it—he had followed Kanashima's team, which had based itself on a small island off Japan and was pursuing its program of research and tests there.

"A modest, not to say pitiful, program, I grant you, compared with yours and the Russians'. But we can launch rockets that reach the high layers of the atmosphere and we hope to put a satellite into orbit by our own means within the next few years."

"A very small satellite," Dr. Kanashima specified.

Each of the *émigrés* mentioned the facilities or the difficulties they had encountered in the country that had harbored him. Schiller, "the Egyptian," disclosed that he had gained Nasser's support and that the years to come would witness some surprising achievements on the banks of the Nile. Stühl, "the Frenchman," complained of the indifference of the successive French governments toward space research.

"When Esnault Pelleterie died," he said indignantly, "only two months after the launching of the first Sputnik, his death passed almost unnoticed in France. The press barely mentioned it and the government did not raise a finger to point out the extent of his work."

"We rendered homage to him in Russia," said Nadia.

"And now," Müller broke in abruptly, "let's talk seriously. This landing on the moon, Stern, when is it going to take place?"

"It's probably Nadia to whom you should put that question," Stern replied with a smile and with no more than a hint of bitterness.

"I don't think Zharov himself could give an exact date. There are masses of problems to be settled beforehand. You know them better than anyone."

Nadia and Stern were sitting next to each other in the middle of the table, opposite Schleuder. Everyone's eyes were now fixed on them, as the two unquestioned celebrities. As the meal progressed, the conversation gradually turned, as it always had

158

at Peenemünde, to the common pole of their dreams, and the talk became more and more vehement. Each person had described his adventures on earth, with good grace but rather as though he were adhering to some formality. Presently, having condescended to sacrifice to petty human curiosity, they all reverted by tacit agreement to the only enterprise they really valued. Satellites were mere appetizers for them. The details of these launchings, the scientific observations they had made possible, all this had been or would be thoroughly discussed in official speeches during the congress. The "lunatics" had other ambitions! Here, among themselves, around this table, it seemed suddenly ridiculous to talk of anything but the moon.

Stern's voice could be heard above the others.

"We're bound to encounter enormous difficulties," he said.

He recalled the main lines of the project that he had conceived in Peenemünde, started to elaborate in detail in the Bavarian Alps, and worked incessantly to perfect ever since: a huge rocket weighing four or five thousand tons, measuring over three hundred feet, and containing in its flanks a smaller rocket for the return. Thus a projectile of about two hundred tons would be liberated, on the outward flight, from the earth's attraction.

Dr. Kanashima gave a whistle of admiration.

"Only in America could projects like this be conceived . . . and also in Russia," he hastily corrected himself, bowing to Nadia.

"It's the return that necessitates such dimensions."

"That's true," the Japanese muttered pensively. "The problem of the return complicates everything."

All the guests were well aware of this. To send an inert load to the moon was almost child's play to them. It would be achieved in the very near future, in a matter of months perhaps. But the moon would not be conquered until a human being had set foot on the lunar dust, and the return of this individual transformed a simple operation into one of unknown complica-

159

tions. All the astronauts dreamed every night of this tantalizing problem, but they did not mind listening while Stern outlined it once again, each of them interrupting repeatedly to suggest his own solution.

The discussion became heated, as it always had during dinner in the Peenemünde mess, where a blackboard was set up to enable them to translate their brain waves into formulas. Here there was no blackboard, but at Schleuder's request the hall porter had sent out for several pads of paper. Sheets covered with figures and rough sketches kept circulating around the table.

In the midst of this excitement, however, Nadia sat in silence and appeared to be wrapped in thought.

"Your project for exploring the planet Mars was admirable," she suddenly said to Stern. "Zharov was fascinated by it."

He could not suppress a surge of pride.

"Really? He liked it?"

"He discussed it with his assistants at several conferences."

"I suppose he also knows my project for the moon?" he asked, as though angling for further praise. "Two rockets, one inside the other . . ."

He felt ill at ease when he fancied he saw a hint of disapproval in her expression. She did not reply to his question, but continued, as though with some secret design:

"He agrees with you completely about Mars. I mean, about the necessity of satellizing big space ships around the planet, from which taxi rockets would be dispatched to make an actual landing."

"I should say so. For a distant planet, that's indispensable; whereas for the moon . . ."

He broke off abruptly. She was still gazing at him and he was now certain he could see the particular gleam in her deep eyes that had always disturbed him. This was how, at Peenemünde, she used to show her reservation on any point with which she did not agree but which she did not presume to criticize openly. How many times had he noticed this expression, and automatically had second thoughts about the question under discussion. For did he not have great confidence in her feminine intuition? Did not the conquest of space demand as much sensibility as reasoning? Thus she had very often prompted the discovery of an error or the elaboration of a fresh theory more fruitful than the first.

After a moment she quickly averted her gaze and her eyes expressed a sort of anxiety mingled with vexation. She seemed to be angry with herself for betraying her own thoughts.

He repeated pensively:

"Whereas for the moon . . . But good heavens!" he suddenly exclaimed, "the moon is a heavenly body like any other . . . and the advantages outweigh the inconvenience. You're absolutely right, Nadia!"

"I never said anything," she protested without resentment.

"But you thought it nonetheless, I know. And you're on the right track, as I said before."

Feverishly he scribbled some calculations on a piece of paper.

"My idea of parent rockets landing on the moon with a child in their bellies—why, it's utter madness! It was stupid of me not to think of it before. This parent rocket merely has to be put into orbit around the moon, as in the case of Mars. . . . It's a considerable saving . . . and the taxi will then leave from this orbit. . . ."

"That's also what Zharov thinks."

She had spoken very quickly, in an almost incoherent tone of voice. Then she added, as though with regret:

"That's what I think, too. . . ."

Thereupon she bit her lip, as though trying to snatch back these words. But he was following his own train of thought and was quite unaware of these subtle inflections.

Why had he allowed himself to be hypnotized for so many years by the big rocket, which was a mistake—of this he was now certain—whereas he had so quickly found the solution for

Mars? Unimaginable. And it had needed only a few minutes' conversation with Nadia—not even that—just a short silence and a look from her. That was what he sometimes missed nowadays.

"Thank you, Nadia," he said in a low voice. "You've suggested the best idea I've had for a long time."

And while she fiercely, almost fearfully, denied this, he continued out loud:

"Of course! It represents a saving of . . ."

He bent over his pad. All the others followed suit, feverishly jotting down equations. The room was soon transformed into a sort of research office where occasional exclamations mingled with requests for advice. Between one scribble and another, Stern kept getting up and wandering around the table to compare results or check a figure. Nadia herself had set to work like the rest of them. All feeling of jealousy seemed to be dispelled. The discovery of the best solution was all that mattered.

"It ought to result in a saving of about thirty tons," said Müller, who was the first to raise his head.

"I make it about the same," Stern declared. "But above all, it's a considerable simplification, and this is an advantage that I can't yet calculate."

Dr. Kanashima leaned toward him and stated in a penetrating voice that impressed Stern even more than the remark itself:

"It's a characteristic of genius, Dr. Stern, always to discover a simpler solution than those preceding it."

TWENTY-THREE

Lunik II reached the moon, Lunik III photographed the moon's hidden face. The President of the United States declared that he saw nothing in these events that constituted a threat to America or could justify the slightest anxiety. His advisers went even further, outdoing him in optimism and adopting a facetious tone when they talked of the Soviet achievements. A dose of sickly sweet bromide was daily administered by the government to appease the outbursts of indignation that each Russian success provoked among the people of the United States. A financial expert explained that the United States ran only one risk in this respect: that of involving herself, through a few hotheads, in a ruinous contest. The day he delivered himself of this statement, fresh tears flowed from Maggie's lovely eyes and young William burst into such a rage that he had to be given a sedative and put to bed.

A little more than a year after the Amsterdam congress, Stern was sitting in his new office in Rockland, in the throes of despair.

It was late. Detained by an appointment with a journalist who wanted to interview him, he had finished work and could not stem the mounting tide of pessimistic thoughts.

163

The Russians were progressing step by step in space, following the rigid lines of a carefully prepared plan, with the support of their government and, it seemed, of the whole nation. It would be some time before they landed a human crew on the moon, granted, but the lead they had acquired was not being reduced—quite the reverse, in fact—and there was no chance of its decreasing so long as the parsimonious policy of the present administration continued.

He looked at the time and sighed. He wondered what on earth he could find to say to the journalist. What was the point of these interviews? Optimism was not only the rule among the governing class, it was also decreed for the whole staff engaged on rocket work, a decree that he, moreover, had so far failed to obey. He had even been taken to task several times for expressing the opinion that America was lagging behind Russia in the realm of space. He and a few others were increasingly looked upon as fanatics whose madness might become dangerous, as amateurs of science fiction who would drive the country to ruin if they were allowed a free hand. He felt he was becoming almost suspect. Had it not been for the services he had rendered the Army he might perhaps have been asked to resign.

What was the point of sounding the alarm, as he had tried to do? The result was nothing, or almost nothing, to his way of thinking. Some satellites had certainly been launched—a shower of small satellites that would provide interesting information, that were marvelously ingenious devices from the mechanical point of view, but miniatures. His personal project, a project on the scale of a nation like the twentieth-century United States, was marking time.

He turned around. Behind him five huge drawings of a rocket, side by side, occupied the whole of the back wall. He gazed at them and sighed again: Phoebe 1, 2, 3, 4, and 5, the last a monster measuring four hundred feet. These were the symbols of his specific program, the one to which he had devoted the best part of his life and that he had not hesitated to work out all over again during the last year, since an obvious simplification had occurred to him.

Phoebe 5 would one day enable a crew to set foot on the moon, he was sure. But when? Where were the means of putting his scheme into effect? It had been approved, in principle, although it was still under discussion at conferences attended by men who had not the faintest idea about rockets. A start had actually been made, an embryonic start. The first stage of Phoebe 1 was taking shape in the workshops at Rockland, to which he had been transferred after finally obtaining permission to maintain a permanent watch on the construction of his missiles. The motor was almost assembled and bench tests could soon get under way. But that was all, whereas a whole succession of investigations and experiments ought to have been undertaken simultaneously for the continuation of the series. There was no money for that, not a dollar. He clenched his fists; what could be done to rouse America?

He noticed he had spoken out loud. Walker, who had just come in unnoticed, replied in his usual way:

"Raise a fuss, smash the windows. That's what I'd do if I were you. Damn it all, it can't go on like this!"

"What's wrong now?"

Walker had left the Navy some months before to come and work with Stern as his personal assistant. He was no less enthralled than his chief by the Phoebe project and railed against anything that retarded its being put into effect.

"A further delay in delivering our special plates."

"Good God! But the firm promised me . . ."

"It's a question of priority. They've got a more urgent Army order."

Priority! This revived his blackest memories of Peenemünde. They were beginning to be treated once again like poor relations. Exasperated though he was himself, he nevertheless did his best to calm Walker.

"Take it easy, old man. It's not worth eating your heart out."

"Have you finished for the day?"

"Yes, but I'm expecting a journalist."

"I know what I'd say to the fellow!"

Stern shrugged his shoulders and looked at him with a disillusioned air.

"Whereas *I* have no idea what I'm going to say to him."

Two days later he was breakfasting with Maggie when she gave a startled exclamation.

"Did you really make this statement?"

"What statement?"

She put down her coffee cup, picked up the newspaper spread out in front of her, and read out loud:

" 'It is stupid to pride ourselves on having several satellites revolving around the earth, whereas the Russians have only one . . .' "

" 'For the Russian satellite,' " Stern quoted, " 'contains far more instruments than all of ours put together.' Yes, I said that."

"And it goes on: 'I am convinced that when our astronauts land on the moon they will be greeted by Soviet air hostesses.' "

"Exactly. And I also added, I remember very well and I hope it hasn't been omitted: 'Now it is too late. We shall never be able to catch up with the Russians in the field of rocketry.' "

"Oh!" Maggie exclaimed indignantly. "That's been headlined in huge letters . . . so big that I hadn't even noticed them. . . . You must be crazy!"

"Lunatic," Stern replied gently.

"You can't really think that," she moaned. "It's not possible! Furthermore, you're going to get yourself arrested, or at least thrown out on your ear."

"I've already been arrested once, by the Gestapo. As for being fired . . ."

He was interrupted by the telephone ringing.

It was not the authorities. It was a long-distance call from the state of Massachusetts.

A politician. A senator? Stern had not caught the name. He wished to meet him? It was not the first time politicians had tried to get in touch with him, out of mere curiosity more often than not. Nothing worthwhile had ever emerged from these meetings. This man, however, sounded young and pleasant. He had just read the interview in the papers. It had made a deep impression on him.

"I can well believe it when you say we're lagging behind the Russians, and I admire you for proclaiming it, Dr. Stern. When I'm not satisfied, I always say so. But when you add: 'Now it is too late. We shall never be able to catch up with them . . .'— is that really your considered opinion? . . . I see. . . . Yes, it's difficult to discuss this on the telephone. But I happen to have some business in Alabama today. I'm catching the next plane. I'll be in Rockland this evening, with a friend of mine who's very interested in space problems and who's better qualified than I am to discuss them. . . . Stewart; I think you may have heard of him. He's a great admirer of yours."

It was the name of a university man who had visited La Grange several times. Stern remembered him perfectly. He was one of the few who appeared to have a thorough knowledge of the subject and whose imagination did not seem circumscribed by narrow specialization.

"I should very much like to meet with you, Dr. Stern."

Stern agreed and made an appointment. Then, as he was about to hang up, he again asked the senator his name, which he had not heard properly. He jotted it down on a piece of paper and came back to Maggie, peering at his scribble and mumbling.

"One of those social politicians, no doubt, who wants to shine in sophisticated circles by pretending to be abreast of the latest technical developments. He's just a name to me. J. F. K. . . . Kennedy. Ever heard of him?"

167

"He has extraordinary presence," said Ruth, rising from her chair to get a light from her husband, who was standing at the far end of the room, although there was a lighter on the table beside her.

Since the beginning of the broadcast she had not been able to keep still, such was her excitement at the television program this evening. She sprang to her feet on the slightest pretext—a guest's glass that needed refilling or a cigarette that needed lighting—to rush across the room with a great flurry.

"Quite extraordinary," Maggie agreed.

This was true. He did have exceptional presence. His personality almost managed to give the little screen a life-size dimension.

He had the good taste, perhaps also the supreme talent, not to trade on his natural charm, appearing even to scorn it. When he talked he did not gesture at all; his lips alone moved. He even disdained this evening to make use of the smile that was his acknowledged weapon, and during this debate that brought him face to face on the screen with his opponent, he had so far maintained a serious, sometimes solemn air that contrasted with his youthful appearance and provided an additional attraction. Since becoming a candidate for the Presidency he had cut off a wayward lock that had formerly fallen over his forehead, but his hair still had an untidy, almost rebellious air that distinguished him at a glance from the professional politicians and contributed to his winning the affection of young people, women, and intellectuals.

He sometimes had strokes of genius. When his rival began singing the praises of the present administration, painting an idyllic picture of America's position in the world, quite simply, and without warning, as though the serious side of his character could no longer withstand such remarks, he started to laugh.

He laughed for a long time and it was a young man's laugh, verging on insolent contempt and affectionate pity, a laugh fraught with hidden meaning that could be sensed from far off and which constituted the best possible refutation, and the most spectacular one, to the description that had just been given.

In the Walkers' living room this impromptu interruption was the sign for a pause, a moment of much needed relaxation, such was the intensity of their concentration; it was an interruption that was appreciated simultaneously by millions of Americans gathered that evening around their television sets, in one another's houses or, in the case of travelers, in hotel bedrooms.

They showed their satisfaction according to their temperaments. Stern had a delighted smile on his face. Walker turned to him and gave a "thumbs up" sign.

"Great!"

As for Ruth, his young wife, she sprang again from her chair and burst into loud applause. She had followed the broadcast with violent exclamations that reflected her admiration or her indignation, according to which of the two opponents was addressed. Maggie, on the other hand, had forced herself to keep calm and betrayed her feelings only by a gesture of approval or an angry shrug. But when the laugh started, she, too, rose to her feet and danced over to clink glasses with Ruth. Then she sat down again, for the oratorical contest was continuing. The young senator from Massachusetts was now speaking.

"I am far from satisfied," he began. . . .

He was indeed far from satisfied. He had already made this clear from his previous remarks, pointing out that the economic situation was chaotic, the housing policy inadequate, the problem of education completely neglected. He had added that American towns were filthy, that juvenile delinquency cost the taxpayers millions of dollars every year, that the racial problem constituted a serious disturbance to the national conscience, and that morality in public affairs left much to be desired.

He now turned to the question of foreign relations and had no difficulty in pointing out further reasons for discontent. To hear him, it appeared that the nation was being driven headlong by the present administration down the road to decadence. He did not actually utter this word, but it sprang brutally to the mind of every listener, gradually creating a vague aura around the sets, a misty specter of indefinite shape, but one more dreadful and more dreaded by American hearts than the most fearful demon.

"He's right," said Ruth, stubbing out her cigarette, "we're becoming a senile nation. We're no longer capable of looking forward."

The others motioned her to keep quiet, for the young senator was embarking on a subject that was of utmost importance to them.

"I was grieved, and I know that every friend of America was likewise grieved, when on several occasions we were faced with the proof that the Soviet Union was ahead of us in the conquest of space. . . ."

They now maintained a complete silence. Ruth herself was holding her breath. Walker again gave the "thumbs up" sign.

"I was upset when, after the exploits accomplished abroad, I heard the Vice President of the United States declare that all

170

was well with us and that our scientific program was progressing in a completely normal manner. I was appalled when I realized that no additional effort had been made to decrease the Russian lead. . . ."

He paused for a moment, during which Ruth recovered her breath while a quiver of indignation swept over America. The voice continued:

"I personally do not believe that everything is normal in this field, as the Vice President asserted, and I do not think that proclaiming this belief is the action of a bad American. *But the facts of the matter are that we have never made the national decisions or marshaled the national resources required for such leadership. We have never specified long-range goals on an urgent time schedule, or managed our resources and our time so as to insure their fulfillment. . . . Now it is time to take longer strides, time for a great new American enterprise, time for this nation to take a clearly leading role in space achievement, which in many ways may hold the key to our future on earth.** I personally believe it is still possible, providing the whole of America makes a gigantic effort, and I think it is the duty of the Government to organize this effort. . . ."

"Was it you by any chance who prepared this speech for him?" Walker asked Stern.

"Space is open to us now; and our eagerness to share its meaning is not governed by the efforts of others. We go into space because whatever mankind must undertake, free men must fully share."

Maggie sprang to her feet, broke into a dance, and cheered. Then she flung herself into her husband's arms.

"We've won, darling!"

"Maybe we have a chance of winning . . . providing he first wins himself."

"He'll win," said Walker, "and then we shall. We'll be the first on the moon."

* See note, page 34.

"I'll leave this country forever if he's not elected!" Ruth exclaimed.

"I'd give ten years of my life for him to be!" cried Stern, unable to contain himself a moment longer and starting to pace up and down the room.

The debate was coming to an end. The young senator had finished talking. Since everything his rival had to say sounded insipid, they switched off the set.

"Seriously, Stern," Walker remarked, "one would think it was you who was responsible for that part of his speech."

"I'd be quite incapable of it, but maybe I unconsciously suggested a few ideas."

"You mean to say you've actually met him?" Ruth asked in amazement.

"I've no reason to hide it. Just a little less than a year ago . . ."

"Just imagine," Maggie broke in, "at that time my genius of a husband had never even heard of him! He couldn't even remember his name!"

Ruth gave an exclamation of astonishment.

"But everybody in America knew about him—and so did the rest of the world."

"I've never dabbled in politics," Stern said by way of excuse.

"Yes, but even so!"

Ruth could not conceal her indignation. She had been married to Walker for a very short time and had only just left the circle of students, intellectuals, and artists with whom she had formerly associated, a circle in which the inertia of the present government was reviled every day and to whom the senator from Massachusetts represented a hope, long disappointed, of vitality and renewal.

"It was the day after his famous interview," Maggie went on vigorously. "He said . . . God, how angry I was with you!"

"I know," Ruth said furiously. "You said, Mr. Stern: 'Now it is too late. We shall never be able to catch up with the Russians . . .' Well, just wait and see, with the new President!"

"He's not President yet."

"He will be in one month from now, and we'll no longer be the laughingstock . . ."

"Let me tell you about it," Maggie went on. "Well, the day after this interview the President rang us up from Massachusetts. He sounded very excited, didn't he, darling? He wanted to see you urgently. He flew straight down with his adviser. . . ."

Stern shrugged his shoulders and burst out laughing.

"Let's get things straight; he had some business in Alabama and he took advantage of the trip to meet me."

"Well, you saw him, didn't you? You spoke to the President?"

"He's not yet President, but I saw him and I spoke to him. He asked me if I still meant what I'd said to the journalist. I said yes, I did, unless . . . unless effective, gigantic, colossal steps were taken (I used all the adjectives I could think of) in the very near future. 'What do you call the near future?' he asked. 'A few months at the outside,' I replied and added: 'Even then I can't guarantee anything. But maybe, if these steps are actually taken, maybe we have a chance of catching up with the Russians in five or six years; not before, and it's only a very small chance. Maybe we could then entertain the hope of being the first to reach the moon; a very faint hope, in my opinion.' "

"And he listened to that without protesting?"

"He protested in his own way, but without getting angry. He said: 'Dr. Stern, I agree with you when you sound the alarm. I agree with you when you say we have to make a colossal effort. But I can tell you this: If there is a small chance, well, we shall seize it, and the colossal effort you mentioned *will* be made in a few months from now. And we *shall* be the first on the moon.' "

"Spoken like a true President!" Maggie exclaimed.

"He's not yet President," said Stern.

"As good as," Ruth asserted. "Then what did he say?"

"Nothing much. I began talking to his adviser, Stewart. I outlined my program to him. He seemed to understand and approve of it. . . ."

"But what about him, the President?"

"You insist on calling him that! Well, the President asked a few questions that showed he had grasped the broad outline even though he did not go into detail. Then he left us to talk it over together. When he said good-by he promised he wouldn't forget me and that I'd be hearing from him in due course. That's all. I'm not sure you can trust the promises of politicians."

"He's not a politician!"

"Yes, he is, in a sense; but what he has said this evening proves he's still interested in space. So long as it isn't just an electioneering speech!"

"He won't forget you," Maggie assured him. "You heard him just now. He was speaking with your voice."

"Unfortunately," said Walker, "there are such things in this world as the national economy, the Berlin wall, Cuba, Laos, and the underdeveloped countries, which for some unknown reason assume far greater importance in the minds of politicians. A President is liable to fall into the temptation of granting them priority and forgetting the essential: the moon."

"He won't forget," Maggie repeated stubbornly.

"He seems to like lost causes," Stern slowly observed. "I have a confession to make: when I gave that interview—the one you consider so scandalous—I was not in a temper that day. It was deliberate. I thought there might still exist a few Americans for whom the word *impossible* was an incentive. He seems to be one of them. If he's elected . . ."

"He will be!" the two women cried with one voice.

"Then I shall begin to believe really and truly that we still have a small chance."

TWENTY-FIVE

One month later, about three o'clock in the morning, after an anxious night spent in front of the television set, Maggie gave a scream of delight, kicked off her shoes, and broke into a wild fandango.

Still up at this unusual hour, young William joined in the frenzy. He scattered on the floor the pieces of a puzzle with which he had been toying for the last two hours, unable to absorb himself in it. Then mother and son clasped hands and danced around in a circle under the excited eye of Stern, who was mopping his brow with a sigh of relief.

"Elected!"

The young senator had won. The waiting had lasted most of the night and the agonizing uncertainty had reigned until the end. The results alternately weighted the scales in favor of one or the other of the two candidates, punctuated repeatedly by exclamations of annoyance and even curses or, on the other hand, by cheers.

The three members of the family had not left the living room. Toward ten o'clock Stern, with a frown, had told his son to go to bed, but the boy had given him such a pleading glance and Maggie, without openly taking his side, had looked so grieved that he consented to make an exception to the rules.

After all, the election of the President of the United States was not an everyday occurrence and this one was fraught with exceptional significance. He allowed his son to stay up, for the boy's attitude proved that he was capable of taking an interest in serious matters despite his youth. Stern knew that he himself would be unable to sleep.

"Elected!"

He allowed himself to be dragged into the frenzied saraband that mother and son danced across the room, knocking into the furniture. He had been living in such a state of tension since the start of the campaign that he felt ready to commit any folly. Maggie suddenly whirled out of the room and came back almost at once with a bottle of champagne. They gaily clicked glasses, William being entitled to a sip after declaring to his father:

"Daddy, at last we'll be able to get to the moon!"

Then he consented to go to bed. He had been gone only a few minutes and Stern was once again telling Maggie what he was hoping for, when he suddenly broke off halfway through a sentence. His face clouded over.

"Maggie, there's a world of difference between a President and a candidate for the Presidency. If only he remembers!"

"He'll remember," said Maggie.

"But he must realize there's not a moment to lose," said Stern in a startled tone. "I imagine a new President must have a mass of formalities to attend to and hasn't time to think of essential things, as Walker said."

"He won't lose any time. He promised you."

They were just going to bed when the telephone rang, giving them both a start. They looked at each other for a moment in silence. It was after four o'clock. A call at this hour was not unprecedented; on the occasion of certain tricky launchings he was sometimes awakened in the middle of the night to give his advice, and sometimes journalists had called him up at unearthly hours to get a statement from him for a special edition.

It was rare, however. The coincidence between this nocturnal call and what they had just been discussing seemed strange to both of them. Maggie held her breath as he walked over to the instrument with a hesitant step, then snatched up the receiver with such nervous eagerness that it almost slipped out of his hand.

"From Washington? . . . Yes, speaking."

Maggie could not contain herself and went and picked up the other receiver.

"Dr. Stern?"

He could hardly reply, he felt so overcome. He fancied he recognized the voice.

"Stewart calling, scientific adviser to you-know-who. You remember me? We had a long discussion some months ago."

"I recognized your voice," said Stern, breathing heavily.

"I knew you wouldn't be asleep. That's why I took the liberty of phoning you at this time of night. Besides, the President's orders are explicit. Extremely urgent. Number one priority."

"I was expecting your call," said Stern after taking a deep breath.

He smiled as he received a violent jab from Maggie, who made a mocking grimace and whispered in his ear:

"Tell him you were expecting the President to call you himself!"

"I don't want to disturb you for long this morning," the voice went on. "It's like this: the President wants to see you as soon as possible; and so do I, of course."

"I'm at the President's service," replied Stern, who was impressed nevertheless, while Maggie kept frantically hammering his shoulder with her fist.

"Today . . . it's after four o'clock . . . it would have been better but I don't think it's possible. The President has a few official obligations that he can't very well put off, you understand?"

"I understand," said Stern, while a condescending pout from Maggie seemed to say that she too understood, if it must be, but that even so . . .

"What about tomorrow?"

This took Stern's breath away again. He stood gasping for a moment. Maggie herself was rooted to the spot. He forced himself to reply calmly:

"Tomorrow suits me perfectly. I'll take the plane this evening."

"I'll expect you at eight o'clock, if that's not too early," said the voice. ". . . Fine. The President will see you at eleven. So there'll be time to have a chat beforehand. He's allowing himself a full hour for this interview."

Stewart told him where to report and hung up.

"Good gracious! Tomorrow!"

There were tears in Maggie's eyes. He felt more moved than he had ever been in his life. They fell into each other's arms, then refilled their glasses.

"We've won!" said Maggie, weeping with joy. "We've won!"

"I think there's some hope. . . . Fancy calling me up on a day like this, less than an hour after the election!"

He felt so elated, he felt such energy bubbling up inside him, that he wanted to get down to work at once. Maggie stopped him. He had to have at least a few hours' sleep. He would need all his mental faculties to converse with the President.

"You're right," he said. "Anyway, all *my* plans are ready. Now it's up to them, up to him."

Before going to bed Maggie glanced into William's room. A pleading voice asked her from whom the telephone call had come.

"It was the President, dear," said Maggie. "He wants to see your father tomorrow and he wishes you good night."

"I was sure it was," the boy said in a relieved tone. "Now I can go to sleep."

Later, as she switched off the light between their twin beds, Maggie caught her breath.

"Darling, you'll never change. You might at least have congratulated him!"

TWENTY-SIX

While flying to the meeting, Stern kept having the strange impression of being carried back eighteen years, to the time when Hitler, at bay, had suddenly pinned all his hopes on the scientists of Peenemünde after ignoring them for years.

Were the men of the Western world unable to think of the conquest of space until the specter of humiliating defeat appeared in the sky? Was it his own destiny never to be taken seriously except when the situation was desperate? For he had barely exaggerated his views in his pessimistic statement to the press. The chances for America to win the Battle of the Moon were infinitesimal, he was sure. With the present Russian lead, the United States would have to make up for lost time and achieve in five or six years what would normally take ten or twelve. This meant a superhuman effort on the part of research workers, experts, and technicians—an effort that the scientific teams would no doubt furnish enthusiastically. But good will alone was not enough. The job of organization must be done first, and this would necessitate mobilizing all the country's resources. Beyond this, the financial problem made his senses reel, although he usually did not allow this question to bother him.

"So long as he realizes," he muttered to himself, "that the profit-and-loss account of the Battle of the Moon should not be reckoned in dollars, either one way or the other! . . . And so long as he has the power to make the others realize it, too!"

Stewart received him at the appointed time. He was not alone. With him was a youngish man whom he introduced as the prospective director of a future space organization that was to embrace all the others. A moment or two later a fourth man was ushered in: it was Meyer, the atomic physicist from Los Alamos. Stern was not surprised to see him here. He knew that Meyer, one of the greatest experts in matters of nuclear energy, had also been in touch with the new team.

As soon as the conference started, the memory of Hitler faded completely from Stern's mind. Though this was also a question of winning a battle, what was at stake in this battle had nothing to do with terrestrial conquests. Not one of these men envisaged the rockets they were discussing falling back to earth and exploding. This was purely a question of space travel. Or, more exactly, as Stewart neatly put it, the specific object of this preliminary meeting between top-level scientists was the moon.

They conferred for three hours without pause. Stern described his project in detail, the broad outlines of which were already known to the rest, including Howard, the director of the new organization. Then Meyer reported on the progress of his research and the hopes that could reasonably be pinned on rockets propelled by nuclear energy in the course of the next few years. For some time Meyer and Stern had kept each other informed of their respective work, examining the possibility of combining both sources of energy in one of the giant Phoebes. But would atomic propulsion be feasible within the time they now had for Operation Moon? This question gave rise to a heated exchange of opinions.

Stern's project also gave consideration to other possible alternatives. Having examined them in detail during their long discussion, they were still not able to agree on a definite choice. It was at this moment that the new President joined them.

Remembering Maggie's advice, Stern this time made sure of congratulating him on his election. The President thanked him with a smile, then sat down and fell silent for a few seconds, making a gesture as though to dismiss a cloud of importunate thoughts by which he did not wish to be disturbed at this moment.

"We have one hour," he said. "Stewart, have you told our friends about the new organization we're planning to create?"

"Not yet. We've spent the morning discussing technical problems."

"Quite right. But the scientists must feel they form a solid front and are supported by the Government. . . . You tell them, Howard; in two words."

Howard explained very briefly the aims of NASA, the National Aeronautics and Space Administration, which would be a civil organization centralizing every aspect of the space problem.

"Have you any comments?" the President asked.

"Only this, Mr. President," Stern replied. "I very much like the word 'National' being included in the name."

"Good. Then let's get down to the essential object of this meeting: the moon, and the means of reaching it. . . . the moon, which you said, Dr. Stern, we could not be the first to reach."

"I now think it's worth making an attempt."

"So do I. Well, now, Stewart and Howard feel, and I agree with them, that Project Moon should be kept separate from the other space projects—separate and on a very high level. The target is too important for us to combine it with secondary objectives. The moon team must deal exclusively with the moon and we mustn't ask anything else of them. . . . I have the impression, Dr. Stern, that the small satellites don't interest you very much?"

"That's not quite true, Mr. President. The information they provide is indispensable to me."

"But you have better things to do than to deal with them directly?"

"Each to his own specialty," the scientist replied with pride. "Mine happens to be power: rockets capable of freeing over a hundred tons from the earth's attraction and sending twenty tons to the moon with a human crew of three. I know I can bring this enterprise to a successful conclusion."

"Fine. Then I'd like you to explain to me, since I'm neither a scientist nor a technician, how you plan to set about sending three men—three Americans—to the moon."

To describe the plan of the Phoebe series to a layman who obviously demanded more than the superficial knowledge of the man in the street was an arduous task, but Stern was prepared for this. He explained with a few details how his project was based on alternating improvements and simplifications, starting with Phoebe 1, whose first stage would yield a total thrust of about six hundred tons, and ending with the supergiant Phoebe 5, whose power would be dependent on the proposed target. When he had finished, the President had another question.

"I suppose these intermediary stages, these stages of substitution, are absolutely essential? Forgive me if my remark makes you smile. As I said before, I'm not a technician and I have to ask these questions. Can't you begin on your Phoebe 5 right away?"

"The stages are necessary. At least, that is the quickest and surest procedure. Why? I can't give you a demonstration here and now, Mr. President. . . . In two words? Because, in a project like this, certain mistakes *must* be made and then corrected afterward."

"I suppose I'll have to be satisfied with that explanation," the President replied slowly. "I'll take it on trust."

He pondered for a moment or two. He was thinking of the imponderables this project still held for him. He had been tempted to look into it in detail, but he quickly realized that such satisfaction was not permissible and such ambition was unreasonable. On the level to which he had risen, his personal actions should be confined more or less to judging his men and selecting them, which was not so easy. Judging them, not on the grounds of their intelligence and professional qualifications, but as human beings—this he could do. The qualities he sought—clarity of mind, sincerity, powers of persuasion—might have little connection with any specific job. In the long run selection almost always boiled down to personal attraction or to his own intuition. In Stern's case, however, intuition was supported by the remarkable results he had already achieved in the realm of space.

"So it's decided that you'll deal exclusively with Project Moon," the President concluded. "You'll be in charge of it from the technical point of view."

Without giving the scientist time to comment on this decision, he continued, "We still have nearly half an hour left. I'm afraid we can't examine today all the proposals I plan to submit to Congress as soon as possible, particularly on the subject of funds, but I'd like to work out the broad outlines. . . . Let's take things in the proper order. To go to the moon means leaving from the earth, from somewhere in the United States. I believe I'm right in saying that Cape Canaveral won't do as a launching base?"

"Cape Canaveral will no longer do when we begin tests on Phoebe 3 and 4," said Stern. "We'd get in the way of the others, they'd get in our way, and it's quite likely there wouldn't be a window unbroken within a radius of several miles. We'll need a vast empty space."

"I know; I read your report. Just tell me again the area you believe will be needed."

"About seventy-five thousand acres."

The President turned with a glance of inquiry to Howard, the Director of NASA.

"I've looked into the matter, Mr. President," Howard said. "We could acquire an area of a hundred thousand acres in Florida, not far from Cape Canaveral."

"I know the place," said Stewart. "I think it will do."

"Do you agree, Dr. Stern?"

"Yes, I agree."

"Price: sixty million dollars," Howard added.

"We must buy it," the President decided, "as soon as possible; I'll ask for the funds immediately. I don't know anything about the mechanics, but I do know that a proper base is essential for any important project. . . . Next?"

Stewart summed up their preliminary conclusions about possible alternatives.

"We're agreed on one point, Mr. President—that there are only three reasonable courses. But which of them is the best, which the quickest, which the ideal course, is still open to discussion. . . . Dr. Stern?"

"Phoebe 4 can be ready by 1967 or '68, I hope. Now, with two of these missiles, we can envision putting two separate projectiles into orbit which, when combined, could reach the moon."

"A space assembly?"

"Exactly. Phoebe 5, which would take at least two more years to build, would then not be necessary."

"Then why don't you agree? We ought to choose the quickest project: the two Phoebe 4's."

"That's what I think," said Howard. "Dr. Stern doesn't agree, but I understand his point of view."

"Why don't you agree?"

"Because I'm not sure that a space assembly is possible for two projectiles of about sixty or seventy tons each. What I'm afraid of is that it might entail a greater delay than the construction of Phoebe 5."

"And I'm not sure," said Howard, "that the construction of this monster is possible, at least within the projected time."

"I think it is, but I can't absolutely guarantee it," Stern admitted.

"To decide with any degree of certainty, Mr. President," Stewart broke in, "we will have to know the results of the tests to be made in the coming years, and also the progress achieved in the construction of big rockets. The data aren't available yet."

"But if you want Phoebe 5 to be ready within the time I indicated, it will be necessary to start on detailed research at once," Stern said.

"I see. In other words, we'll have to make a decision today."

The four scientists fell silent. The President looked at each of them in turn, then asked, "And the last alternative?"

"It has to do with the method of propulsion," Stern replied. "My present project is based on liquid fuel. This is certainly the most suitable source of energy for the lower stages of the rockets, at least for the next ten years. I think we're all agreed on that point."

The three others nodded. Stern continued, "But for the higher stage, there's a further possibility: nuclear energy."

"Dr. Meyer," said the President, "I think this is your department."

The atomic scientist summed up the views he had already given. His conclusion was that it was reasonable to assume propulsion by nuclear energy for the last stage of Phoebe 5; this would give considerable flexibility and increase in power. He hoped the process would be perfected by the given date or thereabouts, but could not give an absolute guarantee on this point, any more than Stern could.

"Let's go over it again," said the President when Meyer had finished. "As I see it, we are faced with three projects that have essential points in common but some differences: two involving propergol—the space assembly and the direct flight—and the third involving an atomic energy boost."

"That's it, exactly."

"And for this final decision, which must be made today, none of you can make a definite recommendation? Is it a responsibility beyond the realm of science? I don't mean this as criticism, but I want to know."

They were all agreed on this point. Then the President pondered the question for some time. It was getting late. The hour allocated for the meeting had almost elapsed. He asked for a few more explanations, then fell silent again for more than a minute. When he raised his head there was a strange gleam in his eye.

"There are a few rare occasions," he said, "when politics have to take precedence over science. I am going to shoulder the responsibility. You must prepare *all three* projects simultaneously: the space assembly, the direct flight, and the possibility of nuclear propulsion. I'll ask for the funds. I'll explain why they're necessary and I'll get them. I honestly and truly believe that the moon is worth it."

WAR OF NERVES

The year 1962 witnessed the birth of a shadow of anxiety among the Soviet authorities engaged in space activities and particularly among the host of scientists directly connected with the conquest of the moon. The fresh impetus given to the American program, the mobilization of an industrial potential that was probably second to none on earth, and, over and above all this, the clearly stated will of the President to reach the satellite in the shortest possible time, began to weaken the conviction of some Russians that they would be the first in this venture, as they had been until now in every space contest.

An uneasy feeling, not yet officially expressed, hovered over the meetings of the men of science, and in their private conversations the boldest of them did not hesitate to mention the nightmare. Nadia was one of those who looked the danger squarely in the face, and she felt nothing but scorn for whoever failed to do so. She often discussed the problem with Nicholas Zharov, her husband and chief. He himself remained calm and confident, but he did not censure her vehemence when she discussed the danger. Their conversation was particularly heated the day after Carpenter's exploit.

"Glenn and Carpenter achieved even less than Gagarin," said Zharov to reassure her. "And they were lucky: it's quite clear that everything didn't go smoothly. This year we'll put inhabited space craft of over five tons into orbit. Theirs are barely one and a half tons. We're still at least a year ahead of them."

"It's not the exploits of Glenn and Carpenter I'm worrying about. I know perfectly well ours are better."

"What is it, then?"

"Stern and his Phoebes. The first model was tested in April, with successful results."

"Only the first stage."

"But he already has further models under construction. The motor of Phoebe 3 is on the test stand. He's not the sort of man to mark time when he's given a free hand; and today he not only has a free hand, he's being urged on."

"By whom?"

"You know perfectly well," she said impatiently.

Zharov shrugged his shoulders and went on with a smile:

"All you can think of is Stern. We also have our own giant rocket program, as you know better than anyone."

Nadia did not reply. It was true. She thought day and night of Stern, picturing him as she had known him in the old days when he gave himself a specific objective—working twenty hours a day, making his presence felt everywhere simultaneously: in the draftsmen's offices, in the assembly workshops, in the blast furnace, on the test bench. And then, where he appeared most formidable of all, sitting alone in his study in the evening, correcting the day's mistakes, searching, always searching for the best solution to a problem, and eventually always overcoming the worst difficulties by the power of his genius, his relentless toil and persistence.

"He has mentioned 1968. That's not a date given out at random. Some people even say he's hoping to succeed in 1967."

"I'd be very surprised if he does. The Americans are always optimists."

"For us, it won't be before 1968."

"Maybe even a little later," said Zharov with a sigh. "It all depends on the funds."

"What! Are they still haggling over them?"

Zharov fell silent for a moment.

"Yes, they are. We held a meeting of the space committee the day before yesterday. The Premier insisted on attending it. The financial aspect was examined with particular care. The president of the Academy pleaded our cause. He spoke up for the estimates that we consider necessary if we are to succeed in 1968. The Premier himself is willing to pass them, but some of his advisers are reluctant. . . ."

Nadia was unable to suppress a gesture of exasperation.

"They argue cold-bloodedly," her husband went on. "One of them said to me—"

"Arguing cold-bloodedly when the stakes are so important!"

"He said to me: 'Do you think, Comrade Zharov, that a nation like ours ought to ruin itself and two hundred million people to land a crew of three on the moon two or three years earlier than a normal program would permit?' At the time I couldn't think of an answer."

"And you believe that their President will hesitate to ruin a hundred and eighty million Americans if he can save two or three years!" exclaimed Nadia, refusing to listen to reason.

"Yes," Zharov calmly replied. "Personally I believe he will hesitate."

"You couldn't have read the speech he made to Congress just after being inaugurated!"

"That's where you're wrong. I did read it."

"Then you must have forgotten it. Do you want me to quote it for you?"

"Only certain passages. I'm not Congress!"

Nadia accentuated her words with a sort of fury.

"He said: *'First, I believe that this nation'*—this nation, do you hear?—*'should commit itself'*—yes, *commit* itself—*'to achieving the goal, before this decade is out, of landing a man on the moon and returning him safely to the earth.'* Then he added: *'But in a very real sense, it will not be one man going to the moon; . . . it will be an entire nation. For all of us must work to put him there.' "*

"And he ended as follows," Zharov broke in, working himself up: " *'New objectives and new money cannot solve these problems . . . unless every scientist, every engineer, every serviceman, every technician, contractor and civil servant gives his personal pledge that this nation will move forward, with the full speed of freedom, in the exciting adventure of space.' "*

"You know it by heart?" said Nadia, lowering her voice in surprise.

"I learned it in order to quote it, at the meeting, to those who are tearing their hair about our expenses. . . . You don't imagine by any chance that I'm not just as keen as you are to win this battle," he exclaimed, clenching his fists.

"What did they say in reply?"

"With the Premier's support, we shall no doubt obtain the funds requested for this year. For next year, it's not so certain. . . . What did the financial advisers say? Just this: 'We were the pioneers in space. In particular, we were the first to reach the moon with our Lunik II and, again, we were the first to fly around it with our Lunik III. These victories will still be ours, even if we don't succeed in landing a crew until 1969 or '70.' "

"After the Americans?"

"Even after the Americans."

Nadia's eyes blazed. She was unable to master her indignation.

"And you know perfectly well," she cried furiously, "you know as well as I do, all that is utterly false! Yes, we launched the first Sputniks; yes, we landed our flag on the moon; yes, we shall be the first to land recording apparatus there; yes, we were the first to send a man into space! But all this, all this will count for nothing in the eyes of the man in the street, the general public, the poets, or even the scientists! And for absolutely nothing in the eyes of Russia and the entire world, the day that a *human being* actually *sets foot* on the moon! I know and so do you, Nicholas, that if this man is a foreigner, all our exploits will be forgotten, wiped out in the memory of mankind! Laika, Gagarin, Titov, our five-ton Vostoks will weigh no more than a straw compared to this one human being. And Stern knows this too, and so does their President!"

"Ours also knows it," said Zharov. "With his support, we'll no doubt obtain the funds requested for this year; but for next year, as I said, it's unlikely."

"How do you know?"

"He told me; he also gave me some important advice that I must pass on to you."

It had happened at the conference, at which no action had been taken except to provide for a re-examination of the estimates for the space program by financial experts. Most of the delegates were already on their way out. The president of the Academy and Zharov were also about to leave when the Premier's personal secretary requested them to stay, as the Premier wanted to have a word with them in private. It was in the course of this confidential meeting that they were notified of the probable reduction in the space appropriations for the following years. The president of the Academy pointed out that Operation Moon could then not be carried out within the time laid down. The Premier made a gesture of vexation that he suppressed at once. "No one regrets it more than I do," he said; "but believe me, comrades, there's no other action we can take."

". . . and he was quite sincere," Zharov said to Nadia. "I'm certain of that. He made it so clear that we didn't pursue the question any further. Put yourself in his place. He's elderly. In '68 he'll be an old man. Two or three years' delay gives him little chance of still being in his present position. And from his expression you would have realized, as I did, that he would give anything to be still at the head of the Union the day the moon is conquered. Imagine what a crowning to his career that would be for a politician who has backed all our ventures ever since the first Sputnik. I tell you, Nadia, he'd willingly sacrifice an arm, a leg, or an eye to speed up the operation. But he can't be expected to destroy the entire economic structure of Russia for the sake of the moon."

"It's as bad as that?"

"As bad as that. He sounded tragic when he told us: 'No country in the world can continue to spend what we are sacrificing for the moon without rapidly being reduced to utter ruin.' It's no use getting impatient. As I said, we didn't know how to reply . . . apart from waving the specter of America in his face, which I did."

"What happened then?"

"Then he thought it over. He said: 'If we, of all people, can't pursue our effort at the present pace, I don't think any other nation will be able to. . . .'"

"Not even the Americans!"

Zharov paused for a moment to look at her closely.

"You admire them as much as all that?"

"Who, me?" She made a gesture of indignation, then changed her tone. "If I weren't Russian, I should like to be American."

He shrugged his shoulders without taking offense. Freedom of expression was a rule between them and he knew how attached she was to Russia. He went on with his interview with the Premier.

"Those were his very words: 'No nation will be able to, not even the Americans, who would be obliged to make an even more superhuman effort, considering the lead we have over them—no, not even with the dynamism of their present President. . . .' And here he let me in on a strange secret, Nadia."

"What?"

"He muttered between his teeth: 'To think that the whole of Russia and I myself were pleased with this election; that we hoped for it with all our heart and soul! If only Eisenhower were still in office we should have no anxiety about the moon today.' We all smiled; the moon can't rule everything. But now I'm absolutely certain that it holds as important a place in his dreams as it does in ours.

"Then he became serious again and went on: 'I'm sure of it. The President will never be able to maintain the impetus he gave while he was still elated by the thrill of his election. There'll be an opposition just as strong as the one I'm subjected to here, or even stronger. He'll be obliged to take it into account if he wants to be re-elected. There's been a certain amount of criticism already, I know. . . . And talking of this, comrades,' he added, 'I think Igor's had a good idea.' "

"Who's Igor?"

"His private secretary, the only other person present at our meeting. . . . 'As I told you, we'll probably have to reduce the funds for the next year. Well, we mustn't conceal the fact. On the contrary, we must shout it from the rooftops. Better still, we must give the world the impression that we are no longer in a hurry to reach the moon, that it's a costly fantasy, too expensive for us, and that we have better things to do. A few statements along these lines from you to the journalists, a few official announcements made by me, and I bet the President's task with respect to the moon won't be made any easier.' What do you think?"

"I think his Igor had a real brain storm," said Nadia after thinking it over.

TWENTY-EIGHT

Stern flung the magazine down on the breakfast table with such violence that his coffee splashed onto the tablecloth. Maggie, who was sitting opposite him immersed in the morning paper and whose angry frown betrayed a deep discontent, raised her eyes.

"Twenty-five Nobel prize winners!" he roared. "It needed twenty-five of them to deliver such imbecilities! Have you seen this?"

"Yes. But I'm trying to read something more important."

He was in such a rage that he paid no attention to her remark and went on:

"Listen to this: 'Twenty-five former Nobel prize winners, who held a meeting at Saint Peter, Minnesota, have indicted and condemned the conquest of the moon. . . . Reasons: it's ruinous and not scientific. . . .' *Not scientific,* do you hear! 'It is too high a price to pay for a popular sensation and a week of headlines in the newspapers. . . .' Twenty-five Nobel prize winners, Maggie!" he said again, clenching his fists.

"A lot of nonsense. You can't expect anything else from doddery old Nobel prize winners, as you know perfectly well. But here's a more disturbing article."

"What?"

"The estimates have been cut."

"I've been expecting it," he said, doing his best to maintain his composure. "By how much?"

There was no need for Maggie to specify she was referring to the funds allocated to NASA.

"Five hundred million dollars."

He sighed but did not utter a word of protest. As he said, he had been expecting a reduction and had feared it might be even greater.

"In that case," he merely remarked, "there's no hope for 1968."

He was getting used to the savage attacks provoked by the idea of reaching the moon and only rarely lost his temper about them. It had needed the quality and number of the learned members of the Saint Peter congress to make him really angry. For some months, however, these attacks had been increasing and they now took the form of a relentless campaign.

The most violent opposition came from big business and the Army. The former accused the lunatic scientists of driving the United States to ruin in order to satisfy what they called "an adolescent ambition"; the latter, seeing no strategic advantage in the occupation of such a distant base, reproached the President for granting a number one priority to a useless luxury product, whereas it should have been earmarked for the conquest of space close to the earth, which would enable missiles crammed with nuclear explosives to be fired at a reasonable distance from an enemy country.

"I'd like to know," Stern remarked bitterly, "whether the policy of this country is being dictated by the Russians."

What exasperated him most of all, indeed, was the underhand scheming that he fancied he detected at the root of this campaign: a series of statements made by Soviet scientists, all tending to suggest that for the time being they were not at all concerned with the moon. The latest report, spread by a celebrated English astronomer after a visit to the U.S.S.R., had created

197

a sensation. He had been received by the leading scientific figures and all of them had made disclosures along these lines: "At the present moment the moon affords us neither military advantages nor any real scientific interest. Our present ambitions are confined to putting into orbit around the earth some heavy platforms equipped with instruments, especially telescopes."

This had caused considerable alarm among the American public who, ever since the Sputniks and Gagarin, had passed from one extreme to the other, from complete skepticism to blind confidence, and tended to regard the declarations of Russian scientists as holy writ and to believe, since Soviet academicians said so, that Operation Moon really was unreasonable. The opposition had then had a great time orchestrating this popular mood. The military spokesman made the following statement: "We are a lot of imbeciles. The Russians have fooled us once again. They have insidiously urged us to engage in an extravagant contest from which they are withdrawing craftily. They are watching us ruin ourselves to reach the moon, while they are building up their offensive potential with much more down-to-earth achievements." Big business and Wall Street reacted similarly: "We are a lot of imbeciles. While we are exhausting ourselves in a sterile battle that is draining all the country's resources, the Russians are engaging all their forces in the economic contest, which we shall end by losing if we continue to neglect our classic industries for the moon. Soon we shall have all our technicians mobilized in the service of lunar rockets."

Those defending the project might well rage and, like Stern, sarcastically ask if the American effort depended on the policy of the Russians; their adversaries replied in the same tone that this had been the case, alas, two years earlier, when the United States had launched herself wildly into this venture as a result of misplaced national pride.

The moon, the serene moon, was creating a conflict of opinion in America almost as violent as the racial problem. In September, 1963, a senatorial committee savagely attacked NASA, accusing it of incompetence in the management of its affairs and of squandering public money. NASA retorted with a furious diatribe against the twelve hundred firms engaged in various space projects, blaming them for a host of malpractices that entailed financial outlay. Within the organization itself old jealousies were revived and new quarrels started regarding the distribution of funds among the various sections.

These conditions were hardly designed to encourage the efforts of the technicians. Fanatics like Stern and Walker, however, bore the brunt of the avalanche of criticism, reproaches, and occasional insults and continued, in this heated atmosphere, to work silently and relentlessly for the moon. Phoebe I, the first model in the series of giant rockets, was almost completed, ready to be launched in a few months, this time with a second stage propelled by liquid hydrogen, which for Stern represented the hope of putting a satellite of about fifteen tons in orbit around the earth. Their passion for work was supported by the prospect of this exploit and especially by the fact that the attacks nowadays went over their heads, being aimed directly at the higher authority who was responsible for the project. As long as this authority maintained his position, the conquerors of space felt they could devote themselves to their enterprise without too much anxiety. The only fear they sometimes felt was in connection with the 1964 election.

"Oh!"

Maggie gave an exclamation of indignant surprise. As usual, she had started by reading the middle pages of the newspaper and had only just turned to the front page.

"What is it this time? More bad news? I'm ready for anything."

"Bad? Surprising, anyway. A statement by the President. There's some question about the race to the moon."

:

"It's utter madness!" Walker cried. "If *he* starts talking like this, there's no hope."

"You can't see properly because of your blinders," Ruth reproached him. "I personally think there's a lot of wisdom in what he says."

Maggie pursed her lips with an air of disapproval. Stern looked absolutely distraught. For the first time, in their little group, Ruth seemed to have an opinion different from everyone else. She and her husband had read the President's statement at about the same time as the Sterns. Without even finishing breakfast they had piled into the car to come and discuss the news with their friends. Walker had not unclenched his teeth during the drive.

"It's no use getting into such a state about it, Walker," Stern said. "Granted, it's not very encouraging for us. . . . Just read that part over again for me, will you?"

Walker started reading, stressing certain phrases with a hiss.

" '. . . Space constitutes a particularly favorable realm for cooperation. It is absurd for the United States and the Soviet Union to engage in a relentless contest to land a man on the moon.' . . . Absurd! Surely you can't agree with that!" he cried angrily, as his wife gave a nod of assent.

"Go on," said Ruth, shrugging her shoulders.

" '. . . Close collaboration and unification of our scientific and financial efforts would be infinitely preferable, for the cause must be won . . .' "

"Don't slur over that passage, please," said Ruth. " *'The cause must be won . . .'* "

" '. . . Not only by the representatives of one country alone but by the whole of mankind.' I have no intention of slurring over it. And yet only two years ago he said, and I can remember it word for word: *'But in a very real sense, it will not be one man going to the moon; it will be an entire nation.'* "

"To rise from the national level to the level of mankind, I

200

call progress. And that's what's so admirable. For a man to progress, once he has reached the White House—I wouldn't have thought it possible."

"You and your Village intellectuals, you'll be the death of me," Walker muttered, turning his back on his wife.

Stern, who seemed more grieved than indignant, spoke with a sort of melancholy.

"It's progress, no doubt. I see what you mean, Ruth. It's a long time since I thought of this sort of cooperation. It might have yielded untold advantages; but it would have been necessary to agree to it at the start. Today we've taken up the challenge . . ."

"And we've lost the initial battles," Maggie moaned. "We've been held up to ridicule."

"It's a capitulation," Walker roared. "That's what it is: an appeal to a victorious enemy for an armistice!"

TWENTY-NINE

Strange indeed was the attitude of the Russian and American delegates to the astronautical congress held in Paris the following month: strange to anyone who had followed the lunar adventure from the beginning with the sporting passion of a spectator witnessing a savage tussle between two top-class teams; a vulgar passion, no doubt, but in this case made sublime by cosmic fever.

201

Suddenly the moon had ceased to interest the contestants. The moon seemed to have disappeared from their mental horizons. If, in the course of official meetings, they complacently expatiated on biological phenomena in relation to flights around the earth, if they discussed *ad nauseam* the scientific information provided by various families of satellites, if, even, they spoke about sending a load of instruments and robots into space, the landing of a human being on the moon seemed to be a subject that was taboo or an extravagance over which serious scientists could not linger for long. If a disconcerted journalist ever asked them point-blank: "What about the moon?" after one of these conferences, the Russian and American delegates would duck the question with an evasive gesture or would vaguely mention the enormous difficulties they were encountering, difficulties so great that the inquisitive fellow would withdraw with the impression that the project had now been tucked away at the bottom of a drawer in expectation of better days.

Stern was subjected to an interview on this subject before he had even arrived in Paris. A journalist traveling in the same plane came and crouched for a moment beside his seat.

"Yes, of course, the moon," Stern said with a sheepish air. "It will be reached someday, for sure. When? Not tomorrow, anyway, believe me, or even in the near future. It entails such complex problems that we have had to postpone the date we had somewhat lightheartedly fixed. . . . Postpone it by two or three years, perhaps a little longer. There's no hurry about it."

"But your Phoebe I that is due to be tested shortly—I thought . . ."

"It will enable fifteen tons to be put in orbit around the earth. That's about all we can see at the moment."

"If it's merely to talk twaddle like that," said Maggie indignantly when the jouranlist had moved away, "you would have done better to stay at home."

"You don't seem to realize that it's precisely in order to

talk this sort of twaddle that I'm going to Paris. Stewart calls it counterconfusion. Did I sound convincing, at least?"

Maggie looked at him for a moment and burst out laughing.

"Not at all," she said.

It was Stewart who had persuaded him to take part in the congress during an impromptu visit he had paid to Rockland shortly before the President's statement on the desirability of an agreement with the Russians. During the flight Stern told his wife the details of his interview with the scientific adviser to the White House.

"I won't go," he had declared as soon as Stewart mentioned the congress, suggesting that it offered an opportunity of making certain statements.

"Why not?"

"For several reasons. In the first place, these meetings don't mean anything—a lot of unbearable nonsense, a sheer waste of time. Secondly, Phoebe I is about to be set up and I can't be away when that happens."

"Don't tell me Walker can't take your place for a few days," said Stewart, peering at him. "I bet that's not your real reason."

"All right. So let's assume it's because of Gagarin, who's going to be there and will be the main attraction. My terrible vanity won't allow me . . ."

"I know you're as proud as a peacock," Stewart broke in, "and also as prickly as a hedgehog. But do you want me to give you the real reason?"

"Go ahead."

"You're sulking because your funds have been cut by a few wretched dollars. You didn't care for the President's last speech and you feel betrayed. Am I right?"

Stern shrugged his shoulders and did not answer the question directly.

"Anyway, you, as his adviser, can tell him—"

"—that this sort of talk is hardly designed to encourage the poor wretches who are working like beavers so that an American may be the first to land on the moon. I've told him already."

"Well, what did he say?"

"He told me to reassure you, and that's partly why I've come down from Washington. I know you scientists haven't the faintest idea of diplomacy and that you're more stubborn than a mule when it comes to common-sense questions a child would understand in two minutes. Just the same, listen to me."

It was this touch of diplomacy he now described to Maggie, to whom he had scarcely had time to speak in the haste of their departure.

"Stewart is convinced, and so am I, that the recent Russian statements concerning the moon are intended just to confuse the American public. Some secret reports show that they haven't buried their project by any means. On the contrary, they're out to beat us. Only they're also faced with the financial problem, which is probably even more acute for them than it is for us. The moon is undermining their whole economic structure."

"Does the moon really cost as much as all that?" Maggie asked ingenuously.

"Forty billion dollars," Stern muttered, lowering his voice as though he were afraid of being overheard. "That's our present estimate and it could be a good deal more."

"Those figures don't mean a thing to me."

"They don't mean a thing to anybody. Any more than . . ."

He had suddenly lapsed into thought. He looked out of the porthole for a moment. The plane, flying above a thick layer of clouds, seemed lost among the stars.

"Any more than the figures that measure the distances between the heavenly bodies. All figures lose their meaning once they're divorced from the earth."

"Go on," said Maggie. "So the Russians have a financial problem."

"They won't be able to maintain their present pace and they'll fall behind schedule."

"I was sure of it. So much the better."

"So they're doing all they can to make us slow down, too."

"And they seem to be succeeding."

"The authorities' plan is to make them believe that they're being even more successful than they really are. Do you understand? That we're encountering insurmountable financial obstacles, too; that we're sorry we ever started in on this venture; that the only way to save face is to come to an agreement with them."

"I see," said Maggie. "In other words, the President's proposal is nothing but a trick?"

"A political gesture . . . There's also the election next year. He has to think of that. His best line, so far as I can gather, is to present himself basically as the champion of peace in opposition to the Republican candidate who will probably be a Cold War fanatic. . . . And there's no doubt about it," he exclaimed with sudden vehemence, "he *must* win, Maggie. If the Republican candidate gets in, it will mean a catastrophic reduction of our funds and the burial of Project Moon, maybe for a generation!"

"I've never seen you so interested in politics," Maggie observed as the plane began to lose altitude before touching down at Orly.

THIRTY

Dr. Kanashima bowed ceremoniously to Stern, who was accompanied by Maggie, then to Nadia, and, in impeccable English, taking great care to distribute his praise fairly, congratulated them both on the successes achieved by the United States and the Soviet Union in the course of the last year.

"Amirable," he said. "My colleagues and I were enthralled. No, more than that. The whole Japanese nation reacted with delight to the announcement of these fresh victories."

"I thank you, Dr. Kanashima, in the name of all the American technicians. But personally I took no direct part in Glenn's exploit and had nothing at all to do with Venusik."

"Same here," said Nadia. "The Zharov team participated only very indirectly in the launching of the last Vostoks. It's the body of Soviet scientists, in fact the whole Soviet nation, that you ought to congratulate."

The Japanese smiled. "I suppose," he said, "you're reserving yourselves for other, even more remarkable, exploits."

A curious silence followed, fraught with hidden meaning, during which the eyes of every Peenemünde veteran were fixed on Nadia and Stern. Both of them sketched a gesture of protest, while doing their all too obvious best to maintain an inscrutable expression. Both of them raised their voices in protest, then stopped simultaneously, as though they realized the vanity of their efforts, as though they suddenly saw how ridiculous it was to deny anything at this gathering of old friends, which was quite different from the official meetings. They stood there, feeling sheepish and awkward for a moment; then, looking each other straight in the eye, they were unable to prevent themselves from smiling.

Their smiles grew broader, gradually infected all the other guests, and then a great burst of laughter echoed around the room, punctuated by exclamations uttered in several languages, but mostly in German. They looked like a conclave of initiates, all fully aware of a certain secret, and the perception of the heroic efforts made by the two celebrities to hide their secret filled everyone with joy. The Peenemünde veterans could not be deceived.

"The moon," Müller exclaimed in a sarcastic voice. "Which of us here ever thinks of the moon? Certainly not the representatives of the smaller nations, like Dr. Kanashima and myself. Still less the famous Dr. Stern, who nowadays deals only with the higher atmosphere, and certainly not Professor Zharov and his brilliant assistant, who are only concerned with putting telescopes in orbit around the earth. The moon? Who ever dreamed of such madness?"

The Peenemünde veterans had gathered in a restaurant in Montparnasse. This banquet had become a tradition at every astronautical congress. This time Stühl, who lived in France, had issued the invitations. The only absentee was Schleuder, who had stayed in America. Maggie had been admitted and was the only woman present apart from Nadia.

When the laughter had died down, Stern tried to divert everyone's thoughts from the moon and turned to Dr. Kanashima, who that morning had given an extremely interesting talk on the latest developments in Japan.

"I shall be the first to rejoice, Dr. Kanashima, when you launch the satellite you mentioned."

"In 1965, did you say?" Stühl anxiously inquired.

"Probably in the first part of the year."

"We could have been ready by 1964," Müller broke in, "but we didn't want to take any chances."

"In 1964 we already have the Olympic Games, and that's a heavy burden for Japan. . . . No, Dr. Müller, we acted wisely. In the realm of space one shouldn't be in too much of a hurry."

"One shouldn't be in too much of a hurry," Stern echoed pensively, looking at Nadia.

Stühl grimaced with annoyance.

"Ours probably won't be launched before the last half of the year."

"A few weeks one way or the other don't mean anything," said the Japanese.

"We," said Boehme, "the Englishman," with a touch of disdain, "we have found it simpler and more economical to have our satellites launched by American rockets."

"I'd very much like to know, Dr. Kanashima," Stühl continued, "if the allocation of funds for space research gives rise to as much recrimination in Japan as it does in this country."

All the scientists sighed in sympathy. The financial question was what harassed them most. It did not, however, appear to to be a cause of undue worry to Dr. Kanashima, who replied lightheartedly:

"With us, money is not the major problem, first because we haven't an ambitious program, like yours. . . . And besides, we have a very different financial system. It is not the government that subsidizes us. We are supported privately."

"You mean to say private individuals are prepared to invest . . . ?"

"Rather rich and powerful private individuals," the Japanese said with a smile. *"Trusts* . . . I believe that is the word you use. But they can only do so because the masses are interested in the idea. Every Japanese citizen contributes to our program, by means of the papers, television. . . . A small tax, you understand? I can't explain the system in detail; I don't know anything about these things."

"The faith of a whole nation is necessary for such a project to succeed," Maggie asserted with vehemence. "Yours was the first to have this faith," she added, turning to Nadia.

"Thank you," said Nadia with a smile. "Incidentally, which project can you be referring to?"

"Why, the . . . the satellites, of course," Maggie stammered.

"That's what I thought."

Still smiling at her, Nadia quoted:

" *'In a very real sense it will not be one man going to the moon, it will be an entire nation.'* "

"You know that by heart?" Maggie exclaimed in amazement.

"I know it. . . . But I also know," Nadia added, turning to Stern, "that recently there has been another line of talk."

"What's your personal opinion of cooperation? What does Zharov think about it?"

"We think the principle is splendid. What about you?"

"So do I. I think we shall inevitably be led to cooperate someday . . . with regard to the planets; and no doubt also for the parceling out of the moon."

"In other words," Nadia said, smiling again, "for the initial flight it's out of the question?"

There was no point in trying to deceive her. He did not reply, but went on listening to Stühl's and Dr. Kanashima's conversation.

"Is every Japanese prepared to contribute his share to the conquest of space without a word of protest?"

"Every Japanese is *space-minded,*" the scientist declared proudly. "Of course, we, too, have our critics."

Müller raised his rasping voice. He had kept out of the general conversation, preferring to drink in silence, and appeared to be pursuing a private daydream from which he awoke only to utter some brief remark addressed to no one in particular.

"I've known it since I was a boy. In every branch of society, civil or military, rich or humble, bourgeois or intellectual, there exists a class of contemptible individuals, a certain caste, to whom the idea of the conquest of the moon is unbearable."

"I know them only too well," Stern agreed morosely. "And you forgot to mention scientific circles."

"I know them too, alas!" Stühl muttered.

Müller went on with his bitter monologue:

"You know them, I know them, we all know them. To them, it's not the question of money at all. It's the very *idea* of landing on the moon that they find odious. They begin foaming at the mouth as soon as they hear the moon mentioned other than as our inaccessible nighttime source of light. They pour scorn on us, hate and revile us. They exist in the East as well as in the West. But in Japan their outcry is stifled by the masses."

He was about to continue in this vein when Dr. Kanashima interrupted him with a little cough and calmly remarked:

"Besides, Dr. Müller, in Japan there's no question of going to the moon."

"No question," Müller echoed after a short pause, as though he had suddenly come to his senses. "No, of course not. Even less so in Japan than elsewhere."

"I'm delighted to hear that the opposition in Japan is drowned by the masses," said Stühl. "In this country . . ."

He produced a newspaper from his pocket and opened it.

"Listen to this, Stern. Here's the result of a public-opinion poll by the Institut Français. The question was: 'In your opinion, is the exploration of space by a powerful nation a worthwhile way of spending its resources, yes or no?' *'Worthwhile'* is not very compromising, is it? They're not being asked to ruin themselves or shed their blood! Well, here are the answers:

'Yes, it is worthwhile, thirty-three percent. No, it is not worthwhile, fifty-three percent! Don't know, fourteen percent.' "

"Don't worry," Stern said to him, lowering his voice. "One Frenchman in every three still thinks it's worthwhile. Nowadays, with the campaign that's being waged against us, I don't think we'd find such a high proportion in America."

Maggie indignantly protested. Stern turned again to Nadia and reverted to the subject of cooperation.

"Mind you, there may be no technical difficulty, as some people have suggested. We could make arrangements to share the job. Your plan, I believe, is first to put your big satellites in orbit around the earth, then around the moon, all of them carrying reserves of fuel. Suppose you stick to this . . . while giving us, of course, the keys to your relay stations. Then we would need a far smaller rocket. Phoebe 2 would probably be enough, carrying our capsule . . ."

Nadia burst out laughing.

"And in this way *your* capsule would land on the moon with three Americans inside it. I can see what your offer of cooperation means. You're giving us the role of gas-station attendants!"

"There's nothing to stop a Russian being included in our crew."

"One Russian or two?"

"We could toss for it," said Maggie.

"Seriously, though," said Nadia, suddenly solemn again, "I often regret we never came to some agreement at the start."

"So do I. We'd be there by now if we had."

The feeling of constraint had gradually been dispelled, and, having with one accord refused to get excited, they kept reverting to their main preoccupation.

"In an enterprise of this kind," Dr. Kanashima observed sententiously, "the team spirit, the national spirit, can sometimes be a powerful incentive."

211

"Your misfortune," Müller suddenly said to Stern, "is that you've been under a handicap from the very start."

"A handicap?"

"America only works three-quarters of the time: three years out of four. The fourth year she elects a President."

"I work full time, believe me."

"He hasn't taken a day off in two years," Maggie complained.

"Stay in Paris for a while," Stühl suggested. "You really look as though you could do with a rest."

"Impossible. We fly back tomorrow. Our son can't be left on his own indefinitely," Maggie replied.

"The real reason is that Phoebe I is due to be tested shortly," Stern added.

"Darling, you're giving away secrets . . ."

"I knew it already," said Nadia, shrugging her shoulders. "All your papers have announced it."

"Do you have many days off, Nadia? Does Zharov?"

"Not many," she admitted.

"Maggie," Stern declared, "I promise to take ten whole days off at the time of the next congress."

"Do you hear?" Maggie exclaimed. "He intends taking ten days off at the time of the next congress! A year or eighteen months from now!"

Dr. Kanashima interrupted this friendly argument and put forward a suggestion in a somewhat solemn voice.

"My colleagues and I," he said, "are going to request that the next congress be held in Japan, and I hope this proposal will be accepted. Dr. Stern, it would be a great honor for me if you would be willing to be my guest for those ten days. I have a villa on the seashore of a rather pretty island, the island where we do our rocket tests. . . . Have no fear, Mrs. Stern, my house is some distance from the base and I think it's quite a good spot for a rest. Naturally, the invitation includes you and your son. I solemnly swear, after the congress is over, not to mention rockets, satellites, the conquest of space, or even the moon, except to point out the beauty of its light at night on the seashore and to quote a few stanzas from our poets who have celebrated it."

"Under those conditions it would be a pleasure," said Maggie.

"I accept with all my heart, Dr. Kanashima. I've always been attracted to your country."

He paused for a moment, struck by a curious coincidence.

"Isn't the next congress scheduled for the beginning of 1965?"

"Sometime in May, I believe."

"Isn't that about when your satellite is due to be launched?"

"Exactly," the Japanese replied solemnly. "It would be a great joy for us if we could make the two dates coincide and enable you all, gentlemen, to witness an event that will make its mark on the history of Japan."

THIRTY-ONE

Maggie dangled the prospective joys of this holiday in Japan before her son's eyes as soon as they returned home. Stern had sworn to devote the time entirely to his family and his own relaxation, whatever might be the complications and worries entailed in the realm of space by the vagaries of politics. He kept his promise, but first he had to undergo further ordeals and

213

spend over a year in agonizing uncertainty, expecting at any moment to see the ruin of his ambitions.

As it did everywhere else in America, the assassination of the young President roused indignation, fury, and dismay among the little group in Rockland. The Sterns and the Walkers, who saw a great deal of each other, could not free themselves from the morbid attraction of television. At first they could scarcely believe what had happened, fiercely discussing the improbability of certain details, cursing in turn the multiple organizations that had not been capable of preventing the outrage, and wildly hoping that a voice over the air would come and restore reason by issuing a denial of this infamy.

After the horror and anger of the first few hours, they were overwhelmed by utter gloom.

"This is the end," Maggie cried in despair. "Everything will slide back to where it was before."

"Where it was before," Ruth echoed. "And we'd hardly begun to ascend the slope."

"Where it was before," muttered Walker, who looked utterly dejected. "We'll never land on the moon now."

"You only think of yourself," said Ruth angrily. "As though that was all that mattered! But there are plenty of other problems: the cold war, the witch hunt, the Negro problem."

"All is not lost."

As usual, when faced with grave events, Stern was the calmest of the little group—in appearance, at least. He made a laudable attempt to raise the morale of his assistant.

"He was a symbol, Walker—the symbol of a state of mind that existed outside him and will endure after him. Someone else will take over the torch."

This was the voice of reason, the voice that was heeded by all Americans who could not believe in the total collapse of a great hope. But Walker was inconsolable, and his one and only interest in life made him reduce everything to the problems of space.

214

"Just you wait and see. In no time, I bet you, they'll be closing down our workshops and laboratories."

"Nonsense! Even if the impetus is not maintained, it can't be suddenly withdrawn. It's impossible."

"But in a few months from now?"

"We can't do anything about it. Our job is to push on as though the impulse were still there."

Here again was the voice of reason. Two days later, however, while working late and alone in his office to finish a job he had neglected since the outrage, Stern turned around and gazed at the huge panels of the giant rockets. He sat motionless for some time, feeling utterly forlorn, and suddenly burst into tears.

He sobbed like a child, as his son William had sobbed the night before, after wandering from room to room for forty-eight hours, questioning the grownups with an anguished air, as though he sensed a fearful menace weighing on his future.

Stern was right about one point, at least: the impetus that had been given could not vanish overnight or even peter out in a few weeks. In the particular field in which he was interested, there was no serious alarm throughout 1964. Peremptory voices were still raised, pressing the government to abandon a senseless project, but they did not prevail. The funds were allocated —grudgingly, it seemed—by a small majority, but they were not drastically reduced.

Yet, if the President refused to satisfy the demands of the opposition, he seemed equally reluctant to encourage the projects of the fanatics. Granted, Stern and his team were officially congratulated on the first successful test of Phoebe 1, thanks to which a nine-ton payload was put into orbit. Granted, the White House on that occasion announced its willingness to bring Operation Moon to a successful conclusion within the specified time. But various signs seemed to indicate that the administration was hesitant and was lending an increasingly attentive ear to detractors. The inspiring spirit that had kept them going for three years was no longer evident at Rockland, and Stern had the impression that he was being deliberately neglected. He heard rarely, and then only by telephone, from Stewart, who, retained in his post as adviser—but probably only on a temporary basis—gave him to understand that the President was being hard pressed and that he himself was extremely worried about the decisions that would have to be taken in 1965. The conservative faction, which was clamoring for at least prolonging Project Moon over a greater number of years, seemed to be gaining ground day by day.

At the beginning of 1965, however, the President, who had been maintained in office but who had not yet taken sides, felt obliged to do so. Stewart called to notify Stern that the President wanted to see him personally.

"This sounds healthier," the scientist replied.

"Don't be too sure. Between ourselves, I think he's merely postponed as long as possible the moment of making an unpleasant decision: unpleasant for him, I'm sure, but disastrous for you."

"It's as bad as that?"

"I'm sorry to tell you this, but the atmosphere is worse than ever. I believe your project is due to be abandoned or at least spread over such a length of time that it comes to the same thing. Maybe our children or our grandchildren . . . Don't lose your temper, but hurry up and come. We'll expect you day after tomorrow."

Stern was first received by Stewart and Howard. This reminded him of another meeting, held in the same place only a few years earlier, and the memory, far from encouraging him, accentuated his discomfort. Today both men looked solemn. Stern felt there was even something sinister about their demeanor. As he shook hands with them, he had the impression of having been summoned to attend a funeral.

This time their preliminary talk was extremely brief. Technicalities were not discussed. It was simply a question of seeing if they would be able to persuade the President to lend his utmost support to a venture that was more and more onerous and was opposed by almost all the politicians, economists, and heads of services.

"It's now up to you," Stewart told him. "I've done all I can. So has Howard. We've exhausted every argument—to no purpose, I'm afraid."

"There must be some way, just the same."

Howard suddenly flew into a passion that made his voice tremble.

"And how do you expect to convince a man who's been up to his neck in politics for thirty years and has no other preoccupation? How do you expect to make him understand what the conquest of the moon really means, when most scientists don't even understand it? It's useless to tempt him with the idea that it's an initial step toward the whole universe. It's not a substantial enough argument to make him forget about balancing the budget and the discontent of the opposition. And the President, of all people! You can ask a President to provide for two years ahead, maybe for twenty or even thirty years, but not for two hundred or a thousand!"

"I still believe there must be a way," Stern replied thoughtfully.

"Then find it!"

At this moment the President came in and joined them. Stern gave a slight start as he entered the room. Carried back four years, he had almost expected another figure to appear. His heart missed a beat. The contrast with the other man was striking. This one was solemn; his eyes were unsmiling. Stern again had the impression of having been summoned only to be notified officially of the burial of his project.

Yet, after shaking hands with him, the President asked how his work was progressing. Stern gave him a short account of the results that had been achieved and described the next stages of his project. The President listened politely, but it was clear that his mind was on another subject. This he brought up, without transition, in an almost abrupt manner, as soon as Stern had finished talking.

"What's the point of landing on the moon, Dr. Stern?"

"What's the point?"

"Yes, what's the point? Is it surprising I should ask this question? Surely I'm the first who needs to know."

Somewhat disconcerted by this tone, Stern was momentarily put off his stride. He quickly pulled himself together, however, and began to enumerate the scientific advantages that could be expected from such a conquest. The President did not allow him to continue his argument for long and interrupted him in a tone that betrayed his exasperation.

"I know, I know! I've already had all that dinned into me by Stewart and Howard. And I also know that all these arguments are countered by scientists no less famous than you. . . . Suppose landing some men on the moon does enable us to know more about the origin and history of the solar system—so what? We'll eventually obtain the same information with unmanned projectiles equipped only with instruments. Suppose a big telescope is installed on the moon, much to the delight of all our astronomers, who complain of working as though at the bottom of a well? The same apparatus installed on a big satellite would afford the same advantages. Suppose all our industry does benefit indirectly from the research involved in this undertaking? All our technicians and economists are agreed that more important progress could be made by other means and with infinitely less expense. Well, then? As you see, I've studied the question. At least, I've looked into it personally. Among all your scientific arguments, I haven't found one—not a single one—that for me, the President of the United States, justifies the expenditure of forty billion dollars."

Stern had listened to him without a sign of protest. He was

watching him closely. Oddly enough, he felt none of the irritation that the well-known patter of the opposition usually
aroused in him. Even the President's tone did not disturb him.
He pondered for a moment, then calmly replied:

"Nor have I, Mr. President. I only mentioned these scientific
reasons as a reminder. It was not with them in mind that I
drew up my project. It is not with them that I intend to defend
it."

The President looked surprised. He glanced at him for a
moment, then gave a shrug.

"With what, then? Are you going to tell me that our national
prestige is at stake and that we shall lose face if the Russians
set foot on the moon a few years before us? In the first place, it
seems they have now abandoned the idea, and besides, even
if they haven't . . . Look. Here is the conclusion reached by
one of our best economists, a sober-minded man like myself,
and one I can trust: *'If, at the end of this decade, the Russians
have reached the moon and we have not, but we have instead
succeeded in the renovation of our cities and our transport, in the
virtual elimination of slums and crime, in the creation of the best
system of public education in the world, whose prestige would be
higher, who more admired in the world?'* Well, what do you say
to that?"

"Nothing, Mr. President," Stern replied almost phlegmati-
cally. "Our national prestige doesn't strike me, either, as a sufficient argument."

For the second time the President glanced at him in astonishment. Since Stern had fallen silent and appeared to be
wrapped in thought, he went on in a different voice, as though
he was about to make an impassioned confession:

"Well, then? Don't you understand that for months I've been
trying to find a valid argument? Valid in my own eyes, at
least. Do you think I'm not fascinated by the idea of conquering the moon, too? Do you by any chance think that I'd abandon
it lightheartedly—as I shall do, however, without hesitation, as I

219

shall be obliged to do—if I can't find a proper justification for the expense?"

He lowered his voice still further and went on in a dull tone:

"Forty billion dollars, Dr. Stern, is the amount estimated so that three Americans may set foot on the moon and come back, probably, to tell us that they saw nothing of interest. I know, and so do you, that these estimates will be exceeded, as all estimates are. It will probably be sixty billion, maybe eighty. Do you question these figures? Would you like me to quote a few examples of what can be usefully done with all that money?"

"I don't question them," Stern replied, "and I know that many other extremely useful enterprises can be undertaken with sixty billion dollars."

After a glance of inquiry at the other two, who merely looked discomfited and did not utter a word, the President continued in the same mood:

"I'm a hundred percent American, Dr. Stern. I consider myself a typical American; not an American scientist, an American poet, or an American intellectual; just an American. So naturally I would love to conquer the moon. But for that I have to have reasons, or at least one reason—a substantial reason that I can weigh against sixty billion dollars, a reason that's perfectly and immediately understandable to the average, sober-minded, practical American that I am. If no one can provide it, I swear I'll put an end to this crazy venture!"

An expression vaguely resembling a smile suddenly enlivened Stern's face.

"Mr. President," he said, "I think I can give you an absolutely valid reason that will entirely satisfy your American conscience."

"You can?"

The President gave a start. It was obvious he had not expected such a declaration. Equally surprised, Stewart and Howard raised their heads and looked at Stern expectantly.

"I've also given a great deal of thought to this question. I've discovered a reason that's valid to me and that will certainly be valid to you, Mr. President, as well as to many others."

"I'd like to hear it."

"Mr. President," Stern continued after a short pause, "one example will suffice. When, in the fifteenth century, some audacious mariners who had sailed from Europe discovered America, nothing seemed to justify such a venture in the eyes of their contemporaries. Today, however, we can see it has given birth to the twentieth-century United States. Don't you think the existence of the United States constitutes a valid reason for Columbus's wild scheme, and don't you think, Mr. President, that such an outcome would have justified the expense of sixty billion dollars, if the expedition had cost such a sum?"

Stern fell silent. There was a long pause before the President replied, but it was clear that the atmosphere of the meeting had suddenly changed and that a fresh, unforeseen, unexpected element had cleared the air. The expressions of the other men had gradually altered. The funereal air now vanished as though by a miracle. A grimace, which looked prodigiously like an ill-concealed smile, made the President's face look younger.

It was not without reason that he had presented himself as a hundred percent American. This was clear from the next words he uttered, as though relying on a certain national sense of humor to mask some deeper personal feeling.

"Dr. Stern," he replied, "what you've just said deserves consideration, I admit. But you're going to give me a solemn vow here and now. You're going to swear to me never to quote this example, never to mention this justification to our enemies . . . or, above all, Dr. Stern, to our closest friends. Do you understand? Never suggest that reason to the British or to De Gaulle! They'll tell you it's the best argument in the world against the project of conquering the moon! . . . But as for me . . ."

It was a complete transformation. His face was now beaming. His eyes were shining as though from the effect of some

221

deep relief or sudden intoxication. He broke off in mid-sentence to address Stewart and Howard.

"Gentlemen, the average American that I am will always submit to genius. We must submit to Dr. Stern."

Then, turning back to the scientist, with a relaxed expression but in a voice that was once again solemn, he said:

"As for me, Dr. Stern, I think you have indeed found a valid argument for the conquest of the moon."

THIRTY-TWO

Thus it was that Stern took off with his family for Japan at the beginning of May, feeling slightly easier about the future and firmly determined to forget all about the conquest of the moon for the next two weeks.

The astronauts, who had come from all over the world to attend the congress, assembled in Tokyo's most luxurious hotel, which had been put at their disposal and where they were treated like visiting royalty. The congress itself lasted only forty-eight hours, since everyone was anxious to settle the scientific questions as quickly as possible. They were expecting a surprise, which was not long in coming. At the end of the second day Dr. Kanashima, who had never felt happier or prouder in his life, invited his principal colleagues to come the following morning to Koshi Island to witness the launching of the first Japanese satellite, a projectile of modest weight but one that would prove that his country was not uninterested in the great scientific problems of the day.

A special plane flew the astronauts to the island, where Stern and his family were to spend a few days. Before landing, they had a brief overall glimpse of the Japanese base. Koshi was a rather elongated island that could not have measured more than half a dozen miles from one end to the other. A chain of hills divided it into two halves: one reserved for the installations familiar to all astronauts—launching pads, gantries, blockhouses, and workshops; the other, a narrower strip between the hills and the sea, where only a few scattered villas could be seen—the living quarters of the senior staff members, no doubt. Dr. Kanashima pointed out his own.

Maggie and her son were wide-eyed with delight, for this villa looked like a paradise on earth. It was close to the sea, surrounded by flowering trees, on a coast line studded with little creeks, sandy bays, and pebbly beaches.

Koshi was encircled by a belt of arid, rocky islets where there was no sign of vegetation but on which could be discerned a large number of long, primitive wooden buildings. These looked like barracks hastily erected to cater to a large population. Some of the islets, however, had stone buildings resembling hotels. A fairly large crowd could be seen around every one of these constructions. Stern was surprised by this and asked Dr. Kanashima for an explanation. The Japanese smiled.

"There will be many more people by tomorrow morning," he said in an enigmatic manner, "but in normal times those islets are deserted."

The plane was already landing on a strip at one end of the main island. Stern's observant eye just had time to spot in the distance several boats of various sizes that seemed to be making for the islands. He had no time to ask further questions. Dr. Kanashima ushered his guests into a building on the edge

223

of the airstrip where they were offered tea. They were then driven off in coaches to the launching site, which he showed them with manifest satisfaction.

There, in front of the rocket that was to carry the satellite the next day, Stern had his first great surprise. Granted, this missile could not be compared to his Phoebes, but it still seemed to him abnormally large, out of all proportion to the aim in view. He examined it closely; it was not an illusion caused by the contrast between it and the height of the small Japanese bustling about at its base. He gave a little whistle of admiration and conveyed his astonishment to Müller, who was standing beside him.

"You told us your satellite weighed . . . ?"

"Not quite two hundred pounds; one hundred and ninety-four, to be exact."

"And the fuel you're using?"

Müller repeated certain details that he had already revealed. Stern shook his head in perplexity. Dr. Kanashima interrupted them with a smile.

"Dr. Müller, a scientist like Dr. Stern has already guessed our little secret. It would be foolish to try and conceal it from him: With this rocket we could launch a far heavier satellite."

"At first glance I would have said about twice as heavy."

The Japanese clapped his hands, as though he could not restrain his admiration.

"Twice as heavy, *exactly,* Dr. Stern. But for an initial test we preferred not to run the motors to their maximum."

The astronauts continued their tour of inspection and lavished compliments on their host. Koshi Island could not, of course, be compared with Cape Kennedy, still less with the new base in Florida that was beginning to take shape, but it had a number of remarkable features, nonetheless. As he visited the installations, Stern had the strange sensation of having lived for months in a world of highly developed Titans and of finding himself suddenly in the midst of a less monstrous race

224

that had preserved a sort of primitive freshness. This made him feel years younger. Finding himself alone with Müller, he congratulated him sincerely on what had been accomplished.

"I can't take the credit," Müller told him. "I've found ideal working conditions here in Japan and really complete understanding. I've been given all I asked for. Kanashima's the real author of this success. Don't for a moment think he's a mere imitator. He's derived inspiration from other people's experiments, but he knows how to make a synthesis of them and extract all that's useful to us . . . considering the modest means at our disposal."

Stern smiled. He fancied he heard a true Japanese speaking.

"I bet your means aren't as modest as all that," he said, "just judging by what I've seen. . . . And perhaps I haven't seen *everything*—have I?"

He laid emphasis on this last question, looking at Müller directly and gesturing vaguely toward the sea. In the direction he was pointing, well beyond the islets surrounding Koshi, could be seen a coast line with mountains in the background: a fairly big island, no doubt. On their arrival Stern had noticed that the plane made a detour, for no apparent reason, to avoid flying over it. Just before landing, however, while the attention of the other passengers was being drawn by Dr. Kanashima to the installations on Koshi, he had happened to turn his head and had witnessed a remarkable sight. It had lasted no more than two or three seconds, then a barrier of rocky crags had blotted out the view; but he had had time to perceive a fairly broad plateau on which several metal structures stood gleaming in the sun, and he could not be mistaken about these: they were rocket gantries. He fancied he saw some roofs and chimneys in the distance, then everything had vanished. From the ground nothing could be seen but a rocky coast line.

Müller also smiled, but awkwardly, and skirted this last allusion.

"No, our means aren't as modest as all that, I admit. You

know our system, I believe. Our enterprises are financed by 'clans'—'trusts,' I suppose you would call them."

"Are there many of them?"

"Three. They had always been at one another's throats in the past. They came to an agreement for the first time on the subject of space. . . . I think they're fairly wealthy."

"So I should imagine, to be able, just the three of them, to bear the costs of all this . . . and all that we haven't yet seen," he repeated ironically.

Müller looked more and more embarrassed. Dr. Kanashima, who had sidled up without a sound, came to his rescue.

"As I told you, Dr. Müller, we can't keep any secrets from a scientist and observer like our guest here. Nothing escapes him. Yes, Dr. Stern, we see more important launchings than this one in the future. We'll need several years' work, but we're already preparing the ground on that island you can see out there."

"Where I thought I noticed several workshops. . . . Müller was just telling me about your financial backing. I must admit, Dr. Kanashima, I'm full of admiration for the high-mindedness of your patrons and I envy the outcome of their generosity."

"High-mindedness, certainly; generosity, no doubt, when it's necessary," said the Japanese with a smile, "but I'm going to let you in on another secret, Dr. Stern. I believe tomorrow's operation will be a *paying proposition,* as they say in America."

"A paying proposition!" Stern exclaimed in utter amazement.

"You'll see for yourself, Dr. Stern," said the Japanese, gazing out to sea and rubbing his hands together with jubilation.

Stern did not pursue the question but reverted to the subject that fascinated him.

"I suppose, Dr. Kanashima, I ought not to ask you if I could visit that big island?"

226

The Japanese scientist looked disconcerted for a moment and exchanged a glance with Müller. Then he burst out laughing.

"Surely you're not thinking of such a thing? Come now, remember the promise I made to Mrs. Stern: not to talk shop with you or even mention the word rocket after tomorrow's launching. She reminded me of it only this morning. I can't break my word like that!"

This was said with such good humor that Stern had no alternative but to acquiesce. He only asked, without attaching any importance to the question:

"Is that mysterious island known by any name, at least?"

"A Japanese name that you would never be able to pronounce," Dr. Kanashima replied after a slight pause. "It was bestowed on it ages ago by the fisherfolk and we have preserved it, because it's lovely. It is called Moon Island."

"Moon Island?"

"The moon, Dr. Stern, holds an important place in the minds of our poets, and the fishermen of this region are nearly all poets. . . . Now I must apologize for my discourtesy, but I have to leave you for the rest of the afternoon. So must Müller, I'm afraid. We've still got a great deal to do, on the eve of such an important day for us."

"I quite understand. Don't bother about me."

Dr. Kanashima introduced a young Japanese, the director of one of the administrative branches, who was fully conversant with all the installations.

"Moji is at your disposal. I want you to feel completely at home here, Dr. Stern. Look at anything you like. Visit any branch you please, unless you'd rather have a rest. Everything at home is ready for you. My driver is at your disposal."

He went off with Müller. Stern wandered around the rocket for a moment, discussed certain details with the other astronauts, and put a few questions to Moji, who replied with the best will in the world and in excellent English. Then, as they

227

were leaving the site to drive to the villa, he asked him one last question.

"You must forgive the insatiable curiosity of a man of science, Mr. Moji. You're not obliged to answer, and I won't take the slightest offense. But why the devil are you launching a two-hundred-pound satellite with a rocket that could easily put a four-hundred-and-fifty-pound projectile into orbit?"

". . . And do you know what he replied?" Stern said to Maggie that evening as he described this conversation. "He replied right off, in a slightly condescending tone, as though I was silly not to have thought of it myself: 'I wouldn't hesitate to satisfy a curiosity that does us honor, Dr. Stern. It's extremely simple. We're doing this so as not to humiliate other nations, particularly France, which is shortly going to launch a satellite weighing only two hundred pounds. The Board of Directors and Dr. Kanashima felt it would be unbecoming to offend our friends in this respect.' "

"What civilized people the Japanese are!" Maggie said dryly. "It's only in the East you'd find such thoughtfulness and tact."

THIRTY-THREE

On the following day, at dawn, Dr. Kanashima's guests were taken by Moji to the highest point of the island, where an observation post had been installed with comfortable chairs, an arsenal of binoculars, and a host of servants who brought them aromatic tea. They had a splendid view, not only of the launching site but also of the sea and the belt of islets now beginning to take shape in the early morning light.

The astronauts were unable to suppress a gasp of surprise. The object of their astonishment was not the rocket, still illuminated by searchlights that were soon extinguished and whose gantry had just been trundled away. They were all accustomed to such ceremonies and were somewhat blasé about them. The real sight, for them, was the sea and the islets. Each of these looked like an anthill. The roofs of the huts, the terraces of the hotels, the rocks, the few trees, the smallest open space, were swarming with people. Stern had never seen anything to compare with such crowds. He now realized that the groups of people he had noticed the day before were simply tourists who had come to witness the event. Their numbers had multiplied during the night, beyond all imagination. It looked as though half the population of Japan had converged on Koshi Island, as though on some site of pilgrimage, and this impression was confirmed by the countless boats lying at anchor or shuttling to and fro between the islets.

None of the visitors remembered having seen such a vast fleet assembled on any sea, except for one who, having witnessed the Allied landing in 1944, declared that he felt he was reliving this event all over again. The armada was as remarkable for the strange variety of its units as for its numbers. It included boats of every shape and size: modest sampans, brown-sailed junks, cargo boats, coasters, a few liners, and even some warships, all proudly flying the Japanese colors. It extended out to sea well beyond the islets, for such a fleet could not come closer with impunity. The astronauts could see through their binoculars that all these vessels, all these ships, were laden with passengers, breathless onlookers who had not been able to find a place on land.

"Quite a crowd, what?" said Moji, whose face was beaming at the sight of this crowd.

229

"If each one of them has paid for his seat, the take ought to be good," Stühl muttered in Stern's ear with a trace of annoyance.

There was no doubt in Stern's mind that they had all paid for their seats. Müller had told him, the evening before, that the organizers were expecting an extremely lucrative operation. The three clans owned not only the main island and the islets, with their hotels and huts, but also the ships and planes carrying the tourists. The fares, in addition to the fixed price for a view of the launching, already ensured a decent return, Müller reckoned. But there were any number of supplementary profits, like the exceptionally large number of television sets purchased since the announcement of the event, by those unable to get away; the prodigious increase in newspaper circulation; and also a mass of small details to which ingenious minds had given their attention, such as the sale of cheap binoculars on the islets and aboard the ships. Television sets, newspapers, and optical instruments were also all owned or manufactured by the three clans.

The crowd was absolutely silent. Only the report on the countdown, broadcast by a loud-speaker system over land and sea at regular intervals, broke the solemn hush that hung over Koshi.

The sun had risen. There were now only a few minutes, a few seconds, to go. Up on the hill Kanashima's guests riveted their attention on the rocket. When the countdown reached zero, the missile rose into the air with the usual roar and then vanished into the sky. Even before it had disappeared, Stern looked back at the crowd, curious to see its reactions. It was still silent and seemed to be holding its breath, in expectation of a confirmation that was not long in coming. The loud-speakers announced that the first part of the program had succeeded. Thereupon Koshi Island became the scene of an indescribable delirium. The roar that rose from sea level reached the scientists' ears with the power of a hurricane and was more deafening than the din of a giant rocket.

"Banzai!"

There was such unity and a note of such passion in this cry that all the astronauts gave a start and trained their binoculars on the crowd, as Stern had already done. An extraordinary commotion reigned on the islets and the sea. In less than a second the onlookers had switched from demure silence to frenzy. A forest of small Japanese flags had blossomed overhead, and every rock and vessel was transformed into a seething mass of color.

"The impassive Asiatic!" muttered Stühl, who seemed to resent this enthusiasm.

"It's a great day for us," said Moji in a somewhat tremulous voice. "You must forgive this popular exuberance."

The commotion had lasted almost a quarter of an hour and there was still no sign of its dying down when Moji, who had gone off for a moment to a telephone near the observation post, came back to Stern and informed him that Dr. Kanashima had something urgent to tell him on the phone.

"Good news?"

"Dr. Kanashima wants to tell you himself," said Moji, who had a curious gleam in his eyes.

"Dr. Stern . . . it's a great, a very great day for us. . . ."

The voice of the Japanese scientist was trembling at the other end of the line. His habitual composure seemed to have deserted him. He had difficulty in expressing himself in English. Stern could tell he was struggling to find the right words.

"Dr. Stern, in memory of our former collaboration at Peenemünde, and all your incalculably valuable instruction, I wanted you to be the first to hear the splendid news . . . I'm speaking from the blockhouse . . . Dr. Stern, it's a complete success! We've attained our objective! The first Japanese satellite is now revolving around the earth! It's broadcasting messages."

Stern himself felt overcome by a curious emotion.

231

"I congratulate you with all my heart, Dr. Kanashima," he said with obvious sincerity. "I'm really extremely happy to be the first to convey my admiration. I rejoice for Japan, for science, and for you."

"Thank you," said the Japanese in a barely audible voice.

There was a strange sound in the earpiece, then the receiver was abruptly replaced. Stern realized that Dr. Kanashima was weeping. This was no cause for derision. He knew from personal experience that the coolest and most calculating mind can be moved to tears on the occasion of an important launching.

He went back to his seat beside Moji and silently shook his hand. On land and sea the loud-speakers were emitting a series of abrupt sounds to request silence. The tumult died down immediately and the crowd paid attention. The total success was then announced, with details of the satellite's characteristics and the trajectory on which it was now set for several years to come.

The crowd waited for the end of the announcement, then gave vent to a fresh outburst of enthusiasm. Firecrackers banged and popped on all the islets. Two small warships patroling just offshore fired several salvos from their guns, while squadrons of aircraft that had miraculously risen above the sea gave a display of extravagant aerobatics, skimming over the rocks and the ships, some of which were listing dangerously since the frenzied passengers all crowded to one side.

"Banzai!"

The delirium reached such a pitch that there was likely to be an accident. The warships lowered some lifeboats so as to prepare for any emergency. This precaution was not pointless: in an excess of enthusiasm several young men had just dived from the deck of a cargo vessel into the water. They were fished out without mishap, luckily.

"What's going on over there?" Maggie suddenly asked, hyp-

232

notized by what she saw through her binoculars. "Are they fighting?"

"Not at all," Moji replied with a gleam in his eye. "Have no fear."

On every islet, on every vessel, wherever the onlookers were gathered, young girls wearing a sort of uniform had started moving from group to group, and the crowd was surging around them in a sort of frenzy, as though intent on tearing them to pieces.

"She's going to be lynched!" Maggie cried.

The girl to whom she referred was being subjected to a particularly fierce attack. Hemmed in, pulled this way and that, with her clothes half torn off, she disappeared completely every now and then in the whirlpool of her assailants.

"On the contrary," Moji calmly remarked, "they're all showing their good will."

Stern eventually discovered the reason for this commotion. The maniacs swarming around the girl had no evil intent— quite the reverse, in fact. She, like the others, was holding in her arms a huge receptable with a slot, like a gigantic money box. The onlookers were fighting to reach her and insert their contributions.

Hysteria reigned. Some people emptied the entire contents of their purses, with such wild gestures that most of the coins were scattered on the ground. Thereupon they would bend to pick them up, only to be trampled underfoot by the others surging around the box. A few, who had given all they possessed, turned their empty pockets inside out in despair, then wrung their hands and burst into tears. Women snatched off their earrings and bracelets and, if these were too big to pass through the slot, picked up rocks and hammered at the settings to extract the wretched stones. Unable to move, the girls had decided to stay on the spot where they were and withstand the assaults. Thus several clusters of swarming human-

233

ity had formed here and there, linked together by columns of people who had lost their heads completely and kept running from one group to the other without being able to make up their minds.

"As you see, they're anything but reluctant," said Moji, who seemed delighted with this sight. "Those girls won't have much difficulty in collecting the small addition."

"What addition?"

"Well, the price of a seat only guarantees the successful launching of a big rocket. There's a small addition in the event of complete success. The sum imposed is very modest. I'm sure we'll collect, on an average, more than twenty times what we're asking."

THIRTY-FOUR

Yielding to his host's urging, Stern spent the rest of the holiday at Dr. Kanashima's villa. He felt he would undoubtedly have an opportunity later on to visit some Japanese cities and villages and show William around them. What he needed for the time being was exactly what the Japanese was offering him here: seclusion, the sea, and complete peace and quiet.

Dr. Kanashima did all he could to make his guests' stay as pleasant as possible and to satisfy all their desires, stretching courtesy to the point of not overwhelming them with too much attention. He was well aware of the criticism that foreigners sometimes leveled at the exaggerated quality of Japanese hospitality and always showed the utmost discretion. He kept out of their way. On several occasions he did not even come back to the villa for the night. He gave them to understand that he had some makeshift quarters on Moon Island, where the work now under way required his frequent presence. But he always turned up, miraculously, whenever a wish was expressed. William had mentioned his interest in boats, and on the day after their arrival they found a small yacht with an auxiliary engine anchored at the dock in front of the house.

The captain put it at their disposal. They spent glorious days sailing between the islets, catching strange fish, and swimming in the creeks. After a few days Stern was a changed man. He had arrived utterly exhausted, showing every sign of worry and overwork. The traces of fatigue gradually disappeared and he even succeeded in forgetting what was most on his mind. Maggie was a great help, and Dr. Kanashima, true to his promise, never mentioned astronautics. Nor did Müller, who sometimes came to spend the evening with them.

This peace was disturbed only on one occasion, about halfway through the holiday, by a sort of roaring noise that made Stern give a startled jump. They were sailing at the time off the extreme tip of Koshi. The sound came from out at sea, most probably from the big island, Moon Island, whose mountains could be seen in the distance. Stern glanced at the captain of the boat, but he appeared not to have heard anything. Maggie and William were too busy hauling in their lines to pay any attention.

He listened closely. This roaring sound was familiar to him and his trained ear automatically tried to analyze it. It lasted several minutes, rising at first to a loud crescendo, despite the distance—even Maggie raised her head for a moment—and then gradually dying down. Stern could not be mistaken: it was the motor of a very large rocket being bench-tested.

The same sound recurred several times during the day. The

last time, he could not prevent himself from making certain comparisons and working out some calculations in his head. Then William called out for help in hauling a huge flapping fish aboard and he forgot the incident.

He thought about it again that evening, however, when the Sterns were dining with Müller. Dr. Kanashima, detained by some important work, was unable to get home that night.

"Müller," he suddenly said, "you've been testing the motor of a rocket on Moon Island today."

Müller looked disconcerted and rather annoyed.

"Who told you that?"

"No one. But if you want to keep it a secret, tell them to fit your motors with silencers."

Müller smiled.

"It's true," he said. "I forget that an expert like you is a sort of Sherlock Holmes when it comes to rockets. I've spent the whole day there myself. Our new installation is progressing rapidly. The bench has just been finished and we've been able to start tests on a new motor. . . . Did Sherlock Holmes make any further deductions?" he added with a somewhat forced laugh.

Stern looked at him keenly.

"It's an extremely powerful motor, much more powerful than the one on the rocket that launched your satellite."

"We've never concealed the fact that we intend eventually to launch slightly bigger projectiles. . . . What else did you gather?"

"Only this: it's probably several motors assembled in parallel—six or even eight sections linked together, as in the first stage of my Phoebe i. What else? I have a fairly sharp ear; I think I can calculate the power of this motor—only approximately, of course. . . ."

Dr. Kanashima's "makeshift quarters" on Moon Island consisted in fact of a house as large as his villa on Koshi. It had only just been completed but he had already furnished it with great care, for the importance of the new base would oblige him to stay here more and more frequently. Dr. Kanashima did not care for improvised encampments or commuting to and fro by speedboat or helicopter, as he was now forced to do.

He was in conference there that evening with three guests who had arrived by the afternoon plane, a Japanese woman and two Japanese men, all of them still quite young but very obviously persons who were accustomed to command, to lead men, and to cope with important business. Mrs. Suzaki, Mr. Okada, and Mr. Yamato were the heads of the three clans, which had decided to put an end to a long rivalry and become partners for the sake of space research. The three visitors and their host were comfortably installed in Western-style armchairs, to which they appeared accustomed. They had simply exchanged their town clothes for kimonos.

The conversation had started with a series of congratulations addressed to Dr. Kanashima, first on the launching of the satellite, and then on the progress achieved on Moon Island. The three directors had not been able to come over the week before, but each had made a point of attending this afternoon's tests, which showed what importance they attached to them. They had taken this opportunity to visit the whole of the new base, paying special attention to the general layout and working conditions—technicalities not being within their province—and they were unsparing in their compliments to Dr. Kanashima. He had apologized for receiving them in this villa, where the paint was scarcely dry, but he had felt the presence of the Sterns might have embarrassed them.

Mrs. Suzaki assured him that she much preferred this house, where they were able to speak and discuss quite freely.

"You were quite right to ask Dr. Stern to Koshi," said Mr. Okada, who appeared to be the oldest of the trio. "It's excellent publicity. I suppose you've been discreet about our projects for the future."

237

A slight shadow passed over Kanashima's face.

"Of course. But he noticed we were doing important work on this island. He caught a glimpse of the gantries, just as we were coming in to land . . . an error on the part of the pilot. . . . Stern is not completely blind. I didn't conceal from him that we intend to launch bigger satellites. We have no reason to hide this."

"Of course not," the three directors replied in unison. "Of course not, there's no reason to conceal the fact that we're preparing to launch bigger satellites," one of them added.

"Have steps been taken against the careless pilot?" Mrs. Suzaki then asked in a dry little voice.

"I merely gave him a reprimand, as I didn't want the business to leak out."

Mrs. Suzaki nodded in such a manner that it was difficult to tell whether she approved or disapproved of this clemency. Dr. Kanashima went on:

"I've had no cause to regret the presence of Dr. Stern. He has given me, as one friend to another, invaluable information, and to Müller as well."

"Talking about Müller," Mrs. Suzaki broke in again, "I suppose, Dr. Kanashima, that you're absolutely certain of his loyalty? He knows all about our projects, including the most important one. I'm sure you've asked yourself this question and that it's only after mature reflection that you often allow him to remain alone with Dr. Stern, a fellow countryman and a former colleague. You've made certain, of course, that he's not the sort of man to give away a secret?"

"That's exactly what I have done," said Dr. Kanashima with a bow. "I have asked myself this question. And the answer is: I guarantee Dr. Müller's discretion."

"Even when he has drunk a little more than is good for him?" Mrs. Suzaki persisted. "They say that sometimes happens."

238

"Never when he's immersed in a job like the one he's engaged in at the moment. . . . I can vouch for Dr. Müller as I would for myself," Kanashima concluded somewhat coldly.

"My dear doctor," said Mr. Okada, "that's exactly what we were hoping to hear. You've set our minds at rest."

Having thus fulfilled their managerial duty, the three directors drew up their chairs and began to discuss the subject closest to their hearts, not without instinctively lowering their voices.

"And now, Dr. Kanashima, can you pinpoint our position? How far along are we with our project?"

The scientist marshaled his thoughts. He was about to reply when a car drew up outside the front door.

"It's Dr. Müller. I asked him to come over if he could get away early enough, for he's at least as qualified as I am to discuss these questions."

A moment or two later Müller entered the room. After being congratulated as warmly as his colleague had been, he said apprehensively:

"Stern heard the noise of our tests this afternoon. It's a little annoying."

"Of course," Kanashima muttered. "I should have foreseen it."

"What disadvantages can this have?" Mrs. Suzaki asked.

"I can't do better, Mrs. Suzaki, than to repeat the remark he made to me. He said: 'This roar could come only from an extremely powerful motor comprising at least six, if not eight rockets in parallel. I'd be very surprised if this motor didn't develop a thrust of at least six hundred tons—if it wasn't capable of putting a seven- or eight-ton payload into orbit.' That's all."

"And . . . in fact?" Mr. Okada asked, after a rather long silence.

"In fact," Dr. Kanashima replied slowly, "our tests have re-

239

vealed a thrust of six hundred and thirty tons, which would no doubt enable us to put a payload of over seven tons into orbit."

A fresh silence ensued, interrupted only by a brief exclamation from Mrs. Suzaki.

"I should like to meet Dr. Stern one of these days," she said. "I admire people who have sharp ears and know how to use them."

"What was your reply, Dr. Müller?" Mr. Yamato asked.

"I told him our tests had not permitted us to determine the exact power of the motor. He smiled and did not pursue the matter."

After the three directors had conferred together in Japanese for a moment, Mr. Okada said:

"We feel there's no advantage in trying to deceive Dr. Stern and no reason not to admit that we're preparing to launch a satellite of seven or eight tons. What do you think?"

Dr. Kanashima pondered for a moment, then spoke hesitantly.

"There may be no reason, but I'm not so sure. . . . Dr. Müller, what do you think?"

"I agree with you: a mind as sharp as his is bound to deduce that we have other ambitions. . . ."

"And is bound to guess the essentials of our Project One. That's exactly my opinion. A satellite of this weight is not an end in itself."

The Big Three conferred together again. This time it was Mrs. Suzaki who acted as their spokesman.

"In the present circumstances, since mistakes have been made, we feel it is preferable to tell Dr. Stern of our ambition to land a man on the moon—in the distant future."

"I think that's the best policy," said Dr. Kanashima. "I even suggest you give me permission to show him quickly around our new installations. However clever he is, the base at the present stage can't give away our intention and hope of forging ahead more quickly. Our most intense effort is only just about to begin, and he'll never discover that. He'll be flattered by our trust and perhaps he'll give us some valuable advice. He's a man of incomparable experience."

After a further exchange of views the three directors approved of this plan. Now that this had been settled, they reverted to their discussion of Project One.

"Can you give us a date?" asked Mrs. Suzaki, raising a tiny teacup to her lips.

"Before answering that question, Mrs. Suzaki, let me once more explain the real difficulty of the problem. A controlled landing on the moon of a projectile carrying instruments is relatively easy. The Americans and Russians will no doubt achieve it this year. If we direct our efforts toward this goal, I'm convinced we can do the same within two or three years."

"Two years," Müller asserted.

"In 1967?"

"Or '68."

"But that's not what interests us," said Mrs. Suzaki with a trace of impatience.

"I know. So we've decided to bypass that stage, merely using the observations of the others, and make a direct attempt with a capsule manned by a crew of two."

"Two Japanese."

"Two Japanese. Well, now, the great difficulty of such an attempt lies in ensuring the return of this crew. . . . As you know, Mrs. Suzaki," the scientist went on with increasing animation, "we're prepared to take certain risks, more risks than the Russians or Americans would take. . . . They both want complete security, and it's precisely this that gives us a good chance of winning. But the risks we take must be *reasonable*. I refuse to listen to the cosmonauts we're already training. They'd personally be prepared to take the most senseless risks."

241

"We're all agreed on that," said Mr. Okada. "Reasonable risks, you said. Well, then? Under these conditions, how soon do you think you'll be ready?"

In turn, Dr. Kanashima and Müller conferred together.

"We think we have a chance of being ready in five years' time," the Japanese scientist eventually stated; "that is, about 1970. Earlier than that is impossible. But I'm also convinced that neither the Russians nor the Americans will be ready before then, considering the difficulties they're encountering in their own countries. Mrs. Suzaki, gentlemen, we are going to set to work with such energy that I have great hopes of beating them to it."

THE COUNTDOWN

One evening in September, 1970, General Schleuder landed in Florida and drove with his luggage to the bungalow occupied by the Sterns on the edge of the site that had been prepared some years previously for Operation Moon. Maggie flung herself into his arms as soon as she saw him and was unable to restrain her tears. She was at the end of her tether.

"Thank you, oh, thank you for coming."

"I had to come, Maggie," he said gruffly. "I want to be here from start to finish, not only at the end. I'm not much good for anything these days, but I wouldn't die happy if I missed this. I'll stay as long as necessary; I applied for an indefinite leave. What's the latest news?" he asked anxiously.

"I don't know, but he's due back this evening from Washington where the final conference is being held."

"And the atmosphere?"

"He called this morning to say he was hoping for a positive decision."

"Good God, Maggie!"

"Since then, nothing. I'm expecting him at any moment."

Only then did Schleuder think of the conventional formalities.

"I'm not going to impose myself on you for a month or more. There must be a hotel in the neighborhood."

"I won't hear of it. There's plenty of room here and we need you. The presence of an old friend like you will help him enormously, even if you don't see much of him. . . . He spends hardly any time at home."

"I can imagine how busy he must be. How is he?"

"Very irritable. He does his best not to show it, but . . ."

"I understand."

"Please stay, for my sake as well. . . . It's terrible at times. Ruth often comes to see me, but she's in the same boat as I am and we don't know what to say to each other."

"Isn't William here?"

"He's at M.I.T. We didn't want him to be here just now; but when the moment comes, nothing on earth will stop him."

"Everything will be all right," Schleuder assured her, giving her hands an affectionate squeeze.

"I'm sorry," said Maggie, trying unsuccessfully to smile and wiping away another tear, "but we're all rather overwrought here at the base."

"I understand," Schleuder murmured again. "It's not an everyday business, landing men on the moon."

"It's all right," said Stern in a rather dull voice. "The decision has been made. The countdown begins the day after tomorrow."

Maggie rushed up and flung her arms around him. When she had first seen him, pale and drawn, she had thought the operation had been postponed again.

"Hurrah," said Schleuder. "This is going to be a triumphant premiere."

"Don't count your chickens . . . The Russians are also ready. We know it."

"We'll be the first," Maggie asserted. "We've been ahead of them for the last two years."

"No one can be sure of that," he retorted with sudden irritation. "Caught up with them? Perhaps. And what if we have?

246

Our programs aren't open to a strict comparison. They already have reserves of fuel around the earth and around the moon. . . . Schleuder, perhaps at this very moment their crew is getting ready; perhaps they've reached the last few seconds of their countdown. The latest information was alarming. And we've been mad enough to announce our progress to the world. They know exactly how far along we are and they are the kind of people who would attempt the impossible in order to beat us. I can feel it; I know it; it's a matter of weeks, of days, maybe only a few hours. But we still have a month to go, probably a little more, perhaps even two!"

"One month," said Maggie. "That's the time fixed for the countdown, isn't it?"

"If there isn't a hitch. But there's *always* a hitch," he went on in a sort of panic. "Even for an ordinary launching, as you know, Schleuder, you've always got to stop and start all over again. And this is no ordinary launching."

"No," Schleuder echoed, "this is no ordinary launching, but I'm sure it's been prepared with more care than any other."

"It's been well prepared, I can vouch for that, but . . ."

He was suddenly ashamed of his irritation and apologized to his wife and friend.

"Don't hold it against me. It's been a harassing day."

The conference held in Washington had assembled the leading figures of NASA under the direction of the President of the United States, who had insisted on attending it from start to finish instead of merely putting in an appearance toward the end, as he usually did. It had lasted the whole of the previous day and part of this morning.

"Two exhausting days," Stern repeated.

But then, the object of this meeting was of supreme importance. The questions to which the answer, yes or no, had to be found, were as follows: Have we provided for everything? Is America really ready to land a crew of three men on the moon and ensure their safe return to earth? Can we begin the count-down, which is anticipated to last one month?

The men primarily responsible for the project had spoken in turn, each of them explaining the degree of accuracy and security reached in his particular field, each asserting that his department was ready for Operation Moon. Meyer, in particular, appeared extremely positive about the last stage of Phoebe 5, which was propelled by nuclear energy.

"But all this doesn't represent the real situation," Stern cried out. "I know the different departments have been ready for some time. But in a project like this what counts most of all is the overall situation, the coordination of the various components, the general harmony. And when that question was asked, it was to me that everyone turned."

"Quite right," said Maggie. "You're the brains of the outfit."

"As if one man's brains could encompass the sum total of such a staggering undertaking! Atomic energy, for instance, Schleuder—I don't know a thing about it! It would need a whole lifetime to master it. I have to rely blindly on Meyer and a handful of others!"

In the conference hall, however, all the participants had felt that he was best qualified to sum up the general conclusions. He belonged in a way to every department. Project Moon was his brain child. It was he who had drawn up the plans, modified them, transformed and perfected them endlessly, who had had them approved after some memorable tussles with almost every scientific body, and who had contributed more than anyone to putting them into effect. A solemn silence indicated the importance they all attached to his opinion.

He had stated, and demonstrated with facts and figures, that the plan was perfected, that America was ready, that no further preparation could humanly be made, that brain, muscle, and machine had completed their tasks on earth and that the moment had come to take action in space.

The President had listened to him gravely, without making a

gesture, without interrupting him once, but he was not satisfied with this deliberately abbreviated summary from which most of the technical details had been omitted. He asked for further explanations and made his advisers submit objections and criticisms to which Stern had to reply point by point. He had emerged from this very creditably, in the general opinion.

"Then the President took the floor," said Stern. "I had never seen him look so pale. The speech he made was not in his usual style. He seemed afraid. Each of his words remains engraved on my memory. This is what he said:

" 'It was a President of the United States who brought this project into being. It is I who pursued and encouraged it. The President of the United States feels no less responsible for its success than those who have been devoting their energy to it all these years. Today I must say this, in all humility, to all of you who are gathered here. I have misgivings. I sometimes have nightmares. I sometimes wonder whether we haven't hypnotized ourselves, you with your calculations, I with the ambition of wanting America to be the first to achieve the event of the century. Today I put this question to you—as men, not as scientists. I put it to you and at the same time implore you to eliminate all consideration of pride from your judgment. . . . Is it really and truly possible, is it *humanly* possible, to land men on the moon, even for Americans to do this?'

"Since no one replied to this question, the President continued in the heavy silence:

" 'At the moment of making a decision that will stamp its mark on the history of mankind, we must banish this competitive spirit that often drives us into risky enterprises. We must dismiss the fear of being preceded by the representatives of another nation. If any one of you thinks that a few months or even a few years of research are still necessary for the absolute safety of our crew, it is his duty to say so. Above all, he must not imagine . . .'

"At this point the President's voice broke slightly.

" 'Above all, he must not imagine that I harbor a personal ambition to see this exploit accomplished during my term of office. No one must be prompted by the desire to belong to the generation that brings about this triumph. No consideration can justify risking the lives of three Americans for a hazardous enterprise. . . . And even if there are some of you who feel . . .'

"He lowered his voice still further and it assumed a strange solemnity.

" 'Even if some of you feel that three human lives can be risked, considering the importance of the stakes, in an enterprise that has . . . let's say, a sixty or seventy percent chance of success, if some of you follow this false argument, you should remember the words we have all heard before: *"In a very real sense, it will not be one man going to the moon, it will be an entire nation."* Well, those profoundly true words should make us ponder on the disgrace and opprobrium that will redound today *on our entire nation* in the event of a failure.'

"He had snapped out the word failure with a violence that made his audience start. Every face was turned toward him. Some of them blanched. Everyone started to examine his own conscience feverishly, with an anguish that deprived each of us of all composure. None of us had the courage to answer the President. He continued further, concluding in a dry voice:

" 'There is still time to tell me. I shall assume all responsibility for the postponement. Gentlemen, you are scientists who are used to dealing in figures. Does anyone feel that the chances of success are less than eighty percent?'

"All eyes were fixed on me," Stern said, "as though begging me for advice.

"It was I who replied for them, Maggie. No one else dared. I said: 'Mr. President, there's not an eighty percent chance of success. The figure, sir, is one hundred percent.' "

THIRTY-SIX

Absolute certainty! An irresistible urge had prompted him to make this proud statement, which he felt was essential in order to provoke a decision. After his reply the President had scrutinized him for a long time. Stern had boldly withstood his gaze. After which the President had pondered only a few seconds; then, raising his head, in a firm voice from which all trace of hesitation had vanished, he declared:

"Very well. In that case the countdown will begin the day after tomorrow, as you suggest. I shall be there."

"You were right," said Maggie. "That was the answer you had to give, because it's true."

He turned pale and mumbled a few incoherent words. Who could presume to calculate the chances of success? Who could give an exact figure, as he had outrageously done? Caught up for the last five years in the machinery of progressive creation, hypnotized by the objective, he had had plenty of time to ponder this question of probabilities!

He tried to dismiss the gloomy thoughts that had assailed him since his return. After all, it was his job to act as he had. The only possible attitude to realize a project like his was to keep the goal in mind every minute, without ever allowing himself to be distracted by the possibility of failure; still less so today, on the eve of realizing the fabulous dream of his youth, a dream that he felt was the justification of his existence. The first men on the moon! A few poets, a few novelists, even a few scientists had predicted the event. But in his heart of hearts none of them had believed in it strongly enough to tackle the *practical achievement* of this adventure, as he himself had done for more than forty years.

The first! This thought brought him abruptly to another aspect of the problem. Another sort of anguish gnawed at him, taking precedence over the scruples that had been harassing him. What were the Russians doing at this moment? What was Zharov doing? What was Nadia doing? His constant nightmare pictured them immersed in work as he himself was, putting the finishing touches to the preparations for departure, striving desperately to save a few precious hours in this crucial period of the final glorious sprint. For they were also ready. As he had told Maggie, it was known from a reliable source that they had reached more or less the same point as the Americans.

Schleuder had been watching him closely for a few moments, without daring to disturb his meditations. Stern fancied he saw a hint of reproach in his gaze and protested vehemently, "It's not what you think. It's not the Soviet threat that prompted me to reply as I did. Another delay and supplementary tests would have added nothing to the safety factor. The conditions are absolutely perfect. I believe this quite sincerely."

"So do I."

"No one can accuse me of acting hastily," he persisted harshly. "Every stage has been carefully developed. Not a step has been taken without mature consideration, without digesting the lessons learned from preceding experiments. In spite of my impatience I never hesitated to increase the time laid down for certain tests, even when it wasn't absolutely necessary. I give you my word, Schleuder, it's conscientious work. Nothing analogous to that wretched Vanguard business."

"I was convinced of that long before you told me."

"Nothing analogous, either, to the risky venture of the Japanese!"

"The Japanese?"

"Of course. I never told you about that. I've hardly seen you in the last five years. Just imagine, on Müller's advice . . ."

Urged on by Maggie, who hoped the subject would change his mood, he described his visit to Japan and the preliminary work he had seen on Moon Island.

In spite of his present worries, he smiled as he remembered the lengths to which Müller and Kanashima had gone to inform him of their secret ambition: that they, too, hoped to land men on the moon. At the time he had taken slight umbrage, but it did not last long. His anxiety had evaporated completely as he gradually pieced together the two partners' plans, assisted by their reluctant explanations and by his own subtle deductions from the work then under way.

In broad outline, their project had been inspired by his own, but theirs was on a more modest scale. Furthermore, hoping to save time, they were planning to use a space assembly of several projectiles in a terrestrial orbit, a method he himself had finally and definitely abandoned. The margin of safety was smaller. They thought they could manage with a payload of less than a hundred tons.

"It's theoretically possible, but it's cutting things fine, much too fine. Nothing is more dangerous than trying to economize in this area."

Above all, he had detected from any number of signs that the Japanese intended forging ahead quickly, more quickly than they admitted. Did they perhaps nurture the hope of catching up with the Great Powers? Who could tell?

"Utter madness, Schleuder! In their case, yes, there were signs of hastiness. Granted, I also saw some worthwhile innovations. I recognized Müller's brilliant genius, all right."

"Brilliant, but not systematic enough and too daring. I remember him well at Peenemünde. The poet in him always prevailed in the end. A poetic mentality is no doubt essential in order to reach the moon, but it is not enough, as the mathematicians say."

"That's it, exactly," Stern muttered. "There's such a thing as the idea, but there's also resistance of materials. And he's rather too scornful of this vulgar science. The missiles he was planning to build might stand up to the strain—in theory, it's not absolutely impossible—but I would consider it rather an extraordinary stroke of luck. Some of his rockets are quite liable to shatter at blast-off. I didn't hide my views from him, either."

He had indeed given his honest opinion to Müller, as one old friend to another, but without mentioning it to Kanashima. He had tried to convince Müller that one could not jump from four hundred pounds to tens of tons without undertaking laboratory experiments and preliminary tests for several years. Müller had looked annoyed, so he had not pursued the matter. After all, it was Müller's business and Japan's. But if they were dreaming of competing with the Great Powers in the race to the moon, as certain indications led him to suspect . . .

"If they were the only ones, Schleuder, I assure you I'd be sleeping more peacefully at the moment! Unfortunately, they're not the only ones."

He relapsed without transition into his morbid anguish and went on in a different tone:

"The Russians, on the other hand, aren't taking any chances, Schleuder. If their technicians consider they're ready—and we know that they do—then it must be true. They can't allow themselves to fail in the eyes of world opinion, any more than we can. . . . And what drives me wild, Schleuder, is that they're going to know, this very evening, that our countdown begins tomorrow. T minus 30 days; T minus 720 hours; T minus 43,200 minutes. Yes, it's the policy of this country; it's got to be done openly. There'll be the press from all over the world, the crowds, the usual circus show. The Russians will be kept informed, hour by hour, of our progress, our hopes, our delays. Do you think that won't impel them to make an additional effort, to attempt the impossible to save . . . a few hours, maybe, and thus carry off the trophy?"

"Our open-door policy is a good one," Maggie asserted.

"I think so, too," said Schleuder. "It has yielded good results, after the setbacks at the start. The Soviets can't attempt anything more than they've already done. You know better than anyone, Stern, that in an enterprise like this you can't improvise, you can't step up the pace or go beyond a certain limit, without taking enormous risks. And they can't take those risks; you said so yourself."

"Let's hope so."

Stern tried again to dismiss his gloomy thoughts. After dinner, which was soon over, he apologized to his guest and turned to Maggie.

"Give me a sleeping pill. I want to sleep tonight and tomorrow night. I don't think I'll have another chance for a month."

THIRTY-SEVEN

In the main room of the control center, a veritable underground city protected by a concrete roof thirty feet thick—the brain box of the boldest operation ever undertaken by man—the President of the United States leaned over his desk and pressed a button with a hand that he tried hard to keep steady. Immediately, on the far wall facing him, three enormous screens lit up.

T — 30 days　　T — 720 hours　　T — 43,200 minutes

At the same time several other smaller screens started flickering on a series of parallel panels arranged in a semicircle, in front of which stood an army of experts.

Outside, the launching pad was also suddenly lit up and through the portholes in the gantry could be seen the mysterious silhouette of Phoebe 5, a monumental metallic body soaring more than three hundred feet above the base, the construction of which had given rise to such arduous problems and which would probably be used only once. The darkness was invaded by a tremor of excitement, muffled like a respectful prayer. Then all those who were privileged to attend the ceremony relapsed into an oppressive silence and nothing could be heard on the site but the buzz of the motors.

Inside the blockhouse, scientists and technicians were now bent over their desks, listening to the loud-speakers giving the directions of the test conductor, the man in charge of this final stage who, every ten minutes for the time being, read out the clauses of a sort of legal code: the list of the checks to be undertaken during the course of the month. All were more intent than they had ever been in their lives on every gesture and on the slightest movements of the pointers on the screens. When the voice fell silent, the hush was almost deathly, barely disturbed by the rustle of a page turned over in the master of ceremony's great ledger.

This silence, this perceptible emotion beneath the apparent calm, had upset Stern. None of his fears had been realized; this time there had been no commotion, none of those noisy outbursts, sometimes verging on hysteria, that almost always accompany the preparations for an important launching. Outside, the onlookers were solemn and silent, visitors and jour-

256

nalists alike; solemn, silent, and also as religiously intent as the participants in the blockhouse. It was as though some sacred rule had forbidden any exclamation, even the merest gesture—as though the slightest movement might jeopardize the success of the enterprise.

The mood of simplicity and dignity had been set by the President himself. He had arrived during the night with a smaller escort than usual. Rapidly shaking hands with a few people, he had made his way toward the control center. Not one of the journalists present had dared put a question to him. One of them, a very young man who had timidly approached an official, encountered such a severe glare that he immediately withdrew, hiding his notebook away. Even the photographers seemed paralyzed and worked with unusual discretion, as though reluctantly. Television equipment had been allowed inside the blockhouse, but reduced to its simplest components: one projector and a single camera. The results on the screen would be less effective, but the President had ordered these arrangements. It was understood that the crew would pack up and leave as soon as the countdown started. They showed more deference than if they had been filming a religious ceremony in a cathedral.

The President's speech was a model of restraint.

"We are embarking on the final stage of a great task," he said, "a task for which we have been preparing for years, one that has been undertaken by the best brains and the best labor in this country, and to which every American has contributed with his toil, with his money, and with his faith. Today we are ready. We have one month left to make the final checks. Once again I ask all Americans to continue, during this month, to help those responsible for this great enterprise, through their composure and their prayers. During this month, I know, every American heart will stop beating. It is with absolute confidence in the pioneers of space and in the nation, it is with absolute confidence but also with deep emotion, that I declare this period of the countdown for the first manned expedition to the moon to be well and truly started."

He had pressed the button and the screens had lit up. Then he took a step backward and stood silent for several minutes, cradling his head in his hands. True to their promise, the television crew had switched off their projector and packed away their camera. No photograph had been taken. Thus, to the rest of the world, was lost the image of the President of the United States uttering a fervent prayer in a low voice before an outlandish altar dominated by three monstrous screens.

T — 43,170 minutes.

The President had left as discreetly as he had arrived, without uttering another word after his speech, merely shaking hands warmly with the principal authors of the undertaking. After seeing him out, Stern came slowly back to the blockhouse, where the test conductor was now reading out in a firmer voice instructions that were broadcast to the control engineers, to the squads working inside the rocket, and to hundreds of stations scattered throughout every part of the world.

The machine was in motion. Stern paused for a moment at the end of the room, watching the technicians immersed in their respective tasks, tripping switches or pulling levers. He felt utterly forlorn. He now had the impression of being a complete stranger to this activity, somewhat like a layman allowed to attend a dress rehearsal and not knowing what expression to assume. He was glad to see Walker moving up and down between the rows of desks, and even happier when he came and joined him. He, too, looked rather strange. He moved furtively, as though afraid of revealing his presence.

"What's the matter, Walker? You look like a hen that's lost her chicks."

"What's the matter? *I haven't anything more to do*. It's a horrible feeling."

Suddenly Stern understood the reason for his own discomfort. That was it, exactly, and he was even worse off than his assistant. There was nothing more for him to do! The task was accomplished. Nothing more could be added to the project; nothing more could be taken away from it; no further correction could be made. And it was these activities that had occupied his mind for years. Today, in an organization comprised of thousands of experts, he was one of the few who had no task regulated by a chronometer.

He regretted not having given himself some specific and absorbing job to do during the countdown. He had to supervise the general activity, an activity no brain on earth could encompass! The best he could do was rely on his intuition and try to guess just where his presence would be most useful . . . or else wait for an accident! He remained some time with Walker, watching the routine gestures of the staff with an envious eye.

"I'm just going up to inspect the top of Phoebe," Walker said suddenly, as though he hoped, without daring to hope too much, that he might be needed there.

"Go ahead. I may join you later."

Stern remained alone, forcing himself to listen closely to the directions of the loud-speakers. After a moment he lost patience, went outside, and made his way toward the rocket. He was only a hundred yards from it when he almost tripped over a trio of men lying on the ground, silently contemplating the great towering shape. They were the three astronauts who were to leave for the moon in a month's time. They had not heard him coming. He watched them for a moment, with the pang of jealousy he always felt in their presence.

He himself would not be the first man to land on the moon! In vain had he requested this glory, striven with all his might to be included in the crew. He knew in advance that this battle would be lost. The directors of NASA felt he was too useful on earth to be allowed to be sent to the moon and that he was not prepared for this expedition. The three astronauts had been preparing for years. Thanks to an admirably ingenious system of training, they knew what they had to do under any given circumstance, but they did it almost instinctively. They had acquired the infallible reflexes of an experienced racing driver. Stern had acquiesced, after managing to elicit the promise that he would take part in a subsequent expedition, once the pioneers had blazed the trail.

"What are you doing here?" he asked.

"Just looking. . . . It's still too early to go to the training center. So . . . We felt we were in the way there," one of them replied, pointing to the blockhouse.

"Same here," Stern muttered with a sigh. "I, too, felt I was in the way. It looks as if I'm out of the game. As for you, your turn hasn't come yet."

He sat down beside them without saying another word and together they waited in silence for sunrise, which presently tinged the apex of the giant rocket.

THIRTY-EIGHT

T — 20 days. T — 478 hours . . .

With her long slender fingers Mrs. Suzaki angrily switched off the radio that was broadcasting the American countdown. Mr. Yamato, who was sitting opposite her, heaved a sigh.

"Twenty days!" he said. "And the Russians, seventeen!"

The Russians had also embarked on the last lap and, determined to take up the American challenge, were also operating openly.

"What does it matter now?" Mrs. Suzaki cried in a furious voice.

She went out onto the terrace of the villa and joined the third director, Mr. Okada, who was observing the launching pad installed on Moon Island through binoculars.

"How much longer?" she asked impatiently.

"Another fifteen minutes. The gantries have been withdrawn."

"Do you think they'll succeed this time? I've never thought much of that fellow, Müller. I trust him still less after last week's failure. And even if they succeed today, what good is it?"

"I'm relying on Dr. Kanashima," Mr. Okada replied solemnly. "He says the project can still succeed with two rockets."

She shrugged her shoulders without answering, sat down, and, like him, trained her binoculars on the launching pad. Mr. Yamato came out and joined them after a few minutes and followed their example.

Dr. Kanashima emerged from the underground room and stood rooted to the spot in amazement, his eyes watering from the smoke of the conflagration. The whole area around the blockhouse was a scene of catastrophe. A thick cloud rose into the air, gradually blotting out the sun, while the mountains on the island began to assume a sinister, coppery hue. A heap of twisted metal lay blazing in an incandescent liquid sheet, and bits of debris were still being thrown far and wide by the final explosions.

No human figure was visible on the pad but some sirens were screaming not far off. Soon the fire engines arrived and, tackling the fire from a distance, gradually managed to bring it under control. Dr. Kanashima still stood motionless and outwardly impassive as he contemplated the disaster through his smarting eyes. Some men emerged from the shelters and gathered in small groups around the pyre, hanging their heads and not saying a word.

"No one hurt?" Kanashima asked one of the engineers in a dull voice.

"No one."

He put the same question to other heads of branches and received the same reply. One of them added tactlessly:

"Only material damage."

"Only material damage," Dr. Kanashima echoed, glaring at him so oddly that the man turned away and abruptly moved off.

"Only material damage, it's true, only material damage!" said a rasping voice.

The Japanese scientist could not prevent himself from giving a startled jump as he detected an unmistakable note of madness in this voice. He turned and saw Müller reeling like a drunken man. He had unbuttoned his collar and was wringing his hands as though he were raving mad.

"It's my fault," he screamed. "It's all my fault. I'm a presumptuous and criminal ass! Stern warned me. My rockets? Two chances out of three of bursting apart at blast-off, he said. Two chances out of three, ha ha! A remarkable statistician!"

"Pull yourself together, Dr. Müller," Kanashima said severely. "It's no good crying over spilt milk, and I'm more to blame than you are. I'm the one who's chiefly responsible."

"It's my fault and no one else's! I'm a drunkard. Worse yet, I'm a poet. Poets aren't cut out to land on the moon. I was the one who drew up this senseless program. . . . Too hasty, far too hasty . . . We had to forge ahead, without thinking, to beat the Russians, to beat Stern. . . . He's going to have a good laugh, Stern is. He told me: several years of preliminary tests . . . and you have to respect the laws of a science known as resistance of metals. But I scorned the materials, and

262

now the materials are taking revenge. I've betrayed Japan. I'm a miserable wretch!"

"Pull yourself together," Kanashima repeated, wrinkling his brow. "You and I have taken risks, risks that were too big."

But Müller was unable to control himself.

"Risks that were too big, ha ha! I tell you, Stern warned me about this. . . . If you proceed like this, there's scarcely one chance out of three of success. . . . And here's our second chance reduced to a cinder! And the third is useless. All I'm good for is launching a kite."

His cries were beginning to exasperate the engineers and workmen, who had now all emerged from the shelter. Dr. Kanashima seized him by the arm, led him to his jeep, and drove him off to the villa he occupied on Moon Island. Müller had fallen silent; he was now prostrated and plunged in despair. They did not exchange a word during the drive. When they arrived Kanashima ordered him to go to bed—he had not slept for several nights—and instructed the one servant who looked after the villa to take care of his master. He himself was about to return to the scene of the disaster when he changed his mind. He went into the living room, picked up the telephone, and dialed his own number. It was the chilly voice of Mrs. Suzaki that answered. He was so disconcerted for a moment that he could not think what to say.

"I'm terribly sorry," he eventually stammered. "The second rocket has also blown to smithereens."

"We saw it."

"I know I have to make a report on this disaster, but I humbly ask you to excuse me until this evening. My presence is needed just now on the site."

"We'll wait for you," said Mrs. Suzaki. "Now we only have a few more hours to go, haven't we?"

Her exaggeratedly calm tone expressed a wealth of insult and reproach. Dr. Kanashima replaced the receiver, closed his eyes, and swayed on his feet, overcome by a sudden spell of dizziness. Alone in the room where no one could see him, he surrendered for the first time to his despair. It did not last long. After a minute he pulled himself together and resumed his rigid mask.

He went and listened at the door of the bedroom; Müller seemed to be asleep. He got into his jeep again, drove back to the site, walked over to the still smoking heap of ruins, and gave instructions in a calm voice.

He spent the whole day on the devastated spot, solely concerned, it seemed, with wiping out the traces of the accident. Moreover, there was hardly any need to issue orders; each man knew his job, since he had already done it only a few days earlier: the first rocket of the Japanese project had burst asunder at blast-off under the same circumstances as this one. A few hundred yards away, a heap of charred fragments bore witness to the previous catastrophe.

After the first accident, Kanashima and Müller had refused to give way to despair and had struggled manfully against fate. Their original project was based on three rockets designed to put a total payload of ninety tons into orbit around the earth, the first two being mere fuel tanks. They had tried to persuade themselves that the payload of two rockets would be sufficient. The first plan had afforded only a slight margin of safety for the return; the new one had afforded none. Even so! . . . The spur of the Russian and American countdown had inspired them with prodigious ingenuity. They had scrapped everything inside their missiles that was not absolutely necessary for the flight. They relentlessly eliminated most of the accessory measuring instruments. They reduced the crew to one man instead of the two for which they had planned and pared down his equipment, leaving him the bare essentials for life. If they had been able to land a man naked on the moon they would have done so, but the protective space suit had to be kept, alas!

Having taken these steps, they resorted to a subtle game of mathematics to prove to themselves that there was still a chance of success. Müller mustered all the resources of his singular genius to demonstrate that the problem was theoretically soluble, even under the new circumstances. In this he succeeded. This new plan presupposed, on the part of the pilot, a miraculous competence during the periods of deceleration, acceleration, and changes of direction, with a constant attempt to economize on fuel. But Kanashima checked to see that his calculations were accurate. In the ideal realm of mathematics, which leaves no margin for error, there was still a chance.

Dr. Kanashima reflected mournfully on those desperate efforts as his teams cleared the ground after the second accident. At present there was not the ghost of a chance. No economy, no calculation, no power on earth could make the attempt succeed. The Americans and the Russians would land on the moon first. Japan was out of the race. He straightened up to look at rocket Number 3, the one that was to transport the crew. Standing isolated now in the middle of the site, it seemed in his eyes to be the only survivor of a family that had been massacred. In line with it, at irregular intervals, there were now only two heaps of twisted girders and charred metal sheets.

This sight induced the second of Dr. Kanashima's dizzy spells that day. He swayed once more, closed his eyes, and put his hand to his forehead. A group of workmen who were taking a break saw him rub his eyelids and heard him emit what sounded like a groan. Once again, it did not last. A moment later he had recovered his composure. Since morning he had not uttered a word of blame, refraining even from mentioning the accident. He confined himself to issuing orders that his subordinates carried out with the same apparent detachment.

Thus they worked until evening, making an almost morbid effort to wipe out all signs of the disaster, clearing away the ashes, even hosing down the site, as though these ludicrous operations could erase the reality of the tragedy.

When everything was restored to order, Dr. Kanashima dismissed his teams, directing them to go and rest until morning. Presently only one man was left besides himself on the launching pad. It was the cosmonaut chosen for the flight to the moon. He lowered his eyes and looked as though he were going to say something, but Kanashima did not give him time to utter a word. In a dry and authoritative tone, which was unlike him, he told him to pack his bags that very evening and go away on a month's leave. The man again opened his mouth as though to protest, then thought better of it and went off without a word, hanging his head.

Left by himself, Dr. Kanashima went back to his jeep, where his driver was waiting for him. He decided to call on Müller again before going home, to see how he was and, if he was in a fit state, drive him back with him to help with the report he had to make to the three directors—a duty that at this moment seemed the cruelest of all tortures.

He was struck by the silence in the villa as soon as the jeep came to a stop. Müller lived alone and entertained no one except an occasional woman flown in from the nearest town. Kanashima sprang out of the jeep and shouted his name. There was no reply. The servant was certainly not there. No doubt he had gone out to the supply center.

"Dr. Müller!"

His voice seemed to echo curiously and he felt overcome by fresh anguish. He glanced at his driver and saw that he, too, appeared uneasy. He called out again; in vain.

"He must have taken a sleeping pill," he said aloud to reassure himself. "I advised him to get some sleep."

He went into the villa, which was unlocked. The living room was empty. He crossed it and knocked on the bedroom door. He received no reply. He knocked again, more loudly.

"Dr. Müller!"

The driver had made so bold as to follow him into the house and was now standing beside him. They looked at each other again intently. Kanashima tried to turn the door handle. The door had been bolted from inside.

"Go get me a tire iron!"

The door gave way after a few seconds. Dr. Kanashima took one step into the room and came to a standstill, while the driver uttered a hoarse grunt. Müller had hanged himself from a beam.

Dr. Kanashima narrowed his heavy-lidded eyes but still remained silent and maintained his composure. He had been a close friend of Müller's but, after the ordeals he had endured, this new stroke of fate appeared almost a triviality. He went slowly over to the poor wretch, climbed up on a chair, and ordered the driver to bring him a knife. With his help he stretched the body out on the bed and examined it. Müller had been dead for some time.

The scientist's reaction to this was extremely odd. He stood motionless for a long while in front of his friend's corpse, frowning and apparently immersed in thought, as though seeking the solution to a difficult problem.

It was almost absent-mindedly that he picked up a letter addressed to himself that he saw lying on a table, glanced through it, and stuffed it into his pocket. With the same absent demeanor he walked out of the room, called one of the staff doctors, and ordered him to do what was necessary. He himself had no time this evening to deal with a dead man. He eventually went back to his jeep and set out for his own villa.

Throughout the drive his face preserved the same odd expression that had come into it when he was contemplating Müller's corpse. His eyes had lost their blank look and a furtive glint came into them every now and then. His features, which had been drawn all day, had undergone a complete transformation and resembled more and more those of a scientist absorbed in some difficult problem, who cannot yet see the solution but feels he is on the right track.

When he reached home a servant told him that his guests had withdrawn to their rooms with orders not to be disturbed until dinner. No doubt they wanted to rest, having also not slept these last few nights. He was delighted with this respite, which enabled him to change before confronting them.

He went into the bathroom and lay soaking for some time in hot water, still immersed in thought, concentrating on the embryo of an idea that was beginning to take shape. He put on clean clothes, still with no change of expression, and glanced at his watch; he still had nearly half an hour. He took out a sheet of paper and embarked on a series of calculations. When he raised his head, at the end of ten minutes, there was a brilliant gleam in his eyes.

While waiting for his guests, whom he could hear dressing, he went out onto the balcony. A thin sliver of moon cast sufficient light on the launching pad to enable him to perceive in the distance the silhouette of the last rocket standing out against the almost white ground. Suddenly the scientist felt invaded by a deep sense of peace. He had found the solution to the problem that had been worrying him for the last few hours, and this discovery gave him a wonderful feeling of elation.

When he went down to welcome his guests—or confront his judges—in spite of the day's disaster, in spite of Müller's tragic end, there was a smile of triumph on Dr. Kanashima's face.

THIRTY-NINE

By the time his guests entered the room, he had resumed his impassive expression. They tried not to show their feelings before the servants, but they were only partly successful. Mrs. Suzaki's face betrayed a mixture of rage and resentment.

Dr. Kanashima asked them if they would prefer having dinner immediately or having a discussion first, without witnesses, on the very regrettable incident that had occurred that morning. On hearing him refer to a national disaster in these terms, Mrs. Suzaki made a violent gesture and almost gave vent to an outburst of temper. It was only the sight of a servant hovering nearby that restrained her, and she merely stated in a dry voice:

"I'm not hungry."

The two others having made the same reply, the scientist gave orders to his butler, who placed some drinks within arm's reach and withdrew after closing the door behind him. Mr. Okada, the eldest of the three, started the attack.

"It's a great misfortune for Japan," he said, raising his thick eyebrows.

Dr. Kanashima poured himself a whisky, after serving his guests, who preferred this drink to any other on such an occasion.

"A great misfortune," he agreed.

"A great misfortune and a great disappointment," said Mrs. Suzaki sourly. "From what you told us, we were hardly expecting this tragedy. How could it have happened?"

Dr. Kanashima lowered his head, but without humility. He was expecting this onslaught. He spoke with a cheerful authority that he had never before displayed before these important people.

"Allow me to sum up the situation," he said. "Then I shall give you all the explanations you're entitled to expect from me. . . . Well now, the second rocket has blown to pieces at blast-off, like the first one."

He said this in a matter-of-fact manner that seemed tantamount to indifference. Mrs. Suzaki could not tolerate his tone of voice and raised her own.

"And why did this rocket blow to pieces? Why did the first one do the same? Were the plans drawn up by pseudoscientists? Wasn't every necessary care taken in the construction of the boosters?"

Dr. Kanashima paused for a moment and replied with his same composure:

"We all took every care in their construction. Not enough, perhaps; this has been proved by experience. In scientific matters it is experience that has the final word. . . . In fact, I now personally think that our ambitions were too great, out of all proportion to the means at our disposal."

"It seems to me we have put enormous means at your disposal."

"Substantial," the doctor corrected her. "We ought to have had even more considerable means, and I'm not talking only of the financial side. . . . I don't say, mind you, that the enterprise was completely senseless, but it entailed a very, very great risk."

"And it's only now you tell us this!" the Japanese woman screamed, beside herself with rage. "I don't understand your behavior, Dr. Kanashima, and still less your present attitude of indifference!"

The wise Okada motioned her to keep calm. He felt that the scientist had much more to tell them.

"I know that I am principally to blame for this failure. I admit I was wrong. I humbly apologize to you and to the whole Japanese nation."

". . . The Japanese nation," said Mr. Okada without raising his voice, "the Japanese nation, which was well aware we were preparing a gigantic enterprise because of certain allusions we made, on your own suggestion; the Japanese nation that, trusting her scientists and engineers, has spared them neither its encouragement nor its contributions."

Dr. Kanashima bowed his head slightly.

"I say again that I have no intention of denying my great responsibility."

"And that fellow Müller," Mrs. Suzaki broke in, "Müller, whom I never trusted in spite of your assurances—isn't he also largely to blame? Wasn't he the first to think of the project?"

"Dr. Müller put an end to his life this afternoon," Kanashima declared gravely. "He left this message expressing his regret and also apologizing to the Japanese nation."

He took the letter out of his pocket and handed it to the Big Three. Mr. Okada put on a pair of thick tortoise-shell glasses and read it carefully but made no comment. Mr. Yamato nodded his head with a vaguely approving air.

"Dr. Müller has finished his own adventure," Mrs. Suzaki eventually said in an icy tone. "We can no longer indict or judge *him.*"

All three of them glared at Dr. Kanashima, who withstood their gaze and appeared in no way put out. He ingenuously agreed:

"Dr. Müller has indeed found an honorable solution."

"And now," said Mr. Yamato, in turn raising his voice

271

slightly, "what are we going to do? Have you a suggestion to make? We are all dishonored. The people of Japan are going to point at us in the street and we'll be the laughingstock of the whole world. You know our real aim is bound to leak out sooner or later—it's already suspected—and also our pitiful failure. Among all the technicians on the island, at least a few are bound to talk."

"It's quite likely. I've thought about this a great deal since this morning. I, too, reached the depths of despair, like Dr. Müller. I hesitated a long time before reporting to you this evening. And then . . ."

"And then what?"

"I came and reported. . . . I dared to come," Dr. Kanashima went on with sudden animation, "because I had an idea. I saw the possibility of escaping disgrace and ridicule. It occurred to me vaguely when I found Müller's body—*at that very moment*—but it was only later that I arrived at a complete solution to the problem. I apologize for expressing myself like this, but it is indeed a problem, a *real problem*. I now realize that we committed a gross error, Dr. Müller and I, but an error that is perhaps excusable because many others have committed it before us."

"There's every reason why you should deplore your errors in calculation," Mrs. Suzaki exclaimed impatiently, "but do you think this is the right moment?"

Mr. Okada, who had kept on his tortoise-shell glasses, was listening with rapt attention and watching the scientist with great curiosity.

"Let Dr. Kanashima explain himself," he said authoritatively.

"I must remind you," Dr. Kanashima went on, "that our project comprised three rockets capable of putting thirty tons each into orbit—a total of ninety tons. These rockets, combined in the first phase on a terrestrial orbit, would have made up a train that would have headed for the moon and started orbit-

272

ing around it. Then, as in the American project, a capsule manned by a crew of two would have detached itself. This capsule would have made the actual landing on the moon, and subsequently rejoined the main space ship. I must point out that the last rocket, the only one now remaining, was to carry the capsule with the crew. The two others, to all intents and purposes, were merely reserve fuel tanks."

"We know all that," Mrs. Suzaki muttered.

"When the first rocket blew up," Kanashima went on without heeding the interruption, "Dr. Müller and I worked out a second plan, which was almost utter madness: two rockets and a sixty-ton payload. Even with a reduced capsule and only one man as crew, this allowed no safety margin for the return."

"Is it really necessary to go into all this today?"

"Yes, it is necessary, Mrs. Suzaki, in order to underline a vital point that every astronaut knows but on which none of them has pondered as deeply as I have today. Namely this: it's the consideration of the *return* that distorts every aspect of the problem. It's the *return* that demands such vast loads of fuel, obliging us to resort to several rockets that are nothing but tanks."

"But we know all this, too! You've told us a thousand times."

"It's sometimes useful to linger over a scientific problem a thousand and one times," Dr. Kanashima gently replied. "That's how we sometimes arrive at the perfect solution, which had escaped us because it was too simple, a solution we only perceive as a result of a random everyday occurrence."

"Too simple?"

"Too simple. In the field of technology, simplification is always an enormous advance. . . . The ideal solution occurred to me when I discovered the death, the useless death, of Dr. Müller."

"I think I'm beginning to see what you mean, Dr. Kanashima," Mr. Okada remarked gravely.

"Well, I don't at all," Mrs. Suzaki exclaimed. "And I must

say, discussing these technical problems at a time like this seems extremely out of place."

Dr. Kanashima looked at her and smiled.

"Mrs. Suzaki," he said, "I'm going to explain myself more clearly. Our essential goal, the exploit that will earn our nation the supreme glory, is landing a man on the moon, isn't it? That, and that alone, is the basic problem. Do you agree?"

"Of course."

"Well, this is perfectly feasible with the last rocket. We can only hope that it won't blow up like the others. But it has been built with even greater care and, as Dr. Stern told Müller, we have one chance out of three."

"But, as I understand it, the return—"

"Mrs. Suzaki," the doctor replied, still smiling, "when, during the last war, our bombers took off from distant bases to attack a particularly important target—the American fleet in Pearl Harbor or the *Prince of Wales*—their target was the essential problem. Many of them didn't have enough fuel to get back. Would you like a more striking example? To our kamikaze pilots, the question of *returning* was never even posed."

Mrs. Suzaki fanned herself with a graceful gesture and fell silent for a long time.

"I think I'm beginning to understand, as well," she eventually said in a softer tone of voice. "I apologize for being so slow, Dr. Kanashima. But, as you say, I'm not familiar with these technical problems."

FORTY

T — 15 days.

"I don't know if I'll be able to hold out until the end," said Stern. "How far are the Russians? Did you listen to the radio?"

"Only half an hour ago. Minus twelve days."

"In hours, Maggie! How many hours?" he asked impatiently.

"Two hundred and seventy-seven, I jotted it down," said Schleuder, taking a notebook out of his pocket. "They haven't gained an hour since the start."

"They haven't lost an hour, either! Everything has gone well with us, it's true, but it also has for them and they're still three days ahead."

"We'll catch up with them in the end, because our procedure is faster than theirs. You've demonstrated that a hundred times," said Maggie.

"Yes, yes, I've demonstrated it," he moaned wearily.

In his present state he was quite incapable of being convinced by a demonstration, even his own.

It was two days after the start of the American countdown that the Russians had begun theirs. They, too, had decided to give it world-wide publicity, realizing that secrecy was of no further use at this stage. Their countdown was due to last twenty-five days instead of thirty, which gave them a three-day lead over their opponent. But their project entailed a double supply system, first around the earth and then around the moon, which would take about three days according to the calculations of the American technicians. As a result there was a difference of only a few hours, perhaps even a few minutes, between the two contestants, and no one could predict the winner.

Stern did his best not to think about them—nothing could or should, at this stage, modify his procedure—but in this he was not always successful. Several times he had had to suppress an impulse that prompted him to fling himself at the test conductor and destroy the endless list of checks. His own copy of this ledger, to which he had contributed more than anyone to drawing up, he inspected minutely every day, tormented by the vague foreboding that some important operation had been left out, striving to discover omissions that, as time passed, he felt more and more convinced of finding.

It was so easy to overlook a detail in a check list that involved more than a million components! And it was often a trivial but indispensable detail that was likely to be overlooked. He remembered with terror when the first cosmonaut had been put into orbit. Everything had been provided for, or so it was believed. The most complicated and delicate instruments had been subjected to detailed examination. At the last moment it was the diesel engine that drove the wheels of the gantry that had broken down. A diesel engine! The most commonplace, most primitive mechanism! He also remembered the fit of hysteria the man responsible for the operation had indulged in when he found that out of the thousands of scientists, engineers, and experts hovering about the rocket, not one was able to discover the cause of the breakdown, still less remedy it. They were too highly trained for this sort of prehistoric machinery. A mechanic had had to be fetched from a nearby haulage outfit. He had repaired the motor in a moment, with the help of a screw driver and a monkey wrench, under the astonished eyes

276

of the conquerors of space. The launching had been delayed several hours as a result.

Yet this time everything seemed to be working perfectly. There had not been a single hitch or setback. It was too good to be true! It was abnormal; it did nothing to dispel his anguish —quite the reverse, in fact. This evening, feeling really at the end of his rope, he had come home, contrary to his habit; since he lived several miles from the site, he usually spent the night in one of the underground rooms adjoining the control center, where he had had a cot set up. There he would snatch an hour or two of fitful sleep, punctuated by nightmares, but he tried to persuade himself that his presence was needed.

From time to time, however, he felt he had to escape. This evening he had gone home, giving orders not to be disturbed unless something really serious happened and to have the daily call from the White House put through to his quarters.

Maggie and Schleuder made a point of not mentioning the operation under way, and applied themselves to taking Stern's mind off it. Maggie even decided not to tell him that she had received a letter from William, since all he could write about was the great adventure. They all went for a stroll in the garden. Maggie tried to interest him in her herbaceous border and he pretended to humor her. She led the way back to the house as soon as it began to get dark, however, on the pretext that she felt chilly. He followed her inside with a faint smile. He knew perfectly well she was frightened, on his account, of the sight of the stars appearing.

She was careful not to switch on the television or radio; there was scarcely a broadcast that did not make some reference to Operation Moon. Schleuder suggested a game of chess and Stern eagerly agreed, glad to recover some sort of mental balance by working out combinations as laborious as they were futile.

A precarious balance! He was brought up with a start by the telephone ringing. Maggie set his mind at rest as she handed him the receiver. It was only the call he was expecting from the White House: mere routine. Stewart was on the other end of the line. Stern started speaking without waiting for the ritual question.

"Everything's going well at the moment. No hitches."

As he said this, he tapped the wooden table top superstitiously. He heard a sigh of relief.

"Thanks, old man—I can imagine how you're feeling. Forgive me for disturbing you. But you're not the only one. . . ."

"Don't mention it. I'm taking a few hours off until tomorrow morning. I feel I really need a good night's rest."

"Quite right, too. You've got to keep your wits about you right up to the end—you, at least—even if everyone else goes crazy, which seems to be happening here. . . . No, I don't want to keep you any longer. . . . By the way, did you hear the news from Japan this evening?"

"No, Maggie has forbidden me to turn on the television."

"Two of their giant rockets have exploded at blast-off. They weren't quite ready."

"I'm not surprised."

"Yes, I remember your telling me something about a possible project of theirs. They announced this very briefly, as though it were an everyday occurrence, but we know it's a hard blow for them."

"It was utter madness. Their plan couldn't possibly succeed. I told Müller so. I had no worry on that score. . . . Stewart," he added vehemently, "couldn't you have told me that the *Russian* rockets had exploded? I should have preferred that."

"So should I, my generous-minded friend. That'll be for the next time. . . . Didn't you mention the name Müller just now?"

"Yes."

278

"It must be the same man. A German adviser of the Japanese. He has committed suicide. Did you know him?"

"Yes, he was one of the old Peenemünde hands."

"I keep forgetting! You're so American! I hope you're not too badly affected by this news?"

"We weren't very close. He must have gone out of his mind. He drank too much."

He replaced the receiver pensively. Müller's tragic end had affected him just the same. He told Maggie and Schleuder what had happened. Maggie was genuinely sorry for Dr. Kanashima, whose kindness and thoughtfulness had touched her heart.

"The moon had sent Müller stark staring mad," Stern declared somberly. "He was trying to jump several stages. It can't be done with impunity. His attempt was sheer lunacy."

"Beneath his impassive Oriental exterior," Schleuder remarked, "I wonder if Kanashima was any more levelheaded than he."

They quickly dismissed these gloomy thoughts. Stern once more sought refuge in the homely family atmosphere, assisted in his efforts by his wife and friend. By dinnertime their mood was almost jovial. Afterward they had a game of cards and presently went to bed. Stern was so tired that he fell asleep at once, despite his worries.

He had been asleep for three hours when the telephone rang.

"I knew it! I bet the Russians—"

His constant nightmare was that the Russians were playing a monstrous trick on the whole world and concealing far more advanced preparations by a fictitious countdown.

"Don't move. I'll answer it."

When Maggie came back she was forcing herself to smile, but her face was white and her lips were trembling.

"Nothing to do with the Russians, but . . ."

He realized it was something serious, but felt immense relief: at least it was not what he most feared.

279

"It was Walker calling from the site. The countdown has been stopped."

FORTY-ONE

"I'll come with you," said Schleuder. "You can drop me off at the observation post."

"And how will you get back? I'll be there for the rest of the night at least, maybe even . . ."

He did not finish his sentence. He had grown superstitious and was afraid of attracting the attention of malevolent spirits by his own pessimistic remarks.

"Don't worry about me. I'll stay over there until morning and find some means of transport if you don't come back."

After the telephone call Stern had taken only one minute to dress, but as he came out of his room he found that Schleuder was also ready and was firmly determined not to go back to bed while the crisis lasted.

"If that's how you feel, let's go."

Maggie accompanied them as far as the car and kissed them both without saying a word. They took barely ten minutes to reach the observation post. Stern drove fast, his teeth clenched, his features drawn. Since waking he had not stopped accusing himself of negligence, attributing the cause of this hitch to his absence, knowing full well, however, in his heart of hearts, that he had no more influence on the progress of the operation than the humblest engineer.

"Is it serious?" Schleuder asked.

"From what Walker says, I don't think so. But it means a delay of several hours."

He pulled up to the side of the road, near a row of restaurants and brightly illuminated bungalows.

"Drop me off here," said Schleuder, "and don't bother about me. I'm going to join my 'friends.' "

In spite of his worry, Stern could not help smiling. They exchanged a brief handshake and he drove off again. Schleuder turned off the main road, away from the lights, and took a path leading up to the top of the hill. This was the observation post overlooking the launching pad a couple of miles away.

Schleuder kept stopping, standing motionless and silent for minutes at a time, desperately hoping that the countdown had been resumed and that the loud-speaker on the summit would soon set his mind at rest. His hopes were not fulfilled. A heavy, almost sinister silence hung over the entire hillside. Moreover, a mere glance around him was enough to reveal the situation and he was deeply distressed by the paralysis that seemed to have struck this center of pilgrimage. Usually, at every hour of the day and night, a noisy crowd surged around the bungalows hastily erected there for the use of the tourists who wanted to see with their own eyes the site on which the most fantastic enterprise of the century was being prepared. The people who used these makeshift accommodations stayed only a couple of days, or merely a few hours, then drove off after indulging in an orgy of photography. They called out to one another loudly and happily. This night these remained silent. Even these; for there were others dwelling on that hill, others belonging to a different race.

These newcomers had settled on the hill at the start of the countdown and were firmly determined to stay until the end. They did not take photographs and they spoke in low voices. They were the out-and-out "lunatics," the people Schleuder called his "friends." Among them could be found melancholic dreamers, Bohemians, artists, poets, amateur astrologers, disillusioned failures, wastrels, and idlers, or else assiduous researchers who spent nights on end in the feverish pursuit of some impossible dream: a demonstration of the Euclidian proposition, the discovery of perpetual motion or how to square the circle. They either scorned the restaurants and bungalows or could not afford them. They had come, frequently by short stages, on foot or hitchhiking or working their way by doing menial tasks on boats or bus lines; they had come from Massachusetts or New York, from Wisconsin or North Dakota, from Arizona or California, from Mississippi or Texas; they had come with all their worldly possessions, which were frequently meager enough, and camping equipment ranging from a proper tent to a tattered old blanket.

They had converged on Florida as soon as they heard the news of the great adventure and had chosen to camp out on the hill overlooking the site of the fabulous departure, the prospect of which obsessed them night and day. Gradually a sort of zone had come into being around the bungalows, a city of ragged canvas and sheets of corrugated iron stolen from the edge of the site. The administration put up with them for the time being, intending no doubt to move them farther off on the eve of the great day. They had become part and parcel of the landscape, and their conversations or solitary ramblings usually formed a constant background noise between the sporadic announcements of the countdown or the barbaric yells of the tourists.

But this noise had also died away, and tonight a complete and agonizing silence hung over the hill. Paralysis had struck even them. They were not asleep, however; in any case they hardly ever slept. But for the last fifteen days they had become so accustomed to the periodic announcements of the loud-speaker that its silence found them suddenly disconcerted, overwhelmed, rooted to the spot, as though time had ceased to pass for them.

Schleuder, General Schleuder who had once commanded Peenemünde, knew them well. He had happened to stop here shortly after his arrival and had subsequently come back several times, taking a bus that ran between the base and the living quarters. He had recognized in them a sort of madness he himself shared, and it was not with derision that he called them his friends. Had he, too, not rushed here from New York, for no other reason than to be here and give himself the illusion of playing some part? In the course of his numerous visits he had made a number of acquaintances among this motley crowd, which even included a few respectable-looking individuals who were not eccentrically dressed.

He searched in the darkness for the secluded corner in which the group of his favorites had settled, a group to which he had been admitted by virtue of a vague sense of fraternity, but access to which was fiercely denied to all intruders. He soon found them, plunged like everyone else in surly silence, lying on bedding made of blankets and old sacks, between two rocks that sheltered them from the wind. All had their eyes fixed on the site where the gantries of Phoebe 5 stood out like cathedral spires. They did not greet him. They did not address a word to him, but a mere glance was enough to show that he was welcome, and two of them shifted their position to make room for him. Old Schleuder, an erstwhile general in the German army, drew his overcoat closer around him, stepped over several bodies, sat himself down, without saying a word, between an illiterate tramp and a former mathematics professor whose mind was slightly unbalanced, and started with his friends on a relentless vigil.

Stern parked the car some distance from the blockhouse and made his way toward it on foot. As he walked along he, too, was struck by the intensity and quality of the silence reigning over the launching pad. Usually Phoebe 5 was the center of intense activity, night and day, and the gantry lifts were constantly in motion. Tonight the searchlights illuminated what looked like a dead world. Somewhere no doubt there was bound to be feverish activity, concentrated on the defective component, but it could not be seen from outside. All movement had ceased. The elevators seemed to have come to a stop at the very point they had reached when a grain of sand had put the mechanism out of gear. Some workmen were standing about, as motionless as the machines, like the minions of a fairy-tale palace spellbound by a magician's wand.

Three figures loomed up in front of him before he reached the blockhouse. They were the astronauts. He was not surprised. He expected to see them there, gnawed by anxiety, begging for information. In spite of the regulations that required them to go to bed early and never emerge at night, whatever happened, they had not been able to restrain themselves. Awakened by an inexplicable foreboding, by some subtle emanation of anguish distilled in the atmosphere of Florida by the stopping of the countdown, they had made their way to the site and were now wandering miserably around the blockhouse.

"We wanted to know, Dr. Stern. Is it going to last long?"

"How do I know? And anyway, you've no business to be out here at this time of night. Good God! You've hardly got anything on and you'll catch cold, or even worse. Do you think your mission is to go and spread microbes all over the moon?"

The astronauts' state of health was one of his daily concerns. He relented, however, in the face of their dismay and contrite demeanor.

"Go back to bed. I promise you'll be given detailed information by telephone in the morning."

They thanked him and went off, although with obvious reluctance. He could not help smiling as he recalled his anger and the way he had cursed and sworn at them a week earlier, when they had come and submitted a request that the countdown be accelerated. As though mere desire could hasten or delay the present pace! He shrugged his shoulders.

"When it's all over," he muttered, "they'll be demigods and I'll be able to go into retirement. In three months the world will have forgotten all about me."

He was stopped at the entrance to the blockhouse by an orderly.

"The White House, sir. They're on the line."

"Tell them I'm busy."

"I think it's one of the President's private secretaries, sir."

"Even if it's the President himself," he screamed, "even if it's the President himself, do you hear, tell him I've got better things to do than waste time chatting on the telephone."

In a fury he entered the control room, where the three screens of motionless pointers appeared like the lugubrious symbol of time brought to a stop.

T – 15 days   T – 343 hours   T – 20,580 minutes.

T – 20,579 minutes.

The minute hand had moved on one unit. The loud-speakers announced the resumption of the countdown. The test conductor started reading again from his ledger. It was two o'clock in the afternoon. Stern stepped out to get some fresh air. His head was throbbing and he ached in every limb. He had not left the place since his arrival; he had spent his time trying to figure out what was happening and talking to Walker and others at loose ends like himself. For the breakdown, caused by defective insulation in the gyroscope circuit, was a job for very specialized technicians. The delay had lasted twelve hours.

T – 20,570 minutes.

At the first crackle of the loud-speakers, the workmen had given a startled jump. Stern had almost expected to see them yawn and stretch, as though another touch of the magic wand had roused them from a lengthy slumber. The machine got under way at once. These were not the same teams as the night before. The others had been relieved at the usual hour, but the new arrivals had instinctively assumed the silence and immobility of their predecessors. As for the latter, they had not left the site. They had simply moved a hundred yards or so away and lain down on the ground, glancing alternately at the blockhouse and the rocket. They had sprung to their feet at the first announcement, but still remained motionless for some time, apprehensive, not yet daring to rejoice. It was only after several minutes, when the rhythm had been re-established, that they consented to go home, talking among themselves in undertones.

The same moods had prevailed some miles away, in the lunatics' encampment. Schleuder, who had spent the whole night and morning there, waited another half hour before leaving his friends and slowly making his way back to the main road.

"You go off and get some sleep," said Stern to Walker, who had joined him outside.

"What about you?"

"I'm going to hang around here a little longer."

"To see if the circuit is working all right, I suppose? You can't do anything about it. None of us can."

"I know. . . . Twelve hours' delay, Walker!"

"Twelve hours, so far."

They both fell silent and listened in anguish, holding their breath as they unconsciously did at the end of each ten-minute interval.

"T — 20,550 minutes," the loud-speakers announced.

They began to breathe again and laughed at themselves.

"We've got to go on like this for another fifteen days," said Stern.

"The Chinese," Walker observed in a weary tone, "the Chinese have invented certain tortures . . ."

FORTY-TWO

"T — 160 hours."

"One hundred and sixty hours," the Soviet Premier echoed. "Just over six days. How is it going with them?"

"Two hundred and thirty-six," Igor, his private secretary, immediately replied.

"You've got the latest news from the base?"

"I called twice this morning. Everything's going well. The countdown has been resumed. Naturally it gave them somewhat of a shock."

"Naturally, as you say!"

"But it wasn't serious and it's been repaired."

"How long was the delay?"

"Eight hours, whereas the Americans were held up for twelve. We've gained an additional four hours."

"And what is . . . I mean, they must have a definite opinion by now. Did you speak to Zharov?"

"No, Comrade Chairman. The first time I called, the breakdown was still on. He sent word to say that he couldn't come to the telephone. They all sounded slightly . . . irritable."

"I understand. So they sent you packing, and me too. That's quite natural. And the second time?"

"The countdown had been resumed, but Zharov had gone

off to bed on strict orders from his doctor. It was Nadia, his wife, who answered. I felt I ought not to wake Zharov. It seems he was in danger of a nervous breakdown."

"Quite right, too. That would be the last straw! But Nadia, she's her husband's right hand, surely she gave you her opinion. . . . Good God, man, speak up!"

"She said: 'I think we have a good chance of getting there first if everything goes smoothly.' "

"She said that?"

"Those were her very words. I jotted them down, Comrade Chairman."

"Say it again," the Premier ordered, unable to conceal his impatience. ". . . 'We have a good chance of getting there first . . . ?' "

" 'I think we have a good chance of getting there first if everything goes smoothly.' "

"That's encouraging. Don't you think so, Igor? Don't just stand there! Say something!"

"Very encouraging, Comrade Chairman."

"That must be Zharov's personal opinion. And he's anything but a boaster, isn't he?"

"Far from it."

The Soviet Premier could stand it no longer. He wanted his secretary to reassure him that the scientists were a hundred percent certain of success. He suddenly realized the childishness of his attitude and dismissed Igor, who was under orders to notify him of the slightest hitch.

Left by himself, he did his best to take his mind off the countdown by trying to concentrate on a delicate point of international diplomacy. He was unsuccessful. After a moment or two he angrily closed the file and sat back in his armchair.

The moon occupied his every thought. The moon imperiously exacted what vital energy he had left. The moon would tolerate no rival. For the last month he had been incapable of making any important decision. He kept putting everything off. He was even unable to take any more interest in the slanders that the heads of certain hostile states were spreading about him.

He mentally reviewed the glorious progress achieved by his country in the race for the conquest of space. They had always been first in the most important stages, and even their opponents had recognized their stature. This had not been achieved without sacrifice. He was well aware that the Russian economy had been somewhat disturbed for several years by the wild expenditures involved in the race to the moon. Agriculture was still in a pitiful state and the country's industrial development had been retarded at several points. They had had to buy wheat from abroad and run into debt. Some people reproached him for this; but he could always retort that he had enabled the Union to maintain her lead in the realm of space, even in face of the gigantic efforts made by America. Granted, this lead had decreased in the course of the last few years. It was now very small, but he was convinced it still existed. A few days, a few hours? . . . A few hours were as good as a few years for a world premiere of such importance.

After such a splendid performance they deserved to win. They could not fail right at the end, with the goal post in sight! He, too, realized that the glorious memory of the Sputniks, the Luniks, and Gagarin would be wiped out, completely effaced by the first man to set foot on lunar soil! The public demands simple exploits, as simple as its own imagination. The moon is a simple goal. The Vostoks? They had created a sensation for a time, but today the peasants of the backward provinces made scarcely any distinction between these missiles and common aircraft. And the Americans, too, realized this—above all, the Americans who had been living all these years in hopes of this dazzling revenge!

. . . And who had caught up with them, give or take a few hours! He tried in vain to persuade himself that success was certain. Was it not Zharov's opinion? What was it his wife, his assistant, had said? He could no longer remember the exact phrase and almost sent for Igor. The fear of ridicule restrained him and the words eventually came back to him: "We have a good chance of getting there first . . ." No, "I think we have a good chance . . ." and she had added: "If everything goes smoothly." . . . Smoothly! How could anything be expected to go smoothly in an enterprise like this? How he wished he could dismiss these last words from his mind!

The previous night's delay had made his heart miss several beats, and since then he had been unable to shed his feeling of foreboding. A few hours' lead? How could one tell if the Americans were not cheating? If they were not deceiving the world with a fake countdown? It was unlike their usual ingenuousness but, for the moon, they were quite capable of such action. No sooner had this suspicion entered his mind than it developed into certainty. It was as plain as a pikestaff. They, the Russians, had been fooled. He almost telephoned then and there to the control center to order the pace to be accelerated.

Just in time he realized the folly of such a move. Decidedly, he must be growing old and his nerves were not as good as they had been. The moon had exhausted him, there was no doubt about it. He was only waiting for the end of the ordeal, and final success, to resign from his post and hand it over to a younger man. To resign after such an exploit! Never would any head of state have known such glory. After this, no one could dream of reproaching him on the subject of agriculture and finance. He would have guided his country to the moon. He would have won the greatest victory of the century. His successors would have all the leisure and all the peace and quiet they wanted to restore order in the other fields.

Three knocks on the door delivered by prearranged signal roused him from this optimistic contemplation of the future, in which he had eventually found refuge. He gave a start and was immediately overwhelmed by anxiety again. It was Igor. He recognized his particular knock. Igor would not dare to disturb him except for something serious. And what other serious subject was there at the moment?

It was in an almost strangled voice that he asked him to come in. A mere glance at his secretary showed that he was not mistaken. Igor's habitually impassive features were distorted. His hands were trembling.

"Com—Comrade . . ."

"What is it?"

Igor was unable to speak. The Premier managed to remind himself of his position. He made a superhuman effort to maintain his composure and said in a kindly but stern voice:

"Pull yourself together, Igor. Bad news? Tell me at once. I am here to receive bad news as well as good. A fresh delay in the countdown?"

"Comrade," Igor stammered, recovering his breath, "we will not be the first."

The old man's shoulders abruptly slumped. For a second his secretary thought he had had a stroke. His head dangled as though he had just been clubbed. Once again, however, he managed to recover his composure, by a miracle of pride and strength of will, and to speak in an almost normal voice.

"Well, we won't be the first, then, Igor. That's all. The Americans . . ."

"It's not the Americans," Igor spluttered. "Comrade Chairman . . . a Japanese landed on the moon this morning."

FORTY-THREE

I drew a large circle in the dust that covers the lunar soil, a circle whose center is the capsule rocket that brought me here. I hoisted the Japanese imperial flag above the capsule. Then I took a step backward and shouted three times: "Banzai!"

Fundamentally I don't really know why I uttered this cry. It astonished even me. It's a romantic, rather military cry, and I'm neither a military nor a romantic. I'm a man of science, a rational human being, who one day had the good fortune to have a fabulous idea. Yet "banzaï" was the first word spoken on the surface of the moon.

I had to stretch the flag between two poles to unfurl it. Otherwise it would droop ingloriously; there's not a breath of wind on the moon. Thus unfurled, the red disk can be seen from far off. Those who come after me will not fail to notice it.

Near the rocket, which is resting on its tripod, I swept an area more or less clear of dust. The layer is scarcely a foot deep. Some scientists calculated that it must be as much as a mile in depth and that the first astronauts would be engulfed in it as in an ocean. They were wrong. It is not the first time scientists have been mistaken about the moon. Under the dust I found a rocky, fairly friable soil. I was able to break pieces off. With these stones I built a little altar, in which I placed a few family relics and the bunch of paper flowers that Mrs. Suzaki gave me before my departure.

Having thus fulfilled my patriotic and religious obligations, I felt I was entitled to think of myself. So I stepped back still farther and, in front of my improvised altar, I traced the following words in the dust:

KANASHIMA
The First Man on the Moon

Then I looked all around me and remained for some time immersed in deep meditation, exalted both by the strange beauty of the lunar landscape and by the sense of my miraculous presence in this setting.

It is night; it will be night for six or seven days. This manner of speaking is rather foolish. Night will last slightly longer than six times twenty-four hours. There is one chance of my seeing the sun again. It is far from certain. Whatever happens, I am happy that the haste of departure obliged me to make a landing by night. I thus escape the dazzling, harmful rays that I am not sure my space suit would be able to withstand. The suit protects me from the cold, but we had no time to equip it against intense radiation. We were in a hurry.

It is night, but I am not plunged in darkness. I touched down on the face perpetually turned toward earth, and the light reflected by the latter, albeit faint, is far more intense than the light known on earth when the moon is full and the sky is cloudless. I can see well enough to read, to write, and to paint. The disk of the Japanese flag can be discerned from far away.

It is the other disk that captures my attention, the disk giving off this light that physicists have calculated is about seventy times more intense than moonlight. It is the disk of the earth, a vision that would delight my Japanese brothers, for whom the nocturnal heavenly body has always been an object of enchantment. I don't believe anyone in the world could escape the spell

293

of this vast, gleaming, dilating "moon" thirteen times larger and five times more brilliant than ours, which I can see at an angle of about forty-five degrees above the horizon.

I realize I won't be able to give any description without mentioning figures. Even in my flights of poetic fancy I remain a man of science. I like to know where I am going and to understand the reasons for the phenomena I observe, even if their beauty moves me to tears. That is why I shall give the following details:

I know more or less exactly where I am at the moment. I have marked the spot on a map. I landed in the Sea of Serenity, at its extreme west—that is, at the extreme right of the usual maps of the moon, in which the directions are reversed—at a point almost exactly on the north-south axis of the visible lunar face, in the northern hemisphere, more or less equidistant from the center and from the circumference. On one side, quite close to me, I can easily distinguish the range of the Appenines, which stands between me and the Sea of Showers. On the other, the Sea of Serenity extends its vast surface beyond the range of the human eye. Perhaps another landing spot might have been more picturesque, but I didn't have any choice. Furthermore, I feel utterly intoxicated by the mere idea of having fallen from the sky into the Sea of Serenity, quite close to the Sea of Showers. This has nothing to do with my scientific background.

I must add that I landed, in terrestrial terms, shortly after the new moon—in other words, for me, shortly after the "full earth"; which explains why I can see almost the full disk of our planet. From my position on the moon this disk is more or less equidistant from my horizon and my zenith. It's an admirable position from an aesthetic point of view. It catches the full light from the earth, while distributing light and shade harmoniously.

I am a man of science, but it is not in this capacity that I now gaze at my nocturnal heavenly body. The sight of earth fills me

*with an indescribable ecstasy. I find myself mentally composing
a poem dedicated to its nocturnal glory.*

*The details I have given show my expectation of witnessing
the rising of the sun. Its first rays will reach me in fact in six or
seven days from now; I shall work out the exact figure if I have
time. I hope to be here still.*

FORTY-FOUR

"A Japanese!"

The President of the United States burst out with a shattering
cry. Though he had steeled himself to the possibility that
Americans might not be the first to land on the moon—match-
ing in this respect the courage of the greatest heroes—the news
completely devastated him. This outrageous blow of fate was
beyond endurance. Stewart, looking wan and shaken, also
abandoned all pretense at saving face.

"A Japanese, Mr. President! Not even a trained astronaut,
but a scientist—a physicist, I believe—Dr. Kanashima. He took
the pilot's place for a one-way flight. We just don't deserve
this!"

The President was unable to admit or even understand the
meaning of this new development. He kept fidgeting with the
objects on his desk, picking them up, then angrily thrusting

them aside. He could find no suitable words to express his dismay and kept repeating senselessly: "A Japanese! A Japanese!" like an old mumbling dotard.

His rage eventually was expressed in an extraordinary manner that made his adviser gape.

"A Japanese, Stewart! But, in God's name, what the hell do you think the Russians are doing?"

The Soviet Premier's rage had not lasted long. It had expressed itself in a short outburst; then the old man's shoulders had once again slumped. He was overwhelmed by an immense sorrow. It was in an almost imploring voice, and with an expression like a beaten dog's, that he asked Igor for further details. Then he relapsed into a gloomy reverie and dismissed his secretary, who left the room with lowered head.

He sat there prostrate, stricken by a fatal blow that he had no idea how to parry. He felt he had lost his last reason for governing. He felt debased in his own eyes and in the eyes of the nation. He had the impression that the stigmata of disgrace were inscribed on his face. Not for anything in the world would he have called up the senior officials, who he guessed were all prepared to lavish their condolences on him. On the contrary, he gave strict orders over the telephone that he was to be left alone. He had no wish to expose what he considered a disgrace, and his pride refused all pity from subordinates.

Yet the pain that gnawed at him was such that he would have yielded all his power to lean on and confide in a friend, a friend who was also an equal. Only an equal could understand the extent and violence of his despair. No one in his immediate circle was capable of filling this role. Igor was only fit for performing an underling's specific tasks.

He finally renounced the idea of pouring out his heart. He renounced it after darting a frantic glance all around him, a glance that constantly reverted with yearning to an object standing on the corner of his desk, an object that for a moment seemed to provide a possible solution to the awful problem of his solitude. He renounced it after a few minutes of harassing and incongruous temptation, after hesitations that broke down his remaining powers of endurance. He renounced it with a disillusioned shrug of the shoulders after casting a final, eager, almost tender glance at the telephone, connected directly with Washington, standing on his desk, and regretting with a sob that this instrument could not in all decency be used for expatiating, in a friendly conversation, on the sufferings of a head of state whose heart was overflowing with bitterness.

FORTY-FIVE

I stood for a long time contemplating the disk of the earth. After half an hour it appeared to be still in the same place. I knew in advance that it would be, but I was not sorry to verify this with my own eyes. It will always appear in the same place, motionless, shrinking little by little until, a few days from now, it is no more than a quarter.

Afterward I did what I could to make my domain as pleasant as possible. I went into my pressurized cabin. I opened the parcel containing a few precious personal possessions that I was able to bring with me. My luggage consists of a paint box, some drawing paper, a few gardening implements, three kimonos, two bottles of Scotch, and a few other odds and ends. The whole lot weighs about forty-five pounds. This was possible because I am much lighter than the astronaut who was earmarked for the flight and also, of course, because of the great degree to which the plan was simplified.

I came out again with my tools. I had made up my mind to build a garden within the circumference. I went and fetched my raw materials from outside the circle. I cleared the dust and attacked the soil with a pick. I thus managed to dig up some rocks of various shapes and sizes. I carried them back to my domain without any undue effort, even the biggest ones; they weigh only one-sixth as much as on earth. With these I constructed a few irregularly spaced piles and took great pains to give them a picturesque shape. Granted, my garden cannot compare with that of the Zen temple at Ryoan-ji or any other famous ones. I have neither the time nor, above all, the ability to compose a masterpiece. However, it surpasses them all in one respect: the exceptional nature of the materials. The big blocks of moon that I shifted would be considered treasures in Japan. I also collected some meteorites from other worlds, which are to be found in profusion in the dust. No equivalent collection exists on earth. I decorated my rocky islets with these unusual pebbles. I worked a long time before finding a harmony of shapes and spaces that satisfied me. I am not displeased with the result. It is an honest amateur achievement.

I next unrolled my strips of paper. I chose a green one, the color of underbrush. I cut it into small pieces and inserted the fragments in some of the cracks in the stones. A handful of fine dust made the junctions invisible and brought out further contrasts of color. In the gentle light of the terrestrial disk the paper could easily be taken for moss, and I amuse myself by making believe that this is what it actually is.

Then I started raking. Here again I am a privileged gardener. I didn't have far to go to find some rare sand. The fineness of the lunar dust lends itself admirably to my design.

When I started using the rake to make a series of furrows, un-

consciously remembering the curves and undulations that had impressed me in a garden in Kyoto, I clumsily tried to reproduce them. I quickly gave this up. They did not harmonize with my domain or with my state of mind. I contented myself with tracing some concentric furrows spreading out from the capsule to the circumference of the circle, leaving room only for three radial paths that I bordered with meteorites and where I shall be able to stroll without damaging my work. I amused myself by giving names to these paths. I inscribed these names on some little paper signposts that I planted at the entrance to each path.

I worked like this for several hours and was not disappointed by the final result. Is it a really suitable spot for meditation? Of that I am not certain. I also wonder what possessed me to lay out this garden in Zen style. Is it an instinctive temptation to initiate myself into this doctrine, with which I am not very familiar but which, despite a certain attraction, has always struck me as somewhat suspect? I'm not sure. I shall try to examine my motives more clearly if I have time. For the moment I am rather inclined to believe that my most powerful motive was the desire to create the first Zen garden on the moon.

I went for a short stroll in the garden and suddenly I made a discovery: the poem I had roughed out on arrival, the poem to the glory of nocturnal earth, had composed itself in my head while I was gardening. So I went back to my capsule to write it down, to write it down and also to paint a few water colors. I can't engage in these activities outside, for want of a certain amount of atmospheric pressure. This warrants a word or two of explanation.

Water, like ink, like any other liquid, would not withstand the vacuum that prevails on the moon. I remember, in this connection, an experiment carried out by the Americans during a test of their Phoebe I, one that made a deep impression on me and on which I often ponder. The missile carried several tons of water, which were suddenly ejected into the relative void that exists at an altitude of a hundred miles. Dr. Stern reported that the water had literally exploded, blowing into smithereens in all directions at a speed of more than a mile per second. As a result of this experiment, scientists have maintained that the human body, which contains an enormous percentage of liquid, might disintegrate in the same way if it was abruptly plunged into the absolute void of lunar space. Hence the necessity of a well-designed and absolutely waterproof space suit. Mine is completely satisfactory from this point of view, but I have to go inside my cabin to use my fountain pen or fill my paint cups.

Once inside my capsule, I shed this space suit at once. I donned a kimono, regretting only that I could not take a bath, but this is a minor inconvenience. I switched on my transmitting set and sent a message to earth, a short message. I summed up my flight, the successive orbits, and how the capsule detached itself from the big rocket, carrying the remainder of the fuel in its tank—a small amount, but enough to reach the moon and reduce speed before landing. The main rocket, an inert body, is now gravitating around the moon and will no doubt continue to do so for several centuries. On arrival, my tank was almost empty. My calculations were very exact, and I heaved a sigh of relief on touching down.

I ended my message with best wishes to some of my friends and that is almost all I sent back to earth apart from a few details on how I pass the time. This is nobody's business but my own. I have only a very few instruments with which to make scientific measurements. I have been able nevertheless to calculate exactly the coordinates of the spot where I landed, and these I also transmitted. But this was done primarily from an egotistical motive. Those who come after me will thus have no difficulty in finding my encampment, my garden, the Japanese flag, and my name inscribed in the dust of the moon. I also hope they will read my poem.

*I began to listen to the reply to my message and to the con-
gratulations of the Emperor, who has given me the highest
Japanese decoration. Then, as the announcer began to elaborate on the sensation caused by my exploit, I switched off. I no
longer need these encouragements, and the elation of the
masses would inflame my mind to no purpose. I delight in my
victory more profoundly in seclusion. For what I still have to
do, I need peace and quiet. Could any place be more conducive to this occupation than the Sea of Serenity?*

*I have written down my poem. I read it aloud. I drink a stiff
whisky and decide to allow myself a few hours' sleep before
starting to paint. Whisky is one of my weaknesses. I have never
overindulged in it, but I prefer it to all Japanese drinks. I
drink a second. A feeling of well-being creeps over me. Is it the
alcohol or is it the healthy fatigue from gardening that plunges
me into a state of gentle euphoria punctuated every now
and then by a thrill of exaltation? Yet I'm not drunk. . . .
And why shouldn't I be a little drunk? Why not be the first
man to get drunk on the moon, looking through the porthole at
strange mountains bleached by the beams of the miraculous
terrestrial disk?*

*That would not be reasonable, and I am a reasonable human
being. I carefully put the bottle away. I fall asleep, lulled by the
voluptuous sensation of being the first man to fall asleep on the
moon.*

FORTY-SIX

Stern darted a sidelong glance at the woman reporter whose pen was racing over her notebook.

"So, in your opinion, there's no hope for him?"

"None," he replied curtly. "His fuel is exhausted, he said so himself. He can't rise more than a few feet above the lunar surface."

"And I suppose"—she seemed to hesitate—"I suppose there's no way of . . . of rescuing him?"

He shook his head impatiently and his face became contorted.

"Nothing can save him. In two days, at the most, he won't have any oxygen left. And we can't get there before twelve days. We've had another delay. Even by taking the most outlandish risks we couldn't get there before eight days. It's too late."

"So it seems the possibility of a rescue has been considered," she remarked, looking up from her notes.

"Good God, what else do you imagine we've been thinking of these last few days, we Americans and Russians, the specialists of space? What do you imagine our heads of state have been dreaming about every night? How do you imagine I've been spending every minute of my spare time since that damned little manikin went and crashed into the lunar dust?"

"Really!"

"Don't you see it was the only chance we had left of saving face in the eyes of the universe for generations to come? In a thousand years' time it will still be talked about on earth and on every inhabited star! Don't you see we have been held up to ridicule, we Americans, much more than at Pearl Harbor, and they, the Russians, a thousand times more than when their wretched armada was destroyed by Admiral Togo at the beginning of the century! The White House has called over a hundred times to find out if it wasn't possible to do something for that harebrained fellow. For that, at least, they were prepared to take risks, every risk, and so was I and so were our pilots. And don't imagine, don't for a moment imagine that it was from a feeling of human fellowship! Don't start thinking that the life of that imbecile matters to us in any way whatsoever. It's our honor we wanted to save! And we even considered, seriously and for the first time, of collaborating with the Soviets. Yes. The 'hot' line is constantly busy. But how can one arrange a collaboration of this sort in a few days, a few hours! I tell you, by the day after tomorrow, at the latest, he won't have any oxygen left! . . . The day after tomorrow he'll be the first man dead on the moon, do you hear! After being, as he claims, the first man to set foot on its surface, the first to admire the beams from the earth, the first to sleep on the moon, he will be the first to leave his wretched bones there. No miracle can prevent this happening. . . . And now let me get back to work, unless you want the Papuans as well to beat us to the moon!"

Maggie motioned to the reporter, who withdrew. She accompanied her to the front door, apologizing for her husband's irritability. Then she came back to the living room. Glowering and clenching his jaws, Stern appeared not to hear the soothing words uttered by Schleuder and Ruth, who had witnessed the scene.

"You oughtn't to fly off the handle like that in front of the press," said Maggie.

Since he still did not reply, she added in a graver tone:

"And above all, above all, darling . . . you oughtn't to refer to him as a manikin."

"Do you think I believe a word of what I say to the press?"

"You oughtn't to call him an imbecile, either," Ruth said in a tone of reproach.

"An imbecile!"

Stern was unable to suppress another outburst of temper, one even more violent than the first.

"An imbecile!" he yelled. "Don't you realize that, on the contrary, he's shown supreme intelligence! Marvelous lucidity! Don't you see that in the realm of the intellect he's head and shoulders above us! And for that, for that I'll never be able to forgive him! . . . Schleuder, for forty years I've worried and worried about this exasperating problem of the return. For forty years I've racked my brains, tackling it from every angle. I've thought of the most complicated solutions, the most scientific solutions, the most onerous solutions, the most colossal solutions, solutions of absolute genius, but never, never have I thought of this, the simplest solution of all!"

"True," said Ruth, "but maybe this solution wasn't within reach of our minds."

But Stern refused to calm down before he had exhausted every aspect of the subject.

"He argued like this," he went on feverishly. "He said to himself: 'Here's a difficulty that is beyond me, that I shall never be able to overcome.' Then, instead of wearing himself out by battling against it, as we're all doing, he quite simply eliminated the difficulty. From then on it was easy. . . . Too easy . . . What do you think?"

"Nothing," said Schleuder. "I only remember that Asiatics have the reputation, with us, of having extremely complicated minds."

Stern suddenly got up and apologized to his friends. He had to get back to the base. He did not wish to hear anything more about this feat or to listen to any further news from abroad. Schleuder accompanied him into the garden, slapped him on the back, and clasped his hand. He drew away with a shrug of his shoulders and vanished into the night.

The general slowly went back to the two women. Ruth was sitting in a corner, her elbows propped on a small table and her head cradled in her hands, looking silently at Maggie.

"It's a hard blow, Maggie," he said, "for all of us, but especially for him. But we'll get over it. There's still the planet Mars."

"It's not the same as the moon," Maggie groaned, bursting into tears.

Schleuder, who was himself extremely moved, tried to console her and eventually succeeded.

"After all, Maggie, in this contest it was implicitly understood that it was also a question of the return. We shall be the first to return from the moon after landing there."

"Yes," she said, raising her head. "We'll be the first. We'll beat the Russians."

"We'll beat them," Schleuder asserted. "We have just as much technique, ingenuity, science, will power, money, and all the rest, as they have."

"Much more than they have," Maggie protested, "and we also have genius."

"No one can deny that," Ruth exclaimed, sitting up. "Isn't that so, General Schleuder, isn't it true that we also have genius?"

He paused for a moment without answering, as though lost in a private dream. Maggie went up to him and repeated the question, as though it were of vital importance. "Why don't you answer? Isn't it true, Schleuder, that we also have men of genius?"

"Isn't it true, General, that we are capable of inventing more than electric light bulbs and the telephone?" Ruth asked.

305

The two women were now clutching at his arms, their eyes dilated by a sort of anguish. He looked out of the window at the beacon sweeping the garden.

"Certainly we have men of genius," he said quietly. "We have as much genius as the Russians, more than the Russians, more than the Japanese, more than any other nation. However, Maggie . . ."

The old man lapsed into thought once again, listening to the sound of the car in which Stern was driving away.

"There are certain rare occasions in life, Maggie, when genius isn't enough."

FORTY-SEVEN

I have slept again for a few hours. This makes the fourth time I have slept on the moon and, each time I have awakened, I have been curiously obsessed by the experiment described by Stern, the one where the water was suddenly subjected to the vacuum of space, and by the consequences that can be deduced from this on the behavior of the human body placed in similar circumstances.

I have dismissed this thought from my mind. I shall consider it more seriously tomorrow. When I speak of "tomorrow" I am still referring to the terrestrial length of time, but this word today assumes another meaning for me. Tomorrow is also a lunar tomorrow. Tomorrow the sun will rise. Tomorrow I shall be the first man to contemplate sunrise on the moon. It is high time. My supply of oxygen is running out, but I shall hold out till then.

I have gotten up. I have eaten a little food. I have drunk some cold tea. I still have a little whisky left, which I am saving —for tomorrow.

I glance through the porthole at the now familiar landscape that I never weary of. As I had foreseen, the earth is still in the same corner of the sky, but the disk has shrunk to a quarter. The light has faded, but it is still quite sufficient for me; in any case I do not regret having landed at night. The brilliance of the sun, even if I could have endured its lethal rays, would have prevented me from seeing the gentle luminosity provided by the earth. Nothing can equal, as I now know, the splendor and majesty of our planet when viewed at a distance of two hundred and thirty-five thousand miles.

I examine my water colors. I am not a great painter, never having devoted enough time to this hobby, but I think I have produced a fairly good likeness of certain aspects of the lunar landscape, with its unimaginable profusion of stars sparkling in a black sky. I have taken particular care to render the snowy whiteness assumed by the mountains in the light of the earth. One of them has attracted me especially and I have made several sketches of it. It bears a striking resemblance to Fujiyama. I have given it this name. Perhaps it will be known by it in the future.

I spent some time admiring my Fujiyama. I corrected certain details, then I stopped. I think I have reached the highest degree of perfection compatible with my lack of experience. That is the aim I had in mind. I shall paint no more. It is late. It is T minus eighteen hours. I sometimes amuse myself by calculating in these terms. I shall never be able to break myself of certain professional habits.

I carefully wrapped up all my paintings properly and put

them away. I placed my poem on top of the parcel. I sent a short message to earth. As usual, I switched off before the end of the reply. I heard once again about the wave of enthusiasm roused throughout Japan by my voyage. Fireworks are being shot off all over the country in my honor. I am pleased by this but I prefer to concentrate. This evening I shall have a little fireworks display just for myself. Yes, I brought two rockets with me.

I donned my space suit again. I have carefully checked the pressure and its airtight seams. While doing this, I could not help thinking again for a moment or two of the American experiment with fluids. I stepped through the double doors of my cabin and went down into my garden.

It is just as I left it before going to sleep. Nothing changes here. No breeze ruffles the dust. My traces will be found unaltered, and the name of Kanashima will long remain inscribed in the lunar soil. If the newcomers do not efface it, it could remain here for centuries, until meteorites gradually cover it up.

I bowed before my altar. I smiled as I caught sight of the bunch of paper flowers that Mrs. Suzaki gave me. The colors are lovely but the arrangement of the flowers themselves does not, I think, bear witness to a superior artistic feeling. Yet her intention was laudable. I forgive her for her harsh words.

I stroll along the paths in my garden, reading out loud the names I have given them. At each step I raise a little dust, but it does not hover in the air. It falls back immediately, as fine grains of lead would do. In the vacuum of lunar space a grain of lead and a grain of dust fall at the same speed. I allow myself to philosophize a little. I reflect that it is providential, from a certain point of view, that the moon has no atmosphere. If there were the slightest breath of air this dust would whirl about incessantly and spoil my landscape. I should be blinded by a perpetual cloud. Is there perhaps a harmony decreed by nature

308

in the conjunction of these two phenomena: abundance of dust and absence of wind? Is the moon perhaps the best of all possible worlds, and is everything perhaps for the best, as a Western philosopher once said? If I had had a different education, I think I should have been interested in philosophy as well as poetry and painting.

I spend many a happy hour turning over a mass of ideas new to me as I stroll along, taking short steps—short steps so that I do not fly into the air on account of my relative weightlessness. As a young man I was absorbed by scientific study. These few days, this holiday I have given myself, have opened up new horizons for me. I had to come to the moon to rediscover a certain élan forgotten since my childhood. It is a mixture of emotions rather hard to define, whose source, I believe, is the joy of coming into intimate contact with nature, a contact that cannot be established except in the perfect solitude into which my cosmic adventure has incidentally plunged me.

Am I impelled toward this understanding of the universe by an atavistically Japanese point of view? Quite honestly, I rather doubt it. Now and then I whisper to myself such phrases as: "What can my Fujiyama be thinking?" or "I wonder what the moon's opinion is of my adventure," but immediately afterward I find myself smiling as I hear their echo in my head. Is it through the medium of my Zen garden that my mind turns to this communion? I am obliged to admit the same doubt. In spite of a certain curiosity it has sometimes roused in me, I don't think I could ever subscribe to a system so hostile to intelligence, a system that raises anti-logic to the heights of religious dogma. I have chanced just as frequently to feel attracted, as though by a magnet, toward its opposite, and to adopt this thought as my own even though it comes from the West: "Nothing worthwhile exists apart from intelligence, and the proof is that every imbecile shies away from it in terror." It seems to me, however, that some sort of relationship has become established between me and the things that surround

*me since my arrival on the moon. A professional philosopher
would no doubt laugh at the clumsy way in which I express
these feelings, as a painter would smile at my sketches, an expert gardener at my furrows, and a real poet at my valiant
efforts at verse. But these attempts contribute to the charm of
my sojourn on the moon.*

*A captious mind would also perhaps discern some hypocrisy
on my part in claiming to commune with nature, emprisoned
as I am in my space suit and capsule, necessarily separated
from all external elements by artifices, breathing air manufactured in factories, and, in short, more cut off from the
world than a rich capitalist in his air-conditioned apartment.
This is a valid criticism that I shall take into account when the
time comes.*

*Time flies when one devotes it alternately to work and medi-
tation. I have just noticed it is T minus two hours.*

*I enter my cabin for the last time. I look around to see that
everything is in order. I drink what remains of the whisky, sip-
ping it slowly. I fill the oxygen tank of my space suit. I have to
don it immediately afterward, for the air in my cabin becomes
unbreathable. My supply is exhausted. I go out. I carefully
close my capsule behind me and settle down for good in the garden. I take with me only my two rockets and a little silver-
handled knife, scarcely bigger than a penknife but with a razor-
sharp blade.*

*I have placed the knife on my altar—not with any ritual in-
tention, but simply to make sure of finding it easily. It is time to
start my private fireworks display: the lunar night is about to
end; it will announce the rising of the sun. I have prepared in
advance an ingenious system of lighting the rockets. I am unable to suppress a smile as I see myself handling these toys.*

*I have shot them off. The tradesman from whom I bought
them did not swindle me. It is a less magnificent celebration, no
doubt, than those organized in my honor in Japan, but the*

spectacle is none the less remarkable. They explode and burst in the sky into a thousand glittering stars. I feel deeply moved. I am the first man to witness a fireworks display on the moon.

The stars of my little celebration have vanished. A little terrestrial ash has mingled with the dust of the moon. After the brilliant light, the lunar soil now looks almost black, all the more so since the earth's quarter has shrunk still further. I have nothing more to do but wait for the sun. It is T minus one hour. I am going to start counting the minutes.

I still have time to dream. I say to myself that if I sometimes feel tempted by the arts, basically I do not regret my scientific career. Scientists have now become poets. The proof is that they are beginning to turn their thoughts to the moon.

It is T minus forty minutes. I suddenly feel in a state of extraordinary elation and tears keep welling up in my eyes. This is not due to the rapidly absorbed alcohol, nor to the sensation of living through an hour of triumph. What provokes this sudden emotion is perceiving in the sky the signs I have been waiting for, the silvery gleam announcing the imminent rising of the sun. I don't know if I am more fascinated by the rare beauty of this phenomenon or by the fact that it is happening exactly as I predicted, at the point I had predetermined, and at the very minute I had calculated. . . . Never will I shed my scientific skin!

For I knew. If the moon, as a result of the absence of atmosphere, is deprived of dawns and dusks caused by diffused light, like those on earth, the appearance and disappearance of the terrestrial disk are preceded and followed by even more marvelous phenomena. Nothing like them can be seen on our planet except on the occasion of a total eclipse, and then only for a very short time. What I see now is a zone of the vast silvery corona that surrounds our heavenly body. I also know that this whiteness will soon be streaked with red flames escaping from the chromosphere. . . . And here are the tongues of

311

these flames piercing the horizon above my Fujiyama, like a field of writhing blades of grass. It will not be long before the pink of the chromosphere itself appears.

T minus ten minutes. The disk will appear exactly on time. The countdown for sunrise never suffers a delay. I shall see the sun again in five minutes. I shall probably be able to spend a few moments gazing at it, but only a few. In my space suit the pressure is starting to fall slightly. It is pointless to wait too long.

It is pointless and it would also be fatal to the plan I have made: a scientific plan. I have, in fact, had another good idea, the second in a month, and for this to be put into effect with complete success, the pressure of my space suit must still be fairly high. There again, by dint of searching, I discovered the solution to a problem that has long been tormenting me. It flashed through my mind only a few hours ago and it gave me a deep intellectual satisfaction. Could it be that I am a genius to have had such good ideas? I'm presumptuous, I know, but I'm the first presumptuous man on the moon.

It was the American experiment with tons of water liberated in the vacuum that inspired me with this remarkable solution, which shows, incidentally, that science is truly international. Had it not been for this experiment, I might have opted for the classical method of hara-kiri. In fact I lingered no more than a few seconds over this possibility. I am not an antediluvian Japanese. I am not a samurai. Moreover, I have a horror of pain. I have received a scientific education and it is in a scientific manner, which in no way precludes elegance, that I wish to put an end to my adventure.

In matters of annihilation, each has his own ideal. Sailors wish to dissolve in the sea. Certain pantheists ask to be buried without a coffin, stark naked in the soil, in order to mingle as rapidly as possible with the earth. Others wish to be cremated, so that their elements may be dispersed instantaneously in the atmosphere.

312

So, for the conqueror of space, I don't think there is a more noble and reasonable ideal than the manner of disintegration on which I have decided. In the experiment with water, Stern reported that the substance had literally exploded and that clouds of elementary particles had been hurled in all directions into space at a speed in the neighborhood of a mile per second. A rent in a space suit must produce a similar result for the human body, which is largely composed of liquid.

One mile per second is almost the speed of liberation from the lunar force of gravity, which is far weaker than the earth's. This means that some of my atoms will start orbiting around the moon. Others will even escape its influence. Some of them will be snatched up by planets, and it is not impossible that a few of them will revolve eternally around the earth. Still others, no doubt—"no doubt" is a scientific term—will become satellites of the sun. And perhaps a few—it is not unreasonable to entertain this hope—a few will escape from the solar attraction through the action of cyclonic disturbances and find their way toward other stars and—who knows?—other galaxies. I have no time to calculate the probabilities of these various dispersions. Whatever happens, it is a fine end for an astronaut.

Here is the sun. I was expecting it when the countdown reached zero, but I was staggered nevertheless by the sudden flash of light. It is rising very slowly. It will take an hour for the whole disk to detach itself from the horizon, but the tiny crescent crowning the mountain is enough to illuminate the Sea of Serenity and dazzle me. This will be one of my final memories, and one of the loveliest.

A torrid heat must already have replaced the cold of night—such is the moon, without transitions. I cannot feel it, however. The thermostat of my space suit is functioning perfectly for the time being, but the pressure is falling.

The moment has come. I have approached the altar and

313

picked up the knife. I should never have had the courage to plunge it into my entrails, but what could be simpler than puncturing the material of my space suit, still stretched like a balloon by the internal pressure. I am deeply disturbed, however. I am not frightened, but a sort of timidity paralyzes me. My garden, streaked with a profusion of new colors and shadows, looks alien to me. My plan was conceived and matured in the gentle whiteness of the earth's rays. Certain ceremonies seem less easy to carry out in the midst of this orgy of light.

I feel self-conscious. How should I behave? Should I turn toward the relics on my altar? Toward the thin sliver of the sun? Toward that other faint crescent the earth has become? Should I shout "Banzai!"? Or should I seek a supreme revelation in the contemplation of my garden?

No. I wish to give myself a final respite in order to make a last confession: I have been play-acting slightly to myself since my landing on the moon. The Japanese flag? The altar? The relics? The Zen garden? The poetry? The painting? . . . No doubt. But I've already admitted that I shouted "Banzai" without any enthusiasm and that I tried in vain, while meditating in my garden, to renounce intelligence so as to attain intuition.

So what have I done since my arrival? I have tried out various states of mind, out of sheer curiosity. It was again the spirit of discovery that prompted me. Fundamentally, patriotism, religious observance, Zen, what is conventionally called philosophy, poetry, and painting—all these have always seemed to me, and still seem, futile, as futile as imperialism, communism, or democracy. None of them strikes me as having the quality of consistency. None of these states of mind has given me complete satisfaction. I have been duped by none. But their re-search has elated me right up to this moment. And research is a scientific passion, the only thrill I am really capable of feeling.

At this moment, at this prolongation of the countdown, my ecstasy derives from the fact that I had a better idea than the other scientists, that I have been more intelligent than even

Stern himself. All this does not simplify my final problem. Yet I cannot cry out: "Long live intelligence!" It would be foolish and pretentious.

I have grasped my knife firmly in my hand. I have directed the point toward my stomach. I shall rip the material from bottom to top. I have not fallen on my knees. I have turned toward the sun. Why not? But I can no longer endure its glare; I have had to lower my head. My gaze has thus fallen on the inscription I traced in the dust of the moon. I spell out the words with fervor in my heart and in my soul: KANASHIMA. The First . . .